59372083342199   CAR

D0054281

BEAUTIFUL DAYS

BEAUTIFUL DAYS

A BRIGHT YOUNG THINGS NOVEL

ANNA GODBERSEN

HARPER

An Imprint of HarperCollinsPublishers

alloyentertainment

Produced by Alloy Entertainment
151 West 26th Street, New York, NY 10001

Library of Congress Cataloging-in-Publication Data is available.

ISBN 978-0-06-196268-4

Design by Liz Dresner

11   12   13   14   15   CG/BV   10   9   8   7   6   5   4   3   2   1

First Edition

For Katy

1

IT WAS A MIDSUMMER AFTERNOON ON LONG ISLAND, and the mosquitoes, like the girls who get dolled up at evening time, would not be seen flitting about for hours yet. A lot of noise was made last night in the mansions that lined White Cove, and plenty would be made tonight, but for now the sky was just a wide arc of blue, and three such girls—some of them already much discussed by newspaper columnists and women in hair salons—were browning poolside. One lay facedown, one sprawled on her back, and one curled up on her side, the better to turn the pages of her fashion magazine.

"Darling." The voice of the first cut through the listless atmosphere, ending the peaceful silence.

Cordelia Grey took a breath of sweet, still air as she returned to consciousness. The sun had warmed the skin of her long legs, and the chaise she was lying upon comfortably accommodated her languid pose. June, with its occasionally gloomy weather and mourning clothes, was behind her. She moved her arm so that her eyes were no longer covered; it was another beautiful day.

"Darling?" the voice repeated. It belonged to Astrid Donal, who over the course of a month and a half had become one of Cordelia's closest friends.

Cordelia blinked so as not to be blinded. The sky was very bright and the pool was very turquoise. Even the leaves on the trees at Dogwood seemed to have embraced the indolent spirit of summer; they were thick and mysterious and green, hardly moving even on their high branches.

"I'm sorry." Cordelia smiled. "I guess I must have drifted off."

"It's nearly four o'clock, you know," Astrid replied from the chaise on Cordelia's left. She rolled over and pushed her cartwheel hat, which she wore to protect her creamy skin, back on her head.

"It can't be!" Cordelia laughed, drawing her heaps of sun-streaked dirty-blond hair into a bun at the nape of her neck. "You shouldn't have let me sleep that long."

"We thought of waking you, but you looked so happy,"

said Letty Larkspur, who had been Cordelia's best friend in that other life she'd left behind in Ohio.

Letty occupied the chaise to Cordelia's right, her legs tucked up close to her chest. Both girls wore new navy blue tank swimsuits, although Letty had mostly covered her petite frame in a gauzy robe. Her dark hair was cropped short and she had pushed her bangs to the side so that they revealed a pale triangle of forehead. Even this far into summer, her skin was almost white.

They had all three bought the same suit on a shopping trip into Manhattan the week before—that had been Astrid's idea, she'd insisted it would be great fun if they had a kind of uniform when they went sea bathing—although Astrid had somehow already ruined hers on a trip to the beach and was now wearing an old black one, which was frayed and worn thin in places but nonetheless flattered her girlish frame. Astrid had been born wealthy, and anything she threw on seemed, as if by some magic, deliberate and expensive.

"You were smiling to yourself," Letty went on, in that small, crystalline voice that belied the deep, rich sound her throat produced when she sang, "and whispering something."

"Then you definitely should have woken me!"

"Nonsense." Astrid drained her lemonade glass and put it on the little wood table that separated their chairs. "I know how you like to keep secrets, Cordelia Grey, and I am not above listening to you talk in your sleep to find them out."

3

"Me? I got nothing to hide," Cordelia replied, with a rakish and somewhat disingenuous innocence, and swung her legs over the side of the chaise.

She stood and walked quickly across the hot pool deck. For a moment she paused at the water's edge, gazing up at the main house with its flights of stone steps zigzagging to its back entry. There was a time when that facade only made her think of her father and his sad end and the terrible way she'd betrayed him. But as the days passed, she'd begun to see that he'd died with dignity, happy to have his daughter home, and that the house was a legacy of the fantastical life he had imagined for himself and then made real. It was as shimmering and solid now as on the nights he had thrown his famous parties there, and it remained a safe haven to his two children—Cordelia, who had only been reunited with him in May, and Charlie, who was now running the bootlegging business that had made Darius Grey rich and famous.

A ripple of gratitude passed over Cordelia, and she even smiled a little to think how satisfied Darius would be to know his offspring were still sheltered under that fine roof. Then she sprang forward, arms overhead so that her body went like an arrow into the cool water. Beneath the surface there was true silence, and she sailed forward on the momentum of her dive as long as she could. It was serene and quiet, and she remembered that in her dream she had been flying.

Cordelia came up for air and took three strong strokes to the end of the pool. She breathed in and pushed the strands of her hair away from her face. Then she realized that someone—not one of the girls, for it was a man's voice—was calling her name. As she pushed herself onto the edge and twisted around, she caught sight of him. One of Charlie's men was standing on the other side of the low, white-washed wall that surrounded the pool. He was wearing an undershirt, darkened in places by sweat, and he was trying not to look at the girls in their revealing suits. Astrid was Charlie Grey's fiancée; no one would want to be accused of staring at his girl when she wasn't wearing much clothing.

"Sorry to interrupt, Miss Grey."

"That's all right . . ." She smiled at him, trying to remember his name.

"Victor."

He smiled back, and she realized that he wasn't truly afraid, and that he was taking as much pleasure in the long July day as she was. Charlie's gang had the run of the place—there were always men who worked for her brother in one capacity or another walking the lawns, guarding the gate, smoking around the card table, or sleeping in the attic—but she didn't mind. It was part of the life, and anyway, these men in sweat-stained undershirts had much better stories than the ones where she came from.

"That's all right, Victor."

"Charlie'd like to see you."

Cordelia's eyes drifted to the lush greenery stretching out beyond the pool, the rolling hills and the shadows of trees growing long across the grass. The afternoon had been so tranquil and perfect; there had been no hurry about anything, and she had swum and joked with her best friends since just after breakfast. To go in so abruptly struck her as sad. "Tell him I'll be up in a minute." She sighed and turned toward the chaises.

"What did he want?" Astrid asked, pushing herself up on slender arms when Cordelia returned to their little encampment.

"It's Charlie—I've got to go back to the house now." Cordelia pulled a linen tunic over her head and reached for a towel to wring out her hair.

"I suppose I ought to get out of the sun, too," Astrid said, her tone careless. "I told my wretched mother I'd dine with them, you know, and I'll be late if I spend any more time baking. Let's meet up later though, shouldn't we? Maybe put on something new and shiny and go into the city and dance till dawn. Letty, don't you move, the maid will come down and collect all this." She gestured at the tray of sandwiches and the lemonade pitcher and piles of magazines that lay around their chairs. "You should stay and enjoy the rest of the day."

Then Astrid put her arm around Cordelia's waist, tipped

her hat forward, and the two began to climb the hill toward the house arm in arm.

Letty paused awkwardly—she had half raised herself to go into the house with the other two, but had frozen when Astrid casually instructed her not to move. She watched her oldest friend glide toward the house in tandem with Miss Donal, who always seemed to mean kindly, but whose manner was so detached that it was difficult for Letty not to feel like a simple girl from Ohio in her presence. Even on a day like today when she wore no jewelry, Astrid had a shimmering quality as though she were covered in diamond dust.

Back in Union—the small Ohio town that they'd left at the beginning of the season, only a couple of months before (although it seemed longer ago than that), and where Letty's siblings and widower father still lived—Cordelia had been the one person who made Letty believe that her dreams of singing onstage in New York City were not ridiculous. But in the month since she had come to live at Dogwood, Letty had done little to pursue those dreams, and she couldn't help but worry, every now and then, that the string of gorgeous afternoons spent like this—lazy and happy and well-fed—were ticking by while other girls worked their way up from the chorus line to solo roles not far away on Broadway. These kinds of thoughts agitated Letty, and whenever they arose she buried them quickly, then tried to smile at whoever was nearby and do something delightful, or else help with any household chore that needed doing.

But that agitation was harder to bury when she was alone, and as the figures of Astrid and Cordelia grew small approaching the great house, she couldn't help but notice how much more natural her old friend was in this setting. She had those high cheekbones and long limbs, and that impressive way of carrying herself that had earned her the disdain of many of the small-town folks in Union ("uppity," they called her) but had caused her close friends to hang on her every word. Even next to Astrid, who had grown up around thoroughbreds and china tea services and yachts and couture, Cordelia did not look a tiny bit out of place.

Letty reached under her chair and felt for the head of Good Egg, her greyhound, who was hiding from the heat. The dog whimpered and lifted her head for more scratching. For another minute, Letty obliged. Then she sank back against the cushioned chaise, pulled her soft robe close around her neck, and turned the page of her fashion magazine, which contained any number of handsome things that, remarkably, it might actually be possible for her to acquire. If any of the people back in Union could see her now—the very picture of sophistication, lounging in rich environs with her sleek, long-legged pet—they would be struck dumb by the miracle of it all.

A smile tugged at the corners of her mouth. After all,

tomorrow would be just as lovely as today, and there was lots of summer left, and plenty of time yet for her to go about making a name for herself down in Manhattan.

"Letty's really become one of us," Astrid said as they went up the stone steps to the south-facing terrace. Once, not long ago, Cordelia had stood on that spot with her father while he taught her how to shoot grapefruit out of the sky.

"I know how to pick 'em, don't I?" Cordelia's skin had by then almost dried from the heat.

"She's awfully bright."

They stepped into the ballroom, with its gleaming, rarely used dance floor and white grand piano, and continued on toward the main hallway. The girls let go of each other and Cordelia passed into the unlit hall, where she had to pause so that her eyes could adjust. Although the ceiling soared three stories above and some natural light filtered from the third-floor windows, the dark wood of the stairs and walls could sometimes create a gloomy effect even on the sunniest days.

"Charlie's up in the billiard room." Victor's voice surprised her, and her breath caught in her throat as the outline of his shoulders emerged from the shadow.

"Thank you."

"I had better go," Astrid said. "If I see Charlie he'll be all over me, and then I'll be late, and Mummy will be angry, and before you know it, we *won't* be able to go into the city tonight."

"But your dress is still upstairs in my room," Cordelia said.

"Oh, so what? I have plenty more, you know."

They both laughed, and then Astrid presented her cheek for a good-bye kiss.

"Don't forget there's a party at Cass Beaumont's tomorrow afternoon for the Fourth of July—I want there to be a whole gang of us."

"All right." As the girls parted, Cordelia turned to Victor. "Will you drive Miss Donal home?"

Once he had nodded in agreement, she turned and hurried up the stairs to the billiard room, which Charlie had begun to use as a sort of unofficial headquarters since their father's death. In Dogwood's previous life—when it had belonged to a family that made their money in some respectable way and presumably took tea in the afternoon and no doubt practiced impeccable manners—this room had been used as a parlor. But now it was furnished with three wide, green felt–topped tables and a few Victorian settees. These had been pushed to the walls and were looking a little worse for wear after being handled so often by rough young men.

The door onto the second-floor hall was cracked, so she slipped in without anyone noticing her.

"Oh ho, there's no getting out of this one alive," her

brother was saying to Danny, one of the guards, as he bent forward over the table to take his shot. Charlie's broad shoulders flared like a cobra's hood as he pulled the cue back.

Cordelia rested her shoulder against the wall by the door. An open pack of cigarettes sat on a small antique-looking table, and she reached down and drew one out along with a match from the matchbox that lay beside it. Smoking would never have been allowed in her aunt Ida's house, where she grew up, and probably would have earned her a slap across the face and a sermon about the grim ends that awaited girls who indulged such a filthy habit. But here no one cared and Cordelia had developed a taste for it. Especially when she was nervous, which she sometimes was around Charlie. There was a camaraderie between them, and he was brotherly and protective of her—but there were also times when she reminded him of the way their father had died, and her foolish involvement in the tragedy, and then she saw the anger in his fierce brown eyes.

At the same instant that she struck the match her brother took his shot, and the smack of the cue ball hitting its mark rung out to the high picture moldings. There was crowing from around the room, and Charlie moved busily to the other side of the table. Cordelia inhaled and let her eyes drift up, and then she noticed that Elias Jones, who had been her father's right-hand man, was watching her. He was about the same age as her father, and he had that long, horse face with features that never moved much. He didn't blink, and she became self-conscious of her appearance. Her hair was wavy from the water, her legs naked under the tunic, and her feet were bare. The skin on the bridge of her nose was surely redder than the rest of her face, and her brown eyes probably had that washed-out quality they took on after too many hours in the sun.

There was another loud *thwack* from the pool table, and Cordelia glanced away from Jones.

"Ha!" Charlie said, as the eight ball rolled into the corner pocket.

Danny shook his head and cursed under his breath. He shook Charlie's hand and said "Well-played," but he didn't seem happy about it.

"Cordelia is here," Jones announced.

"Good!" Charlie turned, handing his cue off to Danny and giving his sister a rakish grin. Smiling back, she put out her cigarette. "Cord, come talk with Jones and me. There's something we want you to do for us."

Charlie threw his arm around Cordelia's shoulders, and under that strong shelter she allowed herself to be drawn down the hall. Charlie's office, if one could call it that, was not as grandly kept as their father's had been. There was a large mahogany desk with only a telephone and several empty glasses on it. She had never asked Charlie why he didn't use the library downstairs, where Darius Grey had given his orders, but she felt she already knew the answer. That was where the secret passageway originated from, the one that the gunman who assassinated their father had escaped through. Cordelia couldn't so much as think of it without a shudder running down her spine, because it was she who had made the fatal error of showing the passageway to Thom Hale, back when she was infatuated with him and had not yet come to understand the ugly history between their families.

The makeshift office did the job, and the view through its high, curtainless windows of Dogwood's west lawn, stretching out to the hedge labyrinth, was as impressive as any gold-edged books or satinwood chairs. Charlie pushed a few of the glasses out of the way, propped himself against the desk, and gave Cordelia an intent, twinkling stare.

When Cordelia first met Charlie—by chance, at a place called Seventh Heaven, before she was anybody—she had not liked him, and he had not liked her. A day or two later, when she was restored to her father, he hadn't immediately taken to the idea that she was his half sister, either. On occasion, Cordelia had wondered at them being related at all—but in moments like these she got a glimpse of their shared parentage. He could be hot while she was cool, but they were unmistakably cut from the same cloth. They were both tall with light-colored hair and sweet brown eyes that shone and searched at the same time.

"Smoke?" Charlie took the pack from his front pocket and

Cordelia pulled one out. Jones lit it for her, and then retreated to the edge of the room and leaned against the bare wall.

"Thank you."

"Dad wouldn't like what a tough broad you're becoming," Charlie said, with a smile and wink.

Cordelia inhaled and watched her brother reflectively—he was joking, she knew, but how much she couldn't be certain. "I don't know how tough a broad I can be when I never leave the house."

This was not, of course, the New York life that she'd imagined for herself on those lonely, bleak nights back in Ohio. There had been plenty of trees and quiet there, and she had longed instead for noise. She'd imagined busy, epic evenings during which she would meet a great variety of people. Astrid, meanwhile, was always trying to convince her to go out, but in her grief, Cordelia hadn't felt like having fun, and even if she had, it wouldn't have seemed appropriate. Instead she'd spent her days obsessively going over the hours that had culminated in her father's murder. She played back the reel of those days again and again, trying to locate the moment when she went wrong, imagining that if she closed her eyes and concentrated hard enough, she could return there and make the story come out differently. It had been a sleepless, nervous time, and if Letty hadn't been there, checking in on her with those round blue eyes, gently encouraging her not to drown in grief,

Cordelia might have given up on eating and bathing entirely. Smoking seemed to her the least of the bad little habits she could have picked up.

"Cord, please. You don't have to stay in the house forever, and anyway, you can't live in the past." Charlie smiled at her in a softer way now, bringing her out of her thoughts and back into the spare office. "If Dad thought you weren't having a good time, he'd figure out how to come back to life just to kill me."

"But your absence—that has gotten a lot of attention." Jones leaned forward and put his fist against the desk, watching Cordelia. A few lines emerged in his forehead—the most dramatic facial expression he ever made. "That's why we wanted to speak to you."

"Exactly." Charlie jumped down from the desk and crossed the floor a few times excitedly. "See, Jones and me, we decided not to take vengeance on Duluth Hale for what he did to Dad in any ordinary way. At first I wanted to strike him down, of course, but Jones convinced me it would be better to work slow, methodical. Really hurt him. Hurt him by taking away everything he's got. And we've made progress. We've near edged him out of Manhattan. Only a few speakeasies left get their liquor from the Hales."

"How'd you do that?"

A manic light crossed Charlie's eye. "Don't worry about that, princess. What I want you to worry about is something else. Everyone knows the Greys control New York's hotels. That's because Dad was such a class guy, and because he always knew how to get the real stuff from Europe. We've managed to hold that, even without him as our leader. Now we control most of New York's speakeasies, too . . . and to show how big we're getting, we want to open a place of our own."

"A speakeasy." Jones leaned back, crossing his arms over his chest. "To show the public, not to mention the rest of the bootleggers, we're strong as ever. That we still got class."

"This place will be our gem, Cord."

"I'm glad business is good." Cordelia's eyes went from one man to the other. It felt even more inappropriate to have spent the day lying by the pool after hearing all Charlie had done to get them out of the mess she'd created. "But what does that have to do with me?"

Charlie gestured at Jones, who produced a few newspaper clippings. Cordelia rested what remained of her cigarette between her lips and stepped forward.

GREY THE BOOTLEGGER'S DAUGHTER: AN AMERICAN TALE OF OUTRAGEOUS FORTUNE AND UNBELIEVABLE LOSS, read the headline. Cordelia scanned the page. It contained a rather exaggerated version of her pauper upbringing far away, her coming-out on the charmed lawns of White Cove, and her introduction, shortly thereafter, into the adult world of pain when she watched her father expire with her very eyes.

"They're all curious about you, Cord."

"Me? Why?"

"Because you're interesting to them. You're beautiful, but not the way they are, and something awful happened to you. And, of course, because as of late, you've made yourself scarce."

"People don't want to take their eyes off a thing like that," Jones interjected.

"Oh." Cordelia sighed, exhaling a cloud of smoke that obscured her view, and then put her cigarette out in the ashtray on the desk. How strange, she thought, that the very thing that closed her off from the rest of the world should make her so fascinating to it. "So what do you want me to do?"

"We want you to run the place."

She tried not to look shocked. "The speakeasy?"

Charlie nodded. "We got a lot of power behind this thing. I put my muscle up against the Hales every day—you don't have to worry about nothing like that. You're gonna be the pretty face of the operation."

"We'll find you the place, all that," Jones said. "Don't worry."

"Oh." Cordelia felt a little stunned, but she wasn't worried. For a month now she had wondered what she could ever do that would make right the way she'd betrayed her father. But with his dying breath he'd declared her an heir to his business, too, and now she saw how she was going to get the chance to prove herself. What Charlie and Jones had proposed brought her no anxiety at all; in fact, it sounded like fun. "Of course! I'd be honored."

"Good!" Charlie clapped his hands and wrapped his arm around his sister's shoulders once again. "Now, I want you to go get dolled up. No more pool clothes. We're going to have dinner as a family, just like Dad would have wanted. Leave the details to Jones for now—but be ready. We're going to need the infamous Cordelia Grey working for us soon."

2

NOT FAR FROM DOGWOOD, DOWN THE LITTLE COUNTRY lanes that skimmed the edges of farms, stood a very different kind of house. It looked similar enough from the outside, with its impressive bulk and Tudor flourishes and leaded glass windows, its multiple chimneys just visible above the high hedges that surrounded the property, its lawns sloping down to a well-manicured orchard. But it lay across an invisible line, perceptible only to a chosen few, which separated the old White Cove from the one where the newcomers lived. Marsh Hall was named for the man who had built it, and it was still occupied by his descendents. It was half a mile closer to the White Cove Country Club, and while it may on occasion have been known for a scandalous evening or two, nothing ever happened there to make necessary armed guards.

These were differences that Astrid Donal, riding home to Marsh Hall in one of the Greys' Daimlers, had been trained to see from a young age but chose not to notice. She could be perceptive, and in three years at Miss Porter's, her boarding school in Farmington, Connecticut, she had proved that she could be a good student when she put her mind to it. But among her other talents were forgetting what she did not like and ignoring what she preferred not to see.

As the car sped along the road that ran by the water, she let her eyes close, breathing in the salty air, and did not even bother to open them when the car swerved and went up the gravel drive toward the house. It had been such an absolutely perfect day, and Astrid felt sure that even if she *were* the sort to keep a long memory, she wouldn't be able to recall a time of such contentment. Cordelia was a true friend, and then about a month ago she had multiplied herself, and now there was Letty, who was such a delightful little fairy creature, always entertaining everyone with some silly face or gorgeous gesture. Meanwhile, someday in the not-so-distant future, she and Charlie were to be wed. Charlie Grey was the most exciting person she had ever met—at least, she had thought so until she'd met his sister, Cordelia—and he had been her boyfriend over a year now, and as of a month ago, she'd been calling him her fiancé. This was all a good riot, and a good riot was what she lived for.

Astrid had left Farmington with the notion that she was not to return, and at the end of a day like this one, she felt even more convinced of it. Her home was here in White Cove, and with the golden light warming the skin of her eyelids, she wondered vaguely if summer couldn't just roll on forever.

"We're here."

"Oh!" The car had come to a stop, and when Astrid opened her eyes she saw her mother's third husband's grand house standing stolidly before them. Its high stone walls seemed to offer enduring sanctuary, but Astrid knew from a childhood spent living out of suitcases and hotel rooms that any impression of that kind was illusion. She smoothed her bright yellow hair down over her ears and smiled a thank-you at the young man who'd driven her home. He was wearing an undershirt tucked into brown trousers, and he had a prominent nose and olive coloring, as though his grandfather were perhaps Italian. His lashes were thick and black. "What was your name again?" she asked.

He opened his mouth to tell her, but she laughed before he had the chance to make a sound.

"Oh, never mind, I'll only forget it. Thank you so much for the ride!"

"Victor," he said with a grin. "My name is Victor."

But by then she had jumped out and hurried up the stairs.

The house was quiet as she went through it. She loitered a moment in the hall outside her room, examining her reflection in the large gilt-framed mirror there, taking pleasure in her appearance after an exquisitely lazy day. Her rich yellow hair was cut short, so that its thick strands—a little puffy after drying in the sun—curled in at her cheekbones. She had the soft, heart-shaped face of a girl who is well fed, but the slim limbs of a lady whose clothes are custom made for her. Her old black suit clung to her small waist in a way that she was not embarrassed to recognize as quite fetching.

When she stepped inside her own room, she saw that the maid had been there. The pale pink bedclothes were crisp and smooth beneath the half-moon polished oak headboard, the dresses she'd decided not to wear the night before had been put away, and the windows were open to allow the breeze to pass through. This room—with its walls painted a glacial shade, its cream coved ceiling, its simple handsome furniture with subdued marquetry details—always had a quieting effect on her. It was one of a long string of rooms that she had occupied, not the finest, but far from the worst.

Astrid knew that her mother's dinner guests would be arriving soon, and that she ought to bathe and dress immediately. If she delayed even a moment, it might impede her slipping out early, back to Dogwood. But the laziness of the day was entirely too pleasing, and she decided that it wouldn't matter much if just for a moment she crawled up on the bed and put her face against the cool, clean sheet.

"Astrid?"

The voice belonged to her mother; Astrid grimaced.

A *rat-tat-tat* of insistent knocks on the door followed, after which she rolled over and opened her eyes. The light coming in her window was decidedly more dusklike than when she'd returned to Marsh Hall, and her mouth was chalky and dry. When she realized she had been asleep, she grew cross—she should have said hello to Charlie before she left Dogwood, for at this rate her mother would make her stay all through dinner and she wouldn't get to kiss him again until tomorrow.

"Astrid Donal, they're arriving now," her mother said as she pushed open the door and came into the room.

Virginia Donal de Gruyter Marsh's hair was dark, but otherwise her appearance was not unlike her daughter's— they had the same features, although those belonging to the older lady had thickened with age and her cheeks were more hollowed out. She wore an excessive amount of dark eye makeup, to distract from the ditches her late nights left under her lower lids. It gave her a severe appearance, especially early on in an evening, or when she stood beside her fresh-faced daughter.

For a moment she seemed to be giving Astrid a stare of imperious indignation, but then a small, dry smile began to form at the corners of her mouth. "Come—if you get dressed right now, we shall be just exactly late enough."

Astrid extended her hands reluctantly and allowed herself to be pulled to her feet. It was well known around White Cove that Virginia liked a party just as well as her daughter did, and maybe better. "Interesting" people were her favorite hobby. She collected them: the type who did gay things late at night and smoked cigarettes in mixed company, those who would have most certainly scandalized her own mother. These predilections, however, were not lost on Virginia's third husband, Harrison Marsh II, who was himself no saint and who had also been married twice before, but who shared some of his ancestors' disdain for publicity. Astrid couldn't help but agree with him a little—there was nothing so odious to her as seeing her own mother in the morning, washed up after some all-night revel and demanding to hear the gossip of the younger generation over strong coffee.

But the third Mrs. Marsh had, in truth, been rather well behaved since she'd returned to Marsh Hall following a bad marital spat a month ago and an ill-advised stay at the St. Regis. There was an almost healthy light to her green eyes now and Astrid couldn't—even after trying—remember the last time her mother had done something truly shaming.

"But I haven't got anything to wear," Astrid groaned, which earned her a skeptical glance from her mother, for this particular protest was too absurd to have any teeth.

"Nonsense. You'll wear the black silk from Worth, the sleeveless one with the complicated turquoise and peach pinwheel beadwork, and those little black high-heeled slippers."

This was, in fact, precisely what Astrid would have picked for herself, even though she couldn't help but notice that the prescribed outfit would make her look rather like her mother's twin. The older lady wore a get-up of billowy black chiffon that left her shoulders naked; it was slightly gathered below the hips, and shining here and there with curlicues of jet.

"Oh, all right." Astrid went into the closet, where she kicked off her suit and pulled a black slip over her head. Her skin was dry from lying in the sun, and it smelled slightly of pool water. But there was no time to take a shower, and she secretly liked the idea of wearing such an expensive dress when her skin still bore the dust of the day. Her cheeks and shoulders glowed naturally, and her tousled hair looked much better than anything she could have done sitting in front of her mirror with sprays and tonics.

"Here you go." Her mother appeared in the closet's doorway and pulled the dress from a wall full of frocks.

"Thanks, darling," Astrid said, and then thrust her arms in

the air so that her mother could put it on over her head the way she had when Astrid was a child.

"So," her mother continued, as the dark silk fell over Astrid's face, "you've been spending quite a lot of days at Dogwood, haven't you?"

"Yes." The dress slithered down her body, swinging loosely from her collarbone and skimming the skin just below her knees. When Astrid's eyes were no longer covered, she gave her mother a crooked glance and then proceeded to the dressing table, lowering herself onto the little round chair in front of the vanity. "Of course I am," she went on blithely. "Cordelia Grey is my best friend—and as you yourself often say, a very fascinating creature—and Charlie is my fiancé."

"Of course, darling, it's always a party there, why *wouldn't* you spend your days at Dogwood?" Virginia followed her daughter, taking one step and then another until their eyes met in the big, round mirror. "I'm only wondering because—"

"Oh, don't start that again," Astrid interrupted as she plucked a lipstick from the several gold tubes that occupied her dressing table. At the beginning of the summer, when it had seemed altogether likely that Harrison might demand a divorce, and Virginia had been despairing of what would become of them if they were thrown out of Marsh Hall, she had suggested that Astrid might do well to marry Charlie, whose family was plenty wealthy from the booze trade. Of course, that was before Charlie had proposed to her, when marriage had seemed like something she might do in a hundred years. "We've only just got engaged, and I won't be hurried into anything just because you are worried about who's going to pay for our next trip to Worth's—"

But her mother surprised her by interrupting with a quiet "Oh, good."

Astrid watched her mother's lips soften into a smile in the reflection. The younger girl narrowed her eyes. "Good?"

"I'm glad to hear it," Virginia replied carefully. "You see, I've been feeling guilty about pressuring you at all, and though I think it a fine thing that Charlie is so devoted, I also want to impart to you my belief that there really is no hurry." Virginia pulled an upholstered stool from the corner and dragged it so that she could sit down beside Astrid and take her hand. "In my day, if you so much as kissed a boy, you had to marry him immediately lest you be ruined—barbaric time *that* was. But we live in a more enlightened era, and you have so much of your life before you, and it seems a shame to shackle yourself to one man so soon."

Astrid widened her eyes and fixed them on her own expression as she used her free hand to dab a poppy tint on her full lips. "Everything is all right between you and Harrison, then?"

"Oh, yes!" Virginia let go of Astrid's hand and took the

lipstick to darken her own mouth. "I married too young, that was my problem, when I was still so curious about the world and wanted to see so many things and have a good time and not be weighed down by the keeping of a house and the raising of children. Harrison and I have made our mistakes, of course, but we can be honest with each other in a way we never could have been in our early years. Both of us can admit when we are wrong and forgive one another. *That* is the difference."

Astrid opened her mouth without any idea of what to say, but before her throat could produce sound, they heard the quick blaring of a car horn trumpeting someone's arrival, and her mother stood up and crossed the room to see who it was.

"Ah," her mother announced, "the Duchess of Malden is here."

For a moment Astrid remained at the vanity, drawing her fingers over her wishbone cheeks and along her taut little neck. She *was* especially pretty that summer, and suddenly it did seem a shame—a tiny one—that Charlie should be the only beneficiary of her radiance. Astrid's ears rung and her skin itched, as they always did when her mother said something logical. Then she quickly blackened her lashes and fluffed her hair.

"That is quite a dress," the older woman said, in a tone that was equal parts admiring and disdainful, as she watched the latest arrivals parading from their car to the house. Astrid stood and joined her mother by the window. Already several cars were parked on the front lawn; out beyond them the sun was going down over Long Island Sound. On the first floor of the house, her mother's guests would be ordering their first round of aperitifs and growing rosy as they waited for their hostess. "And that must be the Irish boxer she has escorting her these days."

At first Astrid was disappointed to realize that the boxer in question was a man and not a puppy, but as the couple crossed the lawn, she found that she did want to know more about them both. They were undoubtedly worthy of collection. The duchess was wearing a gown of cerise chiffon, which showed off her calves but trailed behind her almost to her ankles. A gold turban covered her hair. Her limbs were so long and delicate and English that she seemed hardly able to stand up on her own, and she leaned heavily on the large fellow next to her, who was handsome despite the fact that his face appeared to have been rearranged once or twice.

"I thought you would have *wanted* me to marry Charlie," Astrid said quietly as she and her mother watched the couple disappear into the foyer below. It would never have occurred to her to do anything to please her mother, but their conversation by the vanity had left her feeling muddled and confused for reasons she could scarcely understand.

"Oh, darling, I want whatever makes you most happy." Her mother turned from the window, so that the last of the daylight lit up the edges of her features, and sighed. "Only—think about what I said. It has always been my wish that you will benefit from my mistakes."

And there have been a lot of those, Astrid briefly considered replying. But her mother really was being unusually decent, and it seemed unsporting to reply harshly. By now the wheels in Astrid's head were turning, and she was beginning to wonder if a husband wasn't always an encumbrance, no matter how shiny and tall. "Thanks, Mummy, I promise I'll think about it very carefully."

As they descended the stairs toward the party, Astrid even reached out for her mother's hand, and the two exchanged a fleeting smile of understanding. A quarter of an hour ago, all she had wanted was to get the evening over with so she could be with Charlie, but now she wanted to stay here at Marsh Hall as long as there was laughter.

"Ah, you see," Virginia whispered, lifting their joined hands as they descended the final stair. "I needn't have worried about it being too serious. He hasn't even given you an engagement ring!"

Then the third Mrs. Marsh let go of her daughter's hand and stepped forward into the room with her arms raised. "Oh, you've all arrived early, you good little darlings!" she crowed as she began circling the room and planting kisses on her guests' faces.

Astrid hesitated a minute in the door frame, looking at

her naked finger. It was a pretty finger, but now it looked sad and neglected to her.

"And this, I presume, is your beautiful daughter," the Duchess of Malden said in her crisp accent.

Astrid glanced up. The Englishwoman's eyebrows were painted on in high arcs.

"We hear you are engaged to a bootlegger. How entertaining! You must tell us *everything*."

The other faces in the parlor turned toward the doorway, their expressions frozen in happy expectation.

"I am!" Astrid smiled brilliantly, to distract from her lonely finger. She suddenly wondered if other people had noticed and secretly felt sorry for her, calling herself engaged when there was no jewelry to prove it. "But he's a bore. *I'm* the bright one, so you see you are very lucky because tonight I'm not interested in telling you a single thing about Charlie Grey, and all I want to talk about is me, me, me!"

Everyone laughed and raised their glasses to the young girl. At just that moment around White Cove, groups like this one were coalescing, and who knew what modish clothing would be removed or bizarre confessions made in the course of the evening. The Irish boxer cracked a grin, and Astrid caught a flash of gold amongst his disordered teeth. A little steel settled in her heart, for she wasn't the kind of girl who hurried off to anybody, especially if that somebody wasn't in the habit of buying engagement rings.

3

"OH, TERRIBLY SORRY!" LETTY LARKSPUR EXCLAIMED,
even though the man with the straw boater perched far back
on his head had, in truth, knocked into her. Perhaps she
seemed somehow unworthy of acknowledgment; maybe her
lack of height, or something about her dress, marked her as
a humble and inconsequential kind of girl. In any event, he
went on ignoring her, positioning himself so that he separated
Letty from her friend Cordelia. At the center of the circle stood
Cordelia's brother, Charlie, in a lemon yellow suit, loudly telling a story and waving a half-full mint julep around. There was
something she secretly disliked about Charlie's stories, and she
had more or less given up trying to follow this one.

All across the vast, low-lying lawn, young people in summer-weight suits and little white shifts gathered in groups, laughing and eating fried chicken from china plates. It was the Fourth of July, but a Fourth of July party hosted by Astrid's swanky friends was unlike any Independence Day celebration Letty had ever witnessed. The hosts lived in a gigantic white house with tall columns on both sides, and their substantial grounds had been given over to the cause of celebration. A large band played animatedly on a wooden platform, but the sun was still high in the sky and it was too hot for anyone to really consider dancing. A few billowy clouds hung over the reflective water, threatening nothing. The sky was a very rich blue.

Letty leaned forward, trying to catch Cordelia's eye to see if she might want to walk down by the shore and look at the boats. But the man in the pink seersucker was guffawing and slapping his knee now, so it was difficult to get a proper view.

"Oh, well," Letty sighed out loud. And when Cordelia didn't look over, Letty turned and walked down toward the water alone.

She supposed she ought to hang on Charlie's stories the way everyone else did, and of course it was very grand of him to let her live with Cordelia in the beautifully decorated suite on the third floor of Dogwood, and to eat the food and wear the clothes his criminal activities paid for. But she had never been able to shake her first impression of Charlie, when he had mocked her for being surprised by the taste of beer. Of course she had never tasted beer before—up until then, her name had been Letitia Haubstadt, and she had lived according to the strict rules of the dairy-farming Haubstadt family of Union, Ohio, which made no allowances for soda pop, much less alcohol.

She could still hear him as she meandered over the grass toward the high reeds that marked the edges of the estate. Beyond them sand stretched out to the glassy surface of the cove, and she began to smell the salt water and hear the sounds of birds. In this part of the world even the wildness appeared contained and somehow genteel, and when she stood here, alone, with her spectator heels half sunk in the ground and her pleated white skirt blown against her legs by the wind, she was able to imagine, just for a moment, that she was one of those fancy girls who laughed so easily with boys in blazers whom they'd known since childhood.

"Miss Letty, we haven't received your RSVP for the garden party!" she tried to imagine Cass Beaumont (to whom Astrid had briefly attempted to introduce Letty on their way in, before being distracted by a classmate) calling to her. And then Letty would widen her eyes, lower her bottom lip slightly, and gasp that she was *so* sorry, it was only that she'd had such an unusual number of invitations that month—it was an oversight, and she would see to it immediately.

"Letty—is that you?"

It took her several seconds to realize that this time someone really had said her name. Blushing despite her best efforts, she turned to see who might possibly have recognized her among all these fine folks. When she saw him, half of her wanted to leap in joy at the sight of a familiar face, and the other half recoiled in shame for what the writer Grady Lodge, emerging improbably from among the White Cove gentry, knew about her.

The last time she'd seen him was the worst day she had spent in New York yet—she had lost her job and been thrown out of her apartment, her head hurt on account of drinking gin, and she was facing the unhappy prospect of returning to Ohio and all her father's wrath. Grady had been the only person she could think of who was kind, and she had been searching for him to ask for help. But when she found him he'd had a pretty lady on his arm, and she had not had the courage to interrupt. And Grady knew more about her than that—he knew she'd been taken in by a snake in the grass named Amory Glenn, who purported to be a theatrical producer but who was in fact a letch. He also knew that for a while she'd worked as a cigarette girl, which was not something she'd thought to feel ashamed of until she started going to parties like these ones, where everyone belonged to a country club and knew each other from boarding school.

For another few moments she blinked her lashes and straightened her spine and tried to look like a Miss Porter's girl. But then she saw the way Grady was smiling at her, and her face broke into a smile back. They had never so much as kissed, but she'd known from the way he used to watch her from his bar stool at Seventh Heaven that he fancied her, and it was pleasant to be admired again. The sun had turned his fair skin a little pink, which made his hair appear especially light. It was parted down the middle and rose up on either side, and he was wearing an ivory suit not unlike those favored by the other young men at the party. Although his eyes were set deep in his face, they had a fine, clear quality that had always made her trust him. There was no pretending not to know him now, for he had come forward and taken her hand and kissed it.

"Why, Miss Larkspur, I thought we'd lost you for good."

"No, no . . . it's only that I thought I'd try the country for a while."

"It suits you." Grady beamed. "Shall I ask you how you came to be here, or would I be wiser not to count my blessings?"

Letty's little mouth hung open, but before she could begin to explain, she saw a woman approaching over Grady's shoulder. Her thoughts scattered when she realized it was the same woman he had greeted on that cruel sidewalk.

Clusters of diamonds and pearls dangled from her earlobes and shone from her wrists, and her skirt swished confidently over her feminine thighs. Letty stepped backward, thinking that perhaps Grady would not want his new girl to see him talking to his old crush. But this step did not result in her being any less conspicuous. She felt her shoe sinking into the soft, muddy ground at the edge of the reeds and her arms flailed gracelessly.

"Careful!" Grady reached out and pulled her back to more solid ground.

Meanwhile, the woman with russet hair had arrived at his side. Her eyes, wide with curiosity, moved back and forth between Letty and Grady, whose strong arm was still holding her up. Letty's breath began to settle and her heart to slow to normal, and though she knew the appropriate thing to do would be to draw away from him, she remained as she was, leaning on him for support.

"Dorothy, this is a friend of mine." Grady's lady friend did not seem in the least put out by the presence of another female; her red lips bent upward into a sincere smile. The rather pathetic thought that she herself must not look like much of a threat was just beginning to dawn on Letty when Grady announced: "Letty Larkspur, meet my sister, Dorothy Cobb."

"Oh!" A moment ago Letty had been embarrassed by the sight of Grady Lodge—but now the revelation that the girl she'd believed to be the object of his affection was in fact a relation filled her with relief. "It's such a pleasure to meet you," she went on, taking Dorothy's hand and shaking it perhaps more exuberantly than was necessary.

"Not *the* Letty?" said Dorothy.

"Yes." Grady gave Letty a sheepish look. "I've told Mrs. Cobb a thing or two about you, I'm afraid."

"That's all right!" Letty had spent the morning feeling almost invisible amongst the crowd, and being recognized even in this tiny way made her smile genuine and wide. "Grady was one of the first people to be kind to me when I arrived in the city."

"Oh—you're not from New York, then?"

"No, I—" Letty broke off and glanced at Grady, wondering what exactly he'd told her, if the part about running away from Ohio had not been included. "Not originally," she concluded vaguely.

"Well," Dorothy replied, with exaggerated politesse, "it's certainly wonderful to have finally met you."

She bowed her polished head and turned to walk back across the lawn, where she was quickly intercepted by a woman similarly adorned with jewels.

"My sister married Stillwell Cobb, of the logging fortune Cobbs, hence the invitation to this soiree." Only now did he let go of Letty's arm. He put his hands in his pockets and shifted his weight forward and back on his heels. "She's pretty well taken care of, as you can see."

"Yes, I do see." So that was how Grady Lodge, who wrote short stories for little publications, came to be here at the Beaumonts' on the Fourth of July.

Letty averted her eyes self-consciously and pressed her palms into her white cotton skirt, smoothing out wrinkles that may or may not have been visible to the human eye. "Would you like to go down by the shore and watch the boats come and go with me?"

"Nothing would suit me better." Grady laced his arm through hers again and they began to amble slowly along the water's edge. "But you must tell me—and start from the beginning, and don't leave anything out—everything that has happened to you since last we met . . ."

Should she include the part about how Amory Glenn had slapped her face and insisted that she remove her clothes before an audience of howling men, or the long night she had spent alone in Pennsylvania Station wondering what would become of her? A mere glimpse of these memories made her cheeks sting, her pride ache. She took a breath of salty air and changed the subject by pointing at a passing waiter. "Would you like a drink, Mr. Lodge?"

"No, thank you. I am perfectly content with my state of mind as is, Miss Larkspur." Perhaps he saw how this made

Letty blush, for in the next moment he added: "Plus, in my profession, when one is in a new social situation, one likes to have one's wits about them, the better to observe."

They had reached the part of the lawn closest to the water and sat down on one of the beautiful blankets that had been spread out for the after-dark fireworks display.

"Is that what you write about? Rich people spending carefree afternoons . . ." When she heard her words said out loud, they had a harsh sound that surprised her—all afternoon she had been intimidated by the gorgeous opulence of the Beaumonts' party, and she still felt a little like a child staring through the plate glass at a sweet shop display that she hadn't the coins to indulge in.

Grady looked amused. "Among other things. But I'm still learning. I don't know what my subject will be when I become a real writer."

"How do you know when you're a real writer?"

His deep-set gray eyes twinkled and he sighed self-deprecatingly. "I don't know. I certainly spend plenty of time at my writing desk. When people are begging me to let them print my newest story instead of me begging them to read it, I guess."

"I'd like to call myself a real singer . . ." Letty shrugged and turned her eyes toward the blue expanse above them and trailed off. But as she fidgeted with her hem, considering whether to finish the thought, she sensed that he was watching her intently, and this made her feel she really should say something more. "But I can't do that until I have a band to sing with, can I?"

"Ah, but I've heard you sing, and you do it beautifully—a band won't make you any more or less a singer."

Letty smiled faintly and turned her face away from the compliment. "I haven't read any of your stories, but still—I might say the same to you."

"Fair enough." Grady returned her smile. "You are a real singer and I am a real writer—and may we both find grander stages soon."

There was something handsomer in the architecture of Grady's face than the last time she'd seen him, and she wanted to go on staring at it, to pinpoint exactly what that quality was and give it a name. Something inside her, despite her upbringing, even wanted to flirtatiously tell him about it . . . but instead she just smiled.

And then she heard another girl, from quite close range, echoing her thoughts. "Grady Lodge, how very handsome you are this afternoon!"

As the sun-drenched afternoon came back into focus, Letty comprehended first Grady's boyish features and—when she turned her eyes toward the ground—Peachy Whitburn. She had thrown herself down on the blanket in between Letty and

Grady, so that her strawberry-blond hair was fanned around her aristocratic face. Her nose formed a long, straight vertical line, and her lips made a long, straight horizontal one. She'd rested her hands on the chest of her eyelet shift and crossed her ankles so that her high-heeled, tan-and-white oxfords were placed rakishly close together, and there was a hint of amusement lurking below the surface of her expression. It twisted her face on one side, as though she were hiding a sour cherry in the corner of her mouth.

"Letty Larkspur," Grady said, "meet Peachy Whitburn."

Peachy offered a beautifully manicured hand for Letty to shake. "Awfully pleased to meet you," she replied, without a hint of recognition, even though they had already been introduced by Astrid in the Beaumonts' foyer. "How long are you in White Cove?" she went on, returning her attention to Grady.

"Just for the day at Dorothy's request," he said.

Peachy's eyes rolled back and forth between the two people rising above her on either side. Her fingers played a quick melody on her chest. Then, with sudden swiftness, she righted herself and folded her long, tanned legs back demurely and spent a few moments arranging the sweep of her side-parted hair over her lightly freckled forehead.

"You're very pretty," she announced, pointing her pale red lips in Letty's general direction but not quite meeting her eyes.

"Oh." For a moment, all of Letty's concentration was in smoothing her skirt over her thighs. "Thank you."

"He's awfully nice, isn't he?" Peachy went on familiarly.

The large blue discs of Letty's eyes went to Grady and then back to Peachy. "Yes, I guess he is."

"Oh, he is, he is. *I* know. I've known him forever."

"Forever—?" The wrinkles in Letty's skirt were no longer of any concern to her, and her mind bent trying to imagine how Grady, living in his garret on Bedford Street in Greenwich Village, might possibly have encountered Peachy, who surely lived in some massive house down a nearby lane. "But how is that . . ."

"Oh, well—" Grady furrowed his brow at Peachy. "Not really forever, just since my sister married Mr. Cobb and moved into the area. Peachy is a friend of my sister's, you see."

"Among other things." Peachy gave a peculiar laugh and a vague swat of her hand, before adjusting herself, moving her legs to the other side of her body, so that Letty couldn't help but notice how long and finely formed her calves were.

"I also wrote an article about Peachy once."

"Yes, that was when I first realized that Mr. Lodge was delightfully easy to be with." Casting her eyes upward, Peachy began to blithely relate the story of her coming out and an article Grady had written about the debut. Grady interjected a correction here or there, which Peachy followed with uproarious laughter and, once, a slap on his knee. But Letty had ceased paying much attention. The last thing she'd clearly heard Dorothy's friend say was that Grady was easy to be with, and she couldn't stop thinking that this was exactly right. Even around a girl whose excellent breeding and expensive dress would usually have sent Letty into the back rooms of her self-consciousness, she felt at ease, and she knew this was because of the way that Grady's eyes kept searching hers, letting her know that he was thinking of her and that he found her as lovely as any of the girls arrayed on the tapestries spread over the Beaumonts' grass. "Anyway," Peachy concluded. "*That's* why I feel so lucky to know Grady Lodge."

"Mr. Lodge certainly knows a lot of people," Letty said, speaking to Peachy but looking at Grady. It was nice to think that he wasn't intimidated, as she was, by boarding school manners and ready possession of unscuffed shoes that had not been passed down by even one older sibling.

"Oh, yes. He is loved wherever he goes. Unfortunately, this means he is much in demand—Grady, your sister sent me to fetch you." She used his shoulder to push herself back up to her feet, and took several long steps back toward the house, her long frame springy and assured with the expectation that she would be immediately followed.

"I was enjoying myself much more when you and I were talking about art," Grady said softly to Letty as he rolled his eyes.

"I was enjoying it, too."

"Well, perhaps we could continue the conversation soon?" Grady averted his eyes bashfully.

"Mr. Lo-odge," Peachy sing-songed impatiently. She had come to a stop about twenty feet away on the lawn and was regarding them with her hands fixed at her hips.

"What I mean to say is, I'd like to take you out."

Now it was Letty's turn to look away and turn pink in the face. "I would like that," she said.

"Where can I find you?" Grady asked as he stood to go.

"Do you know a house called Dogwood?" Letty replied, trying not to seem disappointed that he was leaving.

"Ah, of course. Your friend Cordelia—I remember reading that she was Grey's daughter. I am glad to hear you two have been reunited." He winked at her and reached for her hand, so that he could brush his lips across the tops of her fingers. "I'll ring you there tomorrow, lovely Miss Letty."

4

"AND WHEN MY SISTER, CORDELIA, FIRST WENT TO THE White Cove Country Club—without my knowledge, of course—she wore red in defiance of their dress code."

As the group surrounding Charlie broke into twitters, Cordelia turned her face up and tried to appear more pleased than embarrassed. The country club was owned by the in-laws of Duluth Hale and was supplied exclusively by him, so Charlie and Darius never went there on principle. But on the morning in question she had been Astrid's guest, and a White Cove resident of only two days, and simply hadn't known any better than to wear red among the sea of club-approved white frocks. That would not have been like her; Cordelia had never been in the habit of drawing attention to herself on purpose. She was clear-eyed and knew things about people, and yet she had never felt particularly comfortable being watched by others. Even now she was a little uneasy as the object of Charlie's storytelling.

It hardly mattered, however, because by now Charlie had brought the group's attention back to himself. He had so many bad things to say about the Hales that sometimes, when he got started, he was unable to stop. And though Cordelia, in his position, certainly would have played her hand a little closer to her chest, there was no way to quiet him, and the group of well-heeled White Cove young people seemed perfectly entertained by his grandstanding.

"You really think old Hale could be that bad?" asked a man with a straw boater propped way back on his head, who had been standing entirely too close to her for some time. The smell of his cheap cologne filled her nostrils, and that wasn't the sort of question Cordelia had any kind of answer to, so she turned her face to the water and stepped away from the group. That was how she noticed that another crowd was forming— this one bigger and more animated—near the shoreline. In the tranquil blue sky above, a silver biplane was twirling out puffy letters. The white plumes the plane left in its wake strung together a jaunty message—THE BEAUMONTS WISH YOU A HAPPY INDEPENDENCE DAY—and as each word was completed, the girls below jumped up and down and squealed.

A dazed smile came across Cordelia's face. She had seen this kind of lettering before—when she had only just stepped off the train from Ohio—and all the wonder of that first hour in New York returned to her. She had observed the same aerial skill once again, from the vantage of nearby Everly Field, and then on another occasion she had witnessed it failing spectacularly. She hadn't seen the daring pilot Max Darby since delivering him to the Rye Haven Catholic Hospital.

Since that night, she'd barely had a moment to wonder how he had fared. Her family had been in mourning, and she had been too preoccupied with all the things she had done wrong to speculate about someone else. But now, on the Fourth of July, when the air was humid and fragrant with grass, she felt a twinge of excitement to recognize his plane up there. Absentmindedly, she put her hands into the deep pockets of her loose-fitting skirt and drifted away from Charlie and his friends, her head bent back so that she could watch the end of the air show. The plane twirled a few more times and zoomed low over the heads of mingling partygoers twice. Once she saw that it was sailing down toward a smooth landing on the far side of the property she set out at a brisk pace across the lawn.

But the other girls were actually running. They mobbed Max Darby when he jumped down from the cockpit and cried out his name.

It was another twenty minutes before he emerged from

the crowd of jubilant young women and she managed to catch his eye. By that time, the color of the sky was already ripening with the suggestion of dusk, and she was holding a pitcher of mint julep in one hand and a glass for him in the other.

"If that's for me," he said when he reached her, his blue eyes pale in contrast to his tanned skin, "I don't drink."

"Oh." She lowered the pitcher. His appearance, like his words, seemed uniquely unadorned against the background of the Beaumonts' party. All across the field were young people wearing the latest thing, but Max's dark hair was so short it was almost a shadow on his forehead, and the light brown color of his leather jacket matched his trousers.

"I'm glad to have run into you here," he said with a formality that made him sound not exactly glad. "Because I've been meaning to thank you for—what you did that night."

"That." Cordelia wrapped one leg behind the other girlishly, and her red-painted lips sprang upward at the corners. The mention of the night she'd seen his plane go down on the field of some Long Island farm made her feel a little dizzy. Suddenly she remembered the way he'd smiled at her, after being so serious, in that empty early-morning hospital, how wonderfully alive he'd made her feel, after days of feeling lost and useless and worse. "Well—here I am."

"Thank you." She waited expectantly for him to go on, but after he looked away toward the place on the lawn where the band was setting up, her expectation began to curdle. There was a sheen of sweat on his forehead, and perhaps on his hands, too, because he paused to wipe them on his white T-shirt. "That's all I've got to say to a bootlegger's daughter."

For many years, Cordelia had hoarded newspaper stories about New York City and longed for nothing so much in the world as to be called a bootlegger's daughter. It was a double shock that Max, when he uttered that phrase, should make it feel like a slap across the face.

"A bootlegger's daughter!" she repeated with cool indignation. Inside, she was the opposite of cool, and only wished that she wasn't holding the stupid pitcher of julep, which was heavy in her hand. "Well, I suppose trick pilots are in the habit of being careless with their lives and indifferent to those who risk their own helping them."

He averted his eyes again and moved to walk past her and up toward the house. Her hands wanted to shake at this final slight, but she commanded them to hold steady as she tipped the pitcher, pouring a drink for herself into the glass that she'd brought for him.

"Is that why you're being so prissy?" she called after him, loud enough for the young girls watching them to hear.

He paused and gazed at her intently, but did not reply. She took a sip of the sweet, heady drink and that quieted her irritation, though she knew some fury lingered in her face. Here was the person whose body she had pulled from the wreckage—but her bravery had not earned his respect. He thought nothing of her, it turned out, and even less of Darius Grey.

"My father has been dead barely a month." Her voice trembled a little, but her words fell with violent precision. "He wasn't a bad man, and he did all he could for himself and his family. He didn't begrudge other people their choices, and he left a life grander than the one he was born into. So you'll not say 'bootlegger' to me in that righteous tone again." She took another sip of the drink, and then thrust both the glass and the pitcher forward with sudden force, so that Max had no choice but to take them. Then, leaning forward, holding his gaze, and almost hissing, she concluded: "Don't expect me to act like some ashamed nothing just because you talk so high and mighty. I know who I am."

They stood facing each other another few moments, their bodies frozen in animosity. Cordelia blinked once, as though to communicate that she had nothing to prove and was not about to be drawn into anything so petty as a staring contest. Then she turned and walked up toward the Beaumonts' Greek Revival mansion, shaken, but not so badly that she was unable to walk confidently in her high-heeled shoes.

As she made her way along a stone path toward the colonnaded verandah, she was conscious—at first vaguely and then most definitely—of other people's eyes on her. Perhaps she was now radiating some of her fury, perhaps it was visible along the high sharp lines of her cheekbones. Or perhaps they were staring at her in the usual way, with some mix of curiosity about her criminal family and pity for the tragedy that had befallen her so soon into her life as a New York girl.

In any event, she *was* being watched. Even as the band struck up behind her and a few girls shrieked happily at their sweethearts to spin them around. Even as a first firework was set off somewhere down the shore, heralding the bigger show to come once the darkness was complete. Their eyes were on her as she climbed the stairs and went through a palatial hall and into the parlor; their eyes were on her as she glanced around for Astrid or Letty. It was perhaps because of the unabashed stares of the Beaumonts' other guests that she was not at first surprised to find that the familiar face her gaze finally settled upon was already gazing right back at her.

Her lips parted and she heard a fragile little "Oh" escape them. There was Thom Hale, who had used her callously and wrecked her family, holding a half-full cocktail by the window and looking as crisp as ever. Her knees went to mush and her throat got hard and tight.

As always Thom's every hair was in place. His white linen suit fit him just loosely enough, and unlike the other young men, the heat of the day did not seem to have caused him to sweat even a tiny bit. The handsomeness of his features was as devastating to her as ever, and he still stood in exactly the same elegant, careless way. Yet there was something changed in him, in the way he looked at her. Maybe in the set of his jaw, or in the light in his eyes. For a moment she wondered if it was unrequited love, but then she reminded herself that he had had plenty of her (how it seared her heart to remember taking him into her bed), and that this quality probably had more to do with lust or hate or deepening enmity or an intention of violence.

The last time they had stood face-to-face had been the night she'd lured him away from his family's party with the idea of killing him. Even now the audacity of this made her feel sick. But in the weeks leading up to that night he had played a wicked trick and convinced her that he loved her and would do anything for her. Then he had managed to extract a secret about Dogwood and how to sneak into it, and someone working for his family had used that secret to murder her father. She had been so stricken with grief and self-recrimination that driving to the Hales' home with a gun in her garter had seemed like quite a logical thing to do, the only thing to do, and it was not until she had seen Thom on the other end of the barrel and imagined his perfect features marred and bloodied that she had faltered, dropped the gun, and run.

A waiter bearing a tray of wide-lipped glasses passed between them, breaking some kind of spell. Cordelia became aware of the room around her: The fine parquet of the floor gleamed and the deep red of the walls went up twenty feet, where it was crowned by elaborate picture moldings. The tall east-facing windows were open so that breezes could rise off the Beaumonts' parterre gardens and soothe young girls who had been overheated by bourbon and dancing in the sun. Five conversations were going on at once, and she could faintly make out the exuberant playing of the band outside on the lawn, a soft wail of trumpet.

Then Thom took a step in her direction with a curl to his lips that was unlike any expression she'd ever seen on his face before. The indifference of the previous few seconds was replaced by a ragged beating of her heart.

But before she got a good look at the twist of his upper lip or had any chance of really knowing its meaning, she felt the touch of a gentle palm at her elbow.

"Darling." It was Astrid at her side, looking as gloriously Astrid-like as ever: Her hair was shiny and buoyant and only half covering her ears, and her smile was as easy and radiant as though all the world were just a little game set up for her amusement. She rolled her eyes in young Hale's general direction. "You know girls like us never wear the same dress twice."

It had been a tumultuous half hour for Cordelia, and she was relieved when her friend drew her away from the parlor before she could be certain whether Thom had been about to come after her or not.

5

BY THE TIME IT WAS DARK ENOUGH FOR PYROTECHNICS, the star pilot had already packed up and gone home. The Beaumonts, who'd paid him handsomely for his show, had insisted that he stay long enough to shake hands with those female members of their extended family who were particularly enthusiastic about aviation, but he did not linger more than necessary. Soon after he departed, his silver plane growing ever smaller in the gathering dusk, most of the stuffier guests went, too, in a caravan of chauffeured limousines driving slowly out along the topiary-lined drive. Meanwhile, the sun had gone down in a swollen red blaze. The sky began to turn purple, and then Cordelia Grey declared that she was going home, and after that Astrid found that the party wasn't quite so fun anymore.

Not that she didn't try to make it so. That morning she had awoken to a vague headache and a dim recollection that her mother had been trying to stir up trouble, and so she put herself together with the conviction that she was going to be especially gay today and make a big show of how perfect her engagement was no matter what poison her mother tried to spread. She chose a skirt of alternating navy and white scallop-edged tiers (a color combination that Astrid knew brought out the rich yellow shade of her hair) and a loose white top with a neckline shaped like a deep V. The Dogwood crew had traveled over in a big, rowdy pack, and when they disembarked from the Daimler, she made sure to do so hanging on Charlie's arm. Later she and Charlie had made themselves conspicuous on the dance floor, trotting slyly and then shaking in a frenzy as though no one else could see them. Of course, other people could see them—including her mother, whom she caught watching from the tables set up on the lawn.

Then Charlie got called off somewhere and she satisfied herself dancing with the Duchess of Malden's Irish boxer. He had come to the Beaumonts' as Virginia Marsh's special guest, along with a few other of her mother's "interesting" friends who'd stayed particularly late the night before. But this was hardly as much fun—she sensed that it didn't excite her mother's jealousy half as much—and she was relieved when the crackling eruption of the first explosive went off over the sound and they could abandon the dance floor to walk toward the blankets, which had been spread out for them along the water's edge.

"I just adore fireworks," Astrid said as she put her small, soft hand in the boxer's big, rough one, the better to balance herself as she lowered herself to the blanket and tucked her legs up under her skirt. "Don't you?"

The boxer answered affirmatively, in that inscrutable and lilting accent, and then he sat down beside her. He had lost his jacket in the course of the afternoon, his ivory dress shirt was rolled to the elbows, and she could see that there were no socks beneath the ankles of his pinstriped trousers. But he would not have appeared well put-together anyhow. His hair was cut close to his head, so that the tough bones of his skull were perfectly evident, and his shoulders were broad and meaty. These were not characteristics that Astrid particularly minded; in fact, there was something about him that rather reminded her of Charlie.

Over their heads, three rockets went skyward and flared out in red, white, and blue bursts that held a few moments, swaying in the heavens like a constellation of giant squid. Some of the ladies on the surrounding blankets shrieked at the noise. But Astrid liked all of it—how artificial and brash the fireworks were at first, and then so delicate as they faded and fizzled down toward Earth—and for a minute nothing else mattered very much.

The boxer, meanwhile, took a silver flask from his hip pocket and swigged before offering it to Astrid.

"Whiskey?"

Here was one word Astrid understood perfectly. "Thanks, you dear."

There wasn't much in the flask, which explained why he already smelled of sweat and liquor, but she just giggled faintly, tipped her head back, and drank the rest. "I'm sorry. I'm afraid I've killed it," she said with an exaggerated little downturn of the mouth to express her regret.

"Not to worry. I know where there's more," he replied, flashing that grin with the gold spots in it.

There was something in that grin that made her hesitate. Flirting was Astrid's favorite sport—she liked it even better than horseback riding, and tennis she only ever favored for the outfits—but there was a fine line separating certain behaviors from other decidedly darker ones, which she was mindful never to cross. When she realized she might have given the boxer the wrong idea by dancing with him, she shook her head kittenishly, demurring. He had her hand firmly, however, and might even have succeeded in pulling her along against her will had they not been noticed, at just that moment, by a familiar face. The face was rather full, and it belonged to Gracie Northrup.

Gracie—the girl she'd found in Charlie's bed one vile night at Dogwood. The big-chested beast who very nearly broke them up was walking along the edge of the blankets, her cheeks pink from who knows what sort of exertion, and she didn't even have the humility to appear awkward when she recognized Astrid. With an expression that was either very stupid or very shrewd, she greeted her former Miss Porter's classmate, her smile wide and her wave ungainly.

She was wearing a red-and-white-striped dress, which Astrid might have advised against if she had any sympathy for the girl, and she tugged at it as she made herself comfortable on the grass. The image of Gracie with her blouse undone on Charlie's bed recurred in Astrid's thoughts, and perhaps in Gracie's, too, because she went on smiling as she asked, "Where's Charlie?"

The gall of this statement lit a fire inside Astrid that threatened to erupt into conflagration. She narrowed her eyes at Gracie and hoped that she saw what an incomparably light and superior creature Astrid was, how delicate she looked beside the Irishman, how universally desired. But Gracie only stared back dumbly. In the next moment Astrid stopped feeling hateful toward the girl in the red stripes and began to wonder where, indeed, Charlie was.

"I haven't the foggiest," she announced. "We aren't one of those couples that cease to function without each other by our side," she added proudly, although the fact that he was not currently at her side was beginning to make her brain tick, and before she knew it she was furious again about the lack of adornment on her ring finger. She still hated her mother for having pointed out his failure, but that did not make it any less humiliating.

"Well, can I sit here with you?" Gracie went on with a simple-minded smile. "Seems my friends have gone off."

Before Astrid had the chance to reply, she caught sight of Charlie. He was ambling through the blankets alongside Danny, the red-haired guard at Dogwood, holding his ridiculous lemon yellow jacket over his shoulder with one finger, his shirtsleeves rolled to the elbow. Her eyes darted from Gracie back to Charlie, and she wondered where he had been.

"You're in luck," she declared coldly as she pushed herself up from the blanket. "There's our darling Charlie now. I hope he's just as sweet with you as he used to be with me."

Without so much as looking at Gracie or the boxer for a reaction, she began to stride away from the crowd clustered at the waterfront. She almost really did wish that Charlie was sweet to Gracie, at least for a little while, and that they ended up together, so that Charlie could spend the rest of his days wondering why he was with such a second-rate cow instead of his first fiancée, the one he'd not bothered to buy a ring for. "Damn him," she muttered, telling herself not to cry as she continued on toward the Beaumonts' big, pompous house, the grand fireworks display illuminating her face as though it were high noon whenever she looked back.

At first she didn't think Charlie had seen her, but when she heard him calling out her name, she kicked off her shoes and began to run. She ran as hard as she could, her feet barely touching the ground, her limbs wheeling around her body. She felt so angry and so light that she almost thought she might break free of the earth and go swinging up toward the pretty lights in the sky. It was not until she reached the top of the Beaumonts' big steps that she realized she had no idea where she was going and stopped. Very slowly, she turned around, panting, her clothes and hair askew, and looked back toward the water, wishing she were anywhere in the world but here.

Charlie had already reached the base of the steps and was standing still with his brown eyes on her. A moment ago she would have liked to yell all manner of invective at him, but now she found she could not remember exactly what it was she had wanted to say. She stared at him and narrowed her eyes and tried to conjure her anger—but he simply didn't seem like the picture of someone who had just done her wrong. For one thing, he was holding her shoes sweetly and carefully against his chest and smiling in a goofy way, his light hair greased back from his forehead, his shoulders broad under his white shirt. Behind him there were colorful eruptions high in the sky, but they seemed more distant and paler now.

"Get me out of here," she said crossly as she began to descend the steps in his direction.

"Here?"

"Yes, you big oaf, here."

"I'll take you—" A hiccup interrupted Charlie's sentence.

"You'll take me—where?"

"I'll take you—"

There was another hiccup and Astrid—who found hiccups appalling, especially in men, but was nonetheless becoming less and less inclined to linger at the Beaumonts'—grabbed for his hand and pulled him in the direction of the driveway.

"You'll take me home? Indeed you will. But not in a car. Not the way you're slurring. We'll just have to walk."

Charlie agreed affably, throwing his arm around her and humming a few bars of "The Star-Spangled Banner." Astrid, who had selected her shoes more for the flattering way they revealed her ankles and exaggerated her height than for walking, was less ebullient. The gravel drive cut against the tender soles of her feet. The humming did not make her happy, either, and she found that being face-to-face with Charlie only led her to reimagine the scene of him leaping off Gracie Northrup, and how soon after that his proposal had come, and what a crummy thing a proposal without a ring was. But those kinds of thoughts caused her to furrow her brow, which could only result in permanent lines, which were also no good. So she was forced to hum along, ensconced in Charlie's embrace, as they shuffled past the big stone gates and out onto Plum Tree Lane.

As they walked—somewhat lurchingly and not at all fast— a few stars emerged in the darkening cloak of purple above them. The air was fragrant and quiet, and there were no silly girls trying to get attention with their antics. By the time they reached Dogwood, Astrid had almost forgotten what it was that had made her run from the Beaumonts' party in such a hurry. As they moved up the hill between the twin rows of lindens, she extracted herself from Charlie's heavy embrace. She walked ahead of him for a few minutes, listening to his feet crunch against the grass, and instead of climbing the stone steps to the entryway, she continued on into the shadow of the house. There she paused, leaning her shoulders against the cool bricks of the south wall, trying to see if she had ever loved him.

As she stared at him, his eyes grew large—there was something murky and different behind them—and then, to her utter shock, he lowered himself onto one knee.

Her first thought was that he might ruin his silly suit and what a blessing that would be. But then she realized he was going to give her something, and she experienced a lovely swelling of the heart.

"Oh, Charlie," she said faintly as he took her hands in his.

The very act of going down on his knee must have been

a sober-making one, because when he spoke it was without a trace of hiccups. "Astrid Donal, will you marry me?"

There was a little light from the house and the stars, but the ring he produced from his inside coat pocket glittered all on its own. It was a giant oval stone rising high on a swirling and very modern platinum setting. There were so many intricacies to the ring—all the other tiny sparkling stones that surrounded the big one, and the beautiful patterns on the band—that she almost wanted to excuse herself for a moment so that she could get a good look. But before she even had the chance to realize that that wouldn't really have been appropriate, the ring was on her finger, and he had risen back to his feet and picked her up in his strong arms.

"Oh, Charlie, oh, Charlie, oh, Charlie!" she exclaimed. "Oh, Charlie, we're going to be married! Really, actually, truly!"

"It's true!" he answered, his voice rising to a slightly lunatic pitch just as hers had.

She gave him three rapid kisses and then peered around his head to get a look at the beautiful piece of jewelry now adorning her finger. All of her body had become tingly and weightless. The dramas of the afternoon now seemed like nothing more than the exact path she'd had to take to arrive at this perfect place. She was almost grateful for the earlier disappointments, and in her gratitude and contentment she let out a sigh of sweet exhaustion.

"Oh, *Charlie*. It fits so perfectly. How did you know?"

He gave her a lopsided smile. "Never ask my methods, doll."

Who would have thought that big, boyish Charlie would know how to do a thing like buy a girl just the right ring in just the right size? He was always buying her nice clothes, of course, but they were usually too big for her and then she had to have her maid take them in, and she suspected the taste of some salesgirl at Bergdorf's was behind most of these gifts, anyway. That he had done everything right for this far more crucial purchase made her wonder if she'd underestimated him all afternoon—and to think how little her mother knew. There was no way a woman with such a black heart could understand a thing like the love between her and Charlie, as he'd just helped her prove. The only way the moment could have been more perfect was if her mother had been there to see how utterly wrong she'd been.

But of course that would have complicated the one thing that Astrid wanted to do next, which was to run her fingers through the strands of hair at the base of her fiancé's neck, and push his head forward until his mouth met hers. "Oh, Charlie, I couldn't be happier," she sighed in between kisses. And how could she have been? There was the delicious smell of dewy grass at Dogwood, and the gentle winking of stars, and as they kissed, it was almost as though a gentle song was playing, as though all of nature had begun to sing for her and

Charlie and the big wonderful life they were going to share together.

Letty wasn't sure if she or Good Egg needed the walk more, but it didn't really matter, because they were both grateful for the relative cool of nighttime and a little companionship as they meandered through the hedge maze that lay beyond the Dogwood swimming pool. In the end, she had greatly enjoyed the Beaumonts' party, because of Grady Lodge. And yet she couldn't help but feel just the teensiest bit disappointed that the person who had made her afternoon so delightful was not someone rich and impressive, or even what Mrs. Marsh would call an "interesting" person.

Plus, she had come home with Cordelia, who had somehow or other gotten into one of her bleak moods again and hadn't wanted to be at a party anymore. After Cordelia's father had died, Letty had attended to these moods and taken care of her friend when she had stopped wanting to take care of herself. She was happy to do this much and didn't mind that Cordelia hadn't thanked her or seemed to notice—but she had in truth believed that that phase had passed, and had felt a smidge sorry for herself when Cordelia went to bed straightaway and Letty was left alone to wish she had gotten to see the fireworks.

"Ah, me," she sighed, her eyes rolling to the stars.

Good Egg, perhaps sensing that her mistress was wallowing, did a few graceful laps around her ankles and cast her concerned almond eyes upward.

"Why don't I just sing the blues then, if I'm going to act so low-down—is that what you mean with that look?" Letty whispered at the creature she was beginning to consider her best friend.

Good Egg dashed forward and ran in a few quick circles before flopping down on the grass near the entrance of the maze. She couldn't be certain if the dog was urging Letty to play with her, or positioning herself as the most eager audience of one Letty had ever had.

"Well—if you insist," Letty gushed as she reached for her dog and bent down to kiss her on the nose. When she stood up again, she opened her mouth to sing one of the sentimental love songs her mother had taught her back in Union. Because she'd done so little singing lately, she was surprised that the song came so naturally and right away. Even though it was not a happy song, the words made her happy as they moved through her, as though she were getting rid of some old, bad feeling. Letty had never felt quite so alive as in those few moments she'd stood onstage before an appreciative crowd, that one time at Seventh Heaven, but she now found that there was a lot of joy in singing for singing's sake, and that an audience of Good Egg and stars was quite nice, too.

As they walked past the swimming pool and up toward the house, Letty's voice grew stronger. Good Egg hurried forward and then hurried back, her tongue hanging out as she panted in time. Letty might have gone on singing all the way into the house and up to the third-story suite where she slept, had a strong male voice that always brought fear into her heart not stalled her in her tracks.

"What's that music?"

It was Charlie's voice, as barking as ever. A few moments followed during which Letty couldn't locate the source of his voice, but then she began to make out two forms in the darkness. Astrid was fixed in his big embrace, her fluffy yellow hair roughed up around her face and her slender body pinned like a doll's against the south wall of Dogwood. A pall of mortification hung over Letty; there was nothing quite so shaming as intruding on a couple in an amorous state.

But it didn't last. Astrid jumped out of Charlie's arms and twirled around, stepping into the bar of light cast by the windows above. When she saw Letty, she shrieked and leapt backward into Charlie. "Oh! *Oh.* Letty, thank goodness, you looked like a ghost standing there so pale and little! You nearly scared me to death."

"I'm sorry—I'm so sorry." Letty smiled feebly in Astrid's direction and kept her eyes averted. Cordelia wouldn't have been embarrassed, of course—back in Union, Cordelia used to practice saying naughty words so that once she got to New York

City, she wouldn't be shocked by anything. But Letty, sadly, had not lost her provincial shame about witnessing another girl being kissed. Especially when the girl in question was being kissed by someone as volatile as Charlie Grey. "I didn't think anybody was here."

"Didn't think anybody was here?" Charlie bellowed. "Stupid!"

Letty's cheeks burned and she turned her eyes toward her shoes. "Yes, I guess it was stupid. I'm sorry!"

"Stop saying sorry. I meant stupid because you sing so pretty. You shouldn't sing for yourself alone, there's no sense in that, you should sing where there's lots of people and you can make some dollars."

"Oh." Slowly, very slowly, Letty summoned the courage to raise her eyes.

Astrid's pupils were large and black, and one of the straps of her dress had slipped down her right shoulder. She looked no less lovely for being slightly disheveled, and her left arm was still thrown back to hang from Charlie's neck. He did not seem to mind this, even though it meant that he had to stoop slightly. He did not seem in a mood to mind anything at all. There was even something almost soft in his wide-set brown eyes, and like Astrid, his hair had been rearranged and was now pointing in several directions, which was somehow comic, and made him less frightening in Letty's eyes.

"I mean—you're good. You're really awfully good."

"Of course she's good," Astrid interjected. "Cord and I wouldn't be such very tight friends with her if she weren't good."

"Well, better than good then. Good enough to sing in clubs."

"Thank you," Letty managed to summon the breath to reply. She badly wanted to believe in Charlie's compliments, but she couldn't help the old suspicion, which she always had around him, that he was only waiting for the right moment to mock her again.

"Darling, aren't you going to have a club soon?"

"Yeah, I guess I am. Letty, not only should you sing in clubs, you should sing in my club!" He beamed, looking pleased with what he'd just said, as well as with the world and everything in it.

"Oh, marvelous!" Astrid exclaimed. "What a perfect Fourth it's turning out to be. Letty's going to sing in the Greys' club, and I'm engaged for real now. Letty—look!"

Letty took a dutiful step forward, conscious of Good Egg politely at her ankles, and bent to see the large, shimmering stone now adorning Astrid's left ring finger and making her hand appear even more graceful and delicate than before.

"Why that's just . . ." she trailed off, unable to summon the right word. She'd never seen a ring so big or with so many stones, and the right word to describe it simply wasn't in her vocabulary.

"Divine? I think it's divine. Isn't that right, Charlie? Isn't it utterly divine?" Astrid went on in a rush.

"It's the ring my girl deserves." Charlie grinned at Astrid as though she were the only woman in the world. "Anyway, enough of that. I'm starved. Aren't you starved?"

"Completely." Astrid threw her arms back up around Charlie's neck and swayed against him. "Completely and entirely starved!"

Sensing that she was about to be forgotten again, Letty took a step backward. It was dark, and the shadows were deep around the house, and it would be easy enough for her to slip away without them noticing.

"Come on, I'll make you eggs." Charlie planted an almost chaste kiss on Astrid's mouth, then turned to Letty. "Are you coming?"

"Me?"

"Yeah, you. Who else would I be talking to? The lady is wearing a big new bauble—we've got to do some celebrating. You're in, aren't you? And maybe you can do some more singing for us while I cook."

Already he had turned and was walking back toward the house when his welcoming words fully settled in with Letty. To her they seemed utterly remarkable. He had barely said ten sentences to her since she'd moved into Dogwood, and now he wanted her to sing at his club and celebrate his engagement over a midnight breakfast in the Dogwood kitchen. Suddenly all the moping she'd done earlier seemed like the emotions of some other time and place, and with a wink in Good Egg's direction, she hurried up and followed Charlie and Astrid as they ascended the stone steps to the stately front entrance of their home.

6

BY TWO O'CLOCK ON THE FIFTH OF JULY, MOST OF THE
young women who lived in the big neighboring estates had
already heard that Astrid Donal was wearing Charlie Grey's
ring, and that apparently it was very large. Several of these
young women—who had gone to dances with Astrid and copied
her irreverent style of dressing for years—went to the White
Cove Country Club for lunch that day in hopes of getting a better look at the thing. But alas, Astrid had other plans.

"Brenda, if you lay them like this, you see, you can get
at least four more pairs in . . ." she was saying as she flitted
back and forth between several open suitcases propped up
on luggage stands across the room. Brenda, Astrid's personal

maid, was accustomed to fixing frayed hems and packing for a few days on a yacht, but was less skilled at fitting every single pair of Miss Donal's considerable shoe collection into the old Vuitton cases that Mrs. Marsh had used when she and Astrid went to live in a string of European hotels following the death of Mr. Donal. The Donal women were in those days accompanied by Mrs. Ransom, who was much better at organizing large quantities of ladies' clothing, but had unfortunately expired in the interim.

Astrid had not dressed in her much-copied style that morning, but in a prim twill suit that fit close to her hips with a high-collared cream blouse. If she had trouble moving in the skirt—and from the look of it, most girls would—she didn't let on. She was not wearing her hair in the usual way, either—it was slicked so that the high yellow shine was muted to a more grown-up shade. The message she was sending—that soon she was to be a married woman, and should no longer be treated as the kind of pleasure-seeking creature one might find swinging from a chandelier—was not intended to be subtle, and the various maids and butlers and cooks that worked at Marsh Hall understood it perfectly.

Word had also spread to her stepsister, Billie, who was sitting in one of the pale pink velvet armchairs in the corner of Astrid's room, an ankle rested against the opposite trousered knee, watching the proceedings. The only person who presumably had no idea of Astrid's change in stature was her mother, who had not yet risen from bed.

"It's going to be lonely around here without you," Billie said, her dark eyes shining. Like her eyes, her hair was black and gleaming, and it was worn in a mannish style just long enough to peek out from behind her ears. She was very much her father's daughter—observant, shrewd, hedonistic, and fond of automobiles—and was known to dress rather like him.

"Aren't you off for London any day now?" Astrid replied distractedly, as she picked up two satin-covered pairs of shoes and tried to assess their respective merits.

"I keep delaying," Billie answered in a faraway voice, as though she were speaking of the actions of some other person.

"And then you'll be back to college in the fall, and you're always out and about, and anyway, you will come to Dogwood often," Astrid went on without breaking her breezy tone. "I would, if I were you. This house is large, but not large enough that I can keep enough distance between Mrs. Marsh and myself."

"Oh, don't let her bother you." Now it was Billie's turn to be breezy. Astrid turned, wearing a skeptical expression, and watched her stepsister as she lit a cigarette. "She's only jealous of you, you know."

"Yes, that's precisely what I find so disgusting. Brenda—these can stay, or you can have them if you like." Astrid went on, changing the subject and thrusting a worn pair of satin heels toward her maid. She had never been a light packer, and the idea of leaving anything behind that her mother might then don for some party or other sickened her. "One can never be too thin or too rich—I still fit in all my daughter's things, you know," she could just imagine the old lady trilling at one of her evenings. But on the other hand, she had to remember that the less treasure she arrived at Dogwood with, the more there'd be for Charlie to buy her.

"Thanks, miss."

Astrid, whose attention had been temporarily diverted by the beautiful new thing on her finger, replied with a distracted, "You're welcome." She was still gazing at her engagement ring, a little misty-eyed, when the door to the hall opened.

"What's all this?"

Astrid rotated toward the entry and her hand went behind her back. Her mother was standing in the doorway, clothed in a white silk bathrobe, her makeup from the night before only partially removed from her face. Her eyes twitched over the scene, taking in the luggage and reading its meaning.

"Going somewhere?" She pushed a fistful of dark hair away from her face.

"Me?" Astrid replied innocently, taking a step toward her mother and keeping her hand resting girlishly at the small of her back. The thrill of what had passed between her and Charlie last night hadn't faded even a tiny bit, but she now found herself even more breathless and proud as she paused, about to reveal it to her mother.

"Yes, you." Her mother took a long sip from her china coffee cup, observing Astrid over its rim. "I assume you aren't sending all your favorite dresses to the Salvation Army."

"Good afternoon, Mrs. Marsh," Billie said, exhaling in her stepmother's general direction, but otherwise not moving a muscle to express greeting.

"Afternoon, Billie." Virginia went slinking across the floor, balancing her coffee in front of her and finding a place on the bedspread, in between the piles of lace undergarments, to recline. "Did you girls enjoy the party?"

With exquisite patience, Astrid put both hands forward and ever so slowly lifted a silk camisole lying near the edge of the bedspread. She picked it up by the straps, folded it neatly, and placed it to the side so that she could perch on the corner of the bed and rest her left fingers over her right, Charlie's ring sitting like a little jeweled crown on her lap.

"What's *that*?" her mother gasped.

"Careful, darling!" Astrid cried out when she saw the sloshing of coffee in her mother's cup. "My prettiest things are out now," she went on in a patronizing tone, "and you'll ruin them if you don't mind your beverage."

"Did Charlie give that to you?" Her mother scowled as she leaned forward to get a better look.

"Yes, of course! Who else would have given it to me? *I* don't have other beaux," she added with such lightness that anyone other than her mother might have missed the point. But Virginia was no fool, even on mornings like these, and she heard the undercurrent of Astrid's statement perfectly. When she turned her green eyes up at her daughter, they had a kind of desperation in them, but Astrid was determined to smile back with nothing but peachy innocence. "Isn't it pretty?" she prodded.

"Very." Virginia took a sip of her coffee before casting her eyes around the room. "Is Charlie taking you on a cruise of the Orient now?"

"No! Nowhere so far as that." Astrid stood and walked over to the shoe suitcase, where Brenda was still standing, looking a little fearful of what might yet happen between her two mistresses. "Only . . . now that we're going to be married, and everyone can see that from the ring I'm wearing, it seemed silly for us to be apart any longer."

"You're not married yet," Virgina replied, rather too quickly.

"Mother—" Astrid's eyes flashed. "I might almost think you're not excited for me."

"Of course I am, dear." Now Virginia began to regain herself. Her voice became smooth, and she even managed to seem disinterested. "Charlie is very exciting and he always gives you the nicest things. But you can't blame me for being a *touch* concerned. It's simply not how things are done."

"Moving in before the wedding, you mean? Well, of course not. But—" She paused and shifted her gaze toward Billie with a conspiratorial twist at the corner of her mouth. Billie only raised her skinny, penciled-on eyebrows and switched the cross of her legs. "But," Astrid continued, undeterred, "you must know how old-fashioned you sound. Of course I'm not going to sleep in the same room as Charlie, and everybody will know that. We *young* people do not share in your foolish prohibitions—we do not go around calling a girl ruined just because she lives under the same roof as her fiancé."

The emphasis she had put on the word *young* was a cruel stroke, she knew, and she felt almost sorry when she saw how stiffly her mother rose to her feet.

"I thought I knew everything when I was your age, too," Virginia said bitterly. If there had been pity in Astrid's heart a moment before, it disappeared when she heard her mother's tone. "And contrary to what you may believe, I am *always* happy when my daughter receives a new piece of jewelry."

Jewelry, she pronounced as though she were speaking of the kind of toys children play with once and then discard. She tightened her robe and gave a slight bob of her head before turning and leaving her daughter's bedroom. Astrid sighed and ran her fingers over her hair. The brilliant mood she'd woken up in was somewhat dampened, but in the next moment Billie let out a loud, blasphemous laugh, which cut away the tension in the room.

"Oh, poor, damned Virginia, who is fated to be always exactly twenty-two years older than her daughter!"

Astrid began to giggle, too, and to realize, somewhat late in the game, how much more tolerable Marsh Hall had always been when her stepsister was there. Billie was in the habit of being right about everything, and yet she never forced her wisdom down anyone's throat. "Oh, please, promise me you'll come visit me often. And when you do you must bring me little shards of gossip so that I don't grow imbecilic and think I miss this place!"

"Cordelia?"

"Yes?" she answered, reluctantly lowering the newspaper so that she could glance over its pages at her brother. Charlie strode out onto the south-facing verandah and pulled up a chair at the large iron table where they had been eating most of their meals lately. He was wearing a white tennis shirt that he seemed on the verge of busting out of, and his hair was pomaded into place.

Cordelia knew from Letty—who had returned to the Calla Lily Suite with a giant smile on her face the night before, bubbling over with new stories—that Charlie had proposed to

Astrid after the Beaumonts' party, this time with a ring, and that that somehow made their engagement more official and thrilling. And she could tell from his face that he was feeling boisterous and happy in the aftermath of his big gesture. This was all very nice, but Cordelia was still reeling from her various run-ins of the afternoon before, and wasn't quite ready to share in anyone else's joy.

"You feeling sore about that pilot?" Charlie asked, his eyebrows drawing together. The concern he wore on his face was kind, but Cordelia didn't want to be pitied. She quickly folded up the paper and put it to the side. "Astrid told me Max Darby slighted you. What scum, acting like that after what you did for him."

"Max who?" she replied, reaching for a cigarette from the pack that lay on the table beside the remainders of her lunch. Her brother returned her grin as he leaned in to light it for her. "I don't believe I know that name," she added dryly.

"That's my girl."

It pleased Cordelia to think that Charlie was proud of her brash reply, just as their father might once have been. Unfortunately, her flip attitude was somewhat contradicted by the morning hours she'd spent poring over the papers for any mention of the pilot.

"He's boring and righteous and you're lucky to be disliked by him," Charlie went on. Cordelia nodded and exhaled a big cloud of smoke.

In fact, several times that morning she'd thought more or less the same thing. As she discovered in the many profiles of him, he was a teetotaler, and he disliked parties, and his patroness was the president of the Suffolk County Women's Christian Temperance Union. All of this only confirmed her impression of the day before: that he had a very dull and narrow view of the world.

And yet even so she couldn't help but notice the mention of a patroness, and read between the lines an implication that he was an orphan, like her.

"I know something that will cheer you up."

"Yeah?"

"Yeah—I found the place. Put something pretty on. We're going to the city—you're about to see the future home of the Grey family's first speakeasy."

By the time Cordelia returned to the foyer—in a smart little jacket over the red boatneck dress she'd worn to such tremendous effect that day at the Country Club, and with her tawny hair mostly tucked under a cloth cloche—a first wave of luggage had arrived from Marsh Hall. It was now arrayed over the dark wood floorboards, somewhat complicating her journey to the front door.

"You're going to have to move a few hoodlums out of the house to make room for this stuff, I think," Cordelia said to Charlie as he emerged from the library in a dark-colored suit.

"Tomorrow. All that's for tomorrow," he said, linking his arm with hers and giving off the air of the sort of blisteringly good mood that no cloud is strong enough to pass over.

Then the two heirs of the Grey bootlegging concern went down the stone steps of their home and into the chauffeured Daimler that would carry them through country lanes, over the broad span of a bridge, toward the big city. Even the glossy water beneath the Queensboro was busy with tugs and barges and pleasure cruises, and by the time they spun off its final curve and onto the streets of Manhattan, they were thoroughly transported from the shady calm of White Cove into a land far more buzzing and cluttered.

Their destination was in the middle of a block in the West Fifties, the floors of which were mosaic swirls of turquoise and gold, far below an arching ceiling that had once been covered with murals of cherubs and clouds. That the paint on the ceiling had begun to chip and fall away and expose the stone and plaster beneath only added to the mystery and beauty of the vast room. Either wall was flanked with windows covered by iron grates that opened onto other darkened rooms, and at the end were elaborate double copper doors.

"What was this?" Cordelia gasped.

"A bank, of course." Charlie's footsteps echoed as he moved across the floor. As soon as he said it, Cordelia found that she was able to identify the smell of money, among the other odors of dust and mildew that permeated the place. "Those were the tellers' windows. Small bank, not very good— they went belly up last year."

"You mean the bank lost their money?" Cordelia couldn't help but smirk at the thought. She understood how a farmer whose crop is ruined can go belly up, or a family that has begun to live far beyond its means. In Union, there had been only one bank, and everybody in town had put their money into it, and so the idea of a bank short on cash seemed to her if not exactly funny, then at least absurd.

"They lost all their money, but you're going to make us lots of money here. I figure we can have the bartenders behind those teller windows—that way, if there's ever a raid, they can just the shut the windows and have enough time to slip out the back way before any seizures are made."

Cordelia nodded. She was listening to him, but also already she was imagining the nights that would be had in a place like this. Girls would dance onstage, and the music would be fast and loose, and the chatter animated and witty and full of the life of the city. She had come a long way to witness nights like those, and now she felt a little rush thinking that she would have some role in creating them. That had been her father's genius—he'd been a master of staging the sort of evenings where people wanted to drink his wares in vast quantities. On one of his final days, he'd told her he wanted to teach her the business. Now she would make good on that wish.

"You really think I can run a speakeasy?"

Her footsteps echoed as she moved across the floor, peeking into corners, imagining where the tables and stage would go, her sense of elation growing the more she explored.

"You'll have help, but one thing you can be sure of, people will come if they know they're going to see you."

Cordelia turned away from this suggestion uncomfortably and did another quick spin through the room, taking in the metallic grates over the windows, the worn colored pieces in the floor, the few old mahogany desks that had been shoved to the corner but looked not so worn-down despite that. The high windows allowed a pale blue light to filter in—there was something almost heavenly in that color—and for a moment, despite herself, she thought Darius might be with them. Something was present, and it sent a shiver rippling across her shoulders.

"We should go have a drink to Dad," she said when she turned around again.

"You're right about that."

So they went to a crooked little place around the corner. Inside it had all the warm décor of a farm shed, and everyone was smoking and talking so loudly that no one voice could be distinguished from another. Cordelia enjoyed her hour there, and when Charlie said it was time to go, they stepped outside to a sky turning a plum shade that made the neon signs glow like magic. Someone must have tipped off the press, for they were photographed jumping into their waiting car. And while this might once have distressed her, she now viewed it as a very good joke, and thought with pleasure of the possibility of Max Darby opening his morning papers and seeing her in her pretty dress over the caption: BOOTLEGGER'S DAUGHTER SEEN OUT ON THE TOWN.

7

FROM THE SECOND FLOOR OF DOGWOOD CAME A
constant ringing of billiards, the cue ball hitting its mark or
scattering the other fifteen. The parlor there was always filled
with Charlie's gang, hanging around in undershirts and running
the electric fans, waiting for night to fall and their real work to
begin. They slept odd hours on old mattresses in out-of-the-
way rooms. Meanwhile, the kitchen was ruled by a one-legged
man whose specialties included egg sandwiches and spaghetti
and meatballs. All of this had always seemed novel and extraordinary to Astrid. Now that she was a resident of Dogwood it
was soon to change, of course.

Already that morning she had convinced Len, the cook,

to wear a hairnet when he was in the kitchen, and had taught him how to cut cucumbers paper-thin for sandwiches with the crusts removed. She had recruited Danny, the sweetest tempered and most impressionable of Charlie's men, to help her investigate an old barn on the property, and then he and the new man, the vaguely Italian-looking one, had set about clearing it of debris and rusted equipment. A quick call to one of her grandmother Donal's charities determined that old brass beds from a nearby home for wayward youth could be had by the dozen, and would be delivered tomorrow free of charge. The boys would be much happier sleeping there than in the main house, she told Charlie (who was on the phone at the time, and may not have heard her). After that, she'd found a handsome white embroidered tablecloth to cover the chipped white paint of the iron table on the south verandah, and also an old wooden bowl that perhaps came from the barn, which, when she filled it with wildflowers, made a lovely sort of rustic centerpiece.

It had been a busy and most satisfying morning—she had woken far earlier than she was accustomed to and dressed in a simple cotton fawn-colored shirtdress, tied low on the hips with a woven belt. For a moment she paused on the threshold of the verandah and gazed out on the sparkling afternoon, the rolling green vistas, and her two best friends, who now also happened to be her roommates, drinking fresh-squeezed juice.

"Lunch!" she very nearly squealed, so pleased was she with the whole scene.

"Oh! How *nice!*" Letty exclaimed appreciatively, taking the platter of little finger sandwiches from Astrid's hands so that the new mistress of Dogwood could arrange herself in the empty chair. Letty wore a sweet sailor-style blouse and white skirt, and her short black hair was still sleek from the shower.

"Thank you, darling," Cordelia added, as Astrid put a kiss on each girl's cheekbone.

"Just perfect." Astrid clapped her hands and sighed with happy purpose and reached forward to take one of the soft, crisp, buttery pieces between her fingers. "Now—what have you been talking about, what did I miss?"

"I was telling her about the club." Cordelia paused to rearrange her sleeveless, square-necked striped jersey dress, which was clinging to her skin in the afternoon heat despite its looseness. "Charlie found the most beautiful place, and I was asking her where she thought the stage ought to go, and imagining how wonderful her voice will sound there."

Letty's slight shoulders rose excitedly toward her ears and her wide blue eyes shone. "Can you imagine?"

"Yes, as a matter of fact." Astrid took another sandwich and gave Letty a steady look. "I can imagine it perfectly. *I* heard you singing the other night. You won't be able to play the bashful ingénue much longer, you know."

"Oh, yes, you're right of course." Letty nodded, the short black curtains of her hair swinging exuberantly. "It's only— you've got no idea how far away Ohio seems right now, and how long I've always dreamed of this."

"Well," Astrid said, smiling lavishly and raising her tall glass of juice, "here's to Letty Larkspur at Grey's Cabaret, or whatever you're going to call it."

"To Letty," Cordelia seconded, clinking her glass with Astrid's, "who I always knew would be a star."

"Thank you," Letty whispered, "that's so—"

"What in the world!" Astrid cut her off. Something very strange on the horizon had stolen her attention and for a moment she could only furrow her brow and let her mouth stand open. "What in the world is that?"

At first it was just a speck, but then it grew larger, and Astrid put her hand against her forehead so that she wouldn't have to squint so much, and then the breathing of the two girls on either side of her ceased, or at least she wasn't able to hear it anymore over the sounds of the engine. The plane whooshed down over the pool, and just as Astrid was about to ask again what it could possibly be about, Cordelia stood and descended the wide steps and strode across the grass. She did not seem in the least intimidated by the frightful metallic whirring on the nose of the plane—Astrid called to her to be careful, but by then she was out of earshot, the blue-and-white leaves of her skirt swishing against her determined calves.

The various men charged with the security of Dogwood had taken note of the disturbance. Windows on the second floor of the main house opened, guns were drawn behind tree trunks, shouting could be heard from the edges of the property as Darius's daughter crossed the lawn. With a gesture of precocious authority, the girl in question communicated that she would be handling the intruder herself.

"What do you think you're doing here?" Cordelia shouted over the roar of the engine, which rippled her skirt and hair. She was so angry that every part of her seemed to almost shake, as though all of her might come undone and float away on the thick summer air. Max cut the engine, and the airplane quieted. He hopped to the ground, but did not seem any more likely to answer her. "Besides ruining my grass," she added sharply.

He pushed back his goggles and stared at her. Then, without giving any indication of having appreciated the surrounding scene, he said: "Don't you think you have enough of it?"

"That's right—I forgot how easy it is for you to be careless with other people's things."

Max averted his gaze. Against her will, Cordelia found herself thinking that he was rather good-looking in a simple way, his plain white T-shirt tucked into the army-style pants, his utilitarian boots, the compact strength of his torso and arms. His features were smooth and symmetrical as though he himself were a flying machine, and though he was barely taller than she, Cordelia felt certain that if he wanted to, he could easily pick her up. There was no way he would ever move silkily across a dance floor, as Thom Hale might, and into some silly slip of a girl's affections, and she couldn't help but grudgingly respect him for that.

"I'm sorry about the grass," he said in a voice that was quieter and less forceful than any she had yet heard him use.

Contrition was not what Cordelia had been expecting. She crossed her arms over her chest and tried to muster an appropriate retort.

"And I'm sorry about the other day," he went on before she could manage one. "I knew we'd meet again. But that wasn't how I imagined it."

"No, I bet not. You'd rather disparage me in my own home, all the better to spit on the spoils of bootlegging, is that it? That's how the truly righteous do it, I suppose."

"I'm not righteous." His blue eyes met hers and didn't flinch. "I just don't care for your kind of fun."

A sigh of disbelief escaped Cordelia's lips and she rolled her eyes. "Perhaps you mean you don't care for fun?"

"Perhaps."

"Well." Cordelia cleared her throat. "Now that we've got

that clear, do you want to tell me why you've used my lawn as a landing strip?"

"I wanted to tell you I was sorry. For the way I behaved on the Fourth. And thank you more properly for saving my life." He glanced up toward the house, where Astrid and Letty were surely gawking. Cordelia refused to look. When he returned his gaze to her, he put his hand out—either pointing at her or reaching for her hand, Cordelia couldn't be sure. "You can't think I take it lightly, and in time I'll make it up to you. I've been turning over what you said to me at the Beaumonts', that you know who you are—I'd be a hypocrite if I didn't respect that, no matter what I think of your family business. You see, I am impressed by what you did."

Cordelia cocked her head back, wishing that she weren't so pleased with that praise. But it didn't escape her that he hadn't actually said he was sorry—he had merely stated his intention to apologize.

"Impressed?" She made a scoffing noise. "I didn't grow up like these White Cove girls, you know." It was the first time she had ever spoken with pride of her other life, and though she had conjured this rougher history as a kind of defense against his judgments, she was surprised to see him soften at the mention.

"I read about that," he said earnestly. "I guess that's partly why I'm impressed."

So the high and mighty Max Darby went to the news-papers to find out things about people, just as she had. The corners of Cordelia's mouth flickered against her will. "You must have very low standards for being impressed."

"On the contrary." He gave a little bow. "So—does this mean you've accepted my apology?"

"Maybe," she answered reluctantly.

"And you'll let me properly thank you for what you did that night?"

Now Cordelia did lose control of her stony facade and a smile crept over her face. He smiled back. It was the same rare smile she'd seen in the hospital waiting room, the beautiful creases emerging perpendicular to the corners of his mouth in his tanned skin, the sincerity in his eyes that seemed also to convey how unusual it was for him to share this particular facial expression with the world.

"I guess it depends how you intend to thank me—I *do* like fun, you know."

"Yes, I know that, too, but I think I am capable of entertaining even the famous Cordelia Grey."

"Is that so?" Cordelia was about to rejoin, but her flirtatiousness waned when she saw her brother.

"This is private property!" Charlie shouted as he approached across the lawn with Jones just behind him.

Cordelia glanced from her brother to Max, who had

stepped back toward his plane and drawn himself up. The metal fuselage was so reflective that she could not make out his expression.

"You're not wanted here!" Charlie's voice reached a fevered pitch.

"Listen, young man, we have armed men all over this property," Jones said, coming to a halt just behind Charlie. "I'd hate to have to shoot you down."

Max glanced at Cordelia. She was tempted to intervene, but the pilot's gaze was preternaturally steady in the face of this threat. She felt awed by his display of grit and didn't want to meddle. "All due respect, I don't think a criminal much wants the attention he'd buy himself by shooting down a national treasure on his property." He blinked once, but the rest of him was unflinching.

"Really—this talk of people shooting each other down!" Cordelia smiled wide and stepped forward, putting herself between Max and the other two men. "Let's stop bluffing, shall we?"

The corner of Max's mouth twitched, and she saw it, and for a moment they were a secret two-man team. "I didn't mean any harm. I only wanted to see if the lady might want to take an airplane ride—"

"No," Charlie shot back hotly. "I don't think my sister wants to fly with you."

"Actually, I'm rather curious." Cordelia glanced at her brother. "I'd like to know what this flying is like."

"Cord," Charlie hissed, snatching her wrist and pulling her away from the pilot. They took several long, fast strides before he stopped and gave her a serious stare. "You can't fly with him."

"Why not?" A disbelieving sigh escaped Cordelia's mouth. "He's not going to hurt me. I saved his life!"

"Yes, but . . ." Charlie sighed and let go of her. He turned, narrowing his eyes against the bright sunlight. "Listen, we've got work to do. After what the Hales did to Dad, why should they not try for you or me, too? And I wish you wouldn't go up in that damn contraption."

"Oh, Charlie!" A genuine laugh bubbled up from her throat. "Is this because you're afraid of heights?"

Charlie's eyes lit up with fury. "No! But it's no time for reckless living, and anyway, we've got to go into the city. We're opening a speakeasy in a few weeks, or don't you remember?"

"Yes, I remember." Cordelia let out a sad breath, and cast her gaze over at Max. He was staring impassively at the grand house behind them as Jones lingered threateningly by his side. A few days ago, she had been so excited to build something that would honor her father and bring her back into life, and she did badly want to grab at that feeling again after her long spell of self-pity. But then she looked at the airplane, and Max's taut stance, and she wanted above all else to see the world as he saw it. Changing tack, she clasped her hands together and opened her eyes wide. "Oh, please, Charlie . . . please?"

The begging must have softened him, and after a glance backward at the intruder, he threw his arm around her shoulder. Together they walked back toward the plane. "Only for an hour, hear me? And when you get back we're going straight to the city, got it?"

"Yes! I promise." She gave Max a sly smile as they returned. "Mr. Darby, I'm yours for exactly one hour."

Max stepped forward and offered his hand to Charlie, who reluctantly shook it. "You have my word I'll take good care of her."

"All right," Charlie said, turning away. "All right."

"That means you can land on our property once more," Jones said. "After that, God help you."

"One hour!" Charlie yelled as both men retreated.

By then Cordelia had climbed into the cockpit, and Max was strapping her in and handing her aviator goggles. A stoniness came into his features as he went to work on a complicated board of levers and dials. The whole body of the plane began to shake and rumble noisily as they sped forward across the lawn. Just when her mind had drifted from the purpose of the thing, she felt the ground drop away, and before she could stop herself, she had reached out for Max's forearm.

Even then he did not look at her. His arm was strong and rigid, and it did not respond to her touch. His concentration was so intent on the operating of the airplane that he almost seemed to have forgotten the presence of another passenger. Cordelia found herself simultaneously insulted and impressed by the narrowness of his focus. There was something ruthless about the way that he brought them up and up; but it was also unmistakably the way a person went about doing something they loved. The noise of the engine was almost deafening, and yet the space they were entering was a quiet one—the cares of men had become quite literally small and insignificant as she rose above them.

"Does this make me your copilot?" she asked with a grin once they had leveled off, shouting to make herself heard above the mechanical roar. For several seconds he gave no sign of having heard her.

"No," he replied eventually and without any reciprocal flirting, so that the word sounded to her like a rebuke. "You are my passenger."

"Oh."

A few minutes before, when he had given her that conspiratorial look, she had wanted nothing so much as to be on an adventure with him. His hardness stung now as it had on the Fourth, and her eyes drifted away from him to the view. She would never have guessed how vast the estates were—huge blankets of green stretching from one grandly roofed house to another, each with its twisting drive, where tiny figures moved back and forth between porticos and polished limousines. There were swimming pools the size of thimbles, and horses the size of ants, and beyond them boats that might have been used as toys in dollhouses floating across the sparkling blue body of water yawning open in the direction of the sea.

"This is what I wanted to show you," Max finally broke their silence. "This is my world."

His voice was friendlier now, but Cordelia's own friendliness had waned. "But this is only the world at a great remove," she replied breezily. "Doesn't it just make you hungry to go down into it?"

"Sometimes. But I've walked around on the ground all my life." His face was still and serious. "Anyway, I don't feel removed here. I see the earth below much more keenly than you do."

"How is that?" Cordelia laughed. "You certainly can't read a face at this distance."

"No, but you can read the geography and the weather, and those things matter to me twice as much as someone on land. To me, night coming on means something. Not just that it's time to change clothes and get ready for a party. It means that if I run out of fuel or my engine quits, I'll have a much harder time finding a place to land. It means being alone in a darkness and a quiet unlike any you've ever known. It means something real—a matter of life or death."

"And you dare to suggest that is more interesting than a new dress and a roomful of people who want to dance?" Cordelia replied archly. Then she winked to show him she knew how ridiculous this sounded.

Max, she might have guessed by then, was not free and easy with winks, and she briefly thought he was going to return to his dismissive attitude about her family's line of business. But he only smiled and said, "Wait. You'll see."

She did not have a chance to return his smile for at just that moment they went headlong into a cloud. A cottony white surrounded them on every side. They were flying blind, she realized, and her stomach dropped. "Oh, God!" she cried out, and tried to quell her instinct to reach for him.

But perhaps that was unnecessary, because he let his hand rest gently on her arm and said, "Everything will be all right," in the most trustworthy tone she had ever heard.

When they emerged from the cloud, Cordelia's gaze settled on a house positioned on the top of a hill, facing down toward the sound. The house itself was stately and white and flanked by several smaller outbuildings.

"My patron's home," he explained.

"That must be very lovely for you." Cordelia smiled faintly. "How does one get himself a patron anyway?"

"As soon as I was old enough to ride the train by myself, I'd come out to the airfields. Mr. Laurel is a Wall Street man, but he's always been an aviation enthusiast, and he noticed me hanging round the local airfield every day. I was skipping school, of course, and he told me I should go back. But when he saw I wasn't going to listen, he decided to recruit me instead. I was eleven."

"He made you, then."

"No." Max shook his head, and brought the plane even higher, as his adoptive home receded. "I made me. But with all Mr. Laurel's done for me, it sure was easier. Not easy. But easier."

Cordelia found herself looking away again, for what was there to say in return? She didn't want to tell him about the dreary place she came from, and she suspected he didn't want to share his history. Meanwhile, her eyes skimmed the shoreline as they moved fast over the miniaturized landscape. Then she felt her heart lurch for another reason: Down below was a house she had been to only once. The large white-shingled structure spread across a low lawn, its two wings reaching out as though in a sickening embrace. There was the spot down by the water where she had danced with Thom—she had pretended to like him for a few awful minutes, when she had still believed herself capable of killing him.

"The Hales' property," she almost whispered. Then

something strange caught her eye, and her tone changed. "What's that?"

Max leaned toward her to see what she was looking at. "Oh, that."

Some yards offshore, the great gray back of a whale had emerged from the water. It lingered there, spouting water, like something from prehistory, huge and dull in the afternoon sun. Men were running toward it, from the shelter of trees onto an old pier. There was no way she could have heard them, over the roar of the engines and at such a distance, but she knew from the way they moved their arms that they were shouting.

"It's the Hales' submarine—German, from the Great War. He was over there, you know. Not as a soldier but as a profiteer. Apparently he came back with lots of that sort of thing."

"Everyone knows?"

"No—it's a pretty well-kept secret, I think. He wanted to add airplanes to his arsenal, so he talked to Mr. Laurel about it once. Mr. Laurel despises that sort of business. But he couldn't resist the temptation of a submarine ride. And, of course, I see things up here others don't."

"Then you've seen it before."

"Oh, yes. Though not usually at this time of day—they must be up to something. I usually see it at dawn, sinking down from here and then emerging near the White Cove Country Club."

Soon the big submarine was behind them, and the silvery

bullet of an airplane had traveled on. A desire to know more about the Hales flared up in her—but with great speed she was carried far beyond those stale thoughts. Max began to point out other, more interesting landmarks: notable houses, particularly ancient farms, places where he had made emergency landings, and the humble homes of kind people who had helped him in times of distress.

By the time he landed back at Dogwood one hour had become many, and Charlie had already departed for the city. But Cordelia was not sorry. The ground beneath her feet seemed to hold less gravity than before; when she climbed down from the airplane she felt positively weightless.

"Thank you for your time, Miss Grey," Max said from the cockpit.

She smiled back at him.

"I hope you'll let me take you up again some time."

That seemed like enough of an assurance that they would see each other soon, so Cordelia replied with nothing more than a little wave and moved away toward the house on impossibly light feet, without looking back.

8

THERE ARE FEW SIGHTS SO PLEASING AS TWO YOUNG
women walking side by side, their short hair mostly covered
by the cloche hats sitting slightly jaunty and irregular on their
heads, their slim arms laced casually at the elbows, their pert
noses pointed upward—which is of course a result of their hat
brims, but also allows them to carefully assess whomever they
may encounter when they enter a room. Astrid had, by now,
become effortless at participating in such scenes, although
when she stepped into the White Cove Country Club's luncheon room in the company of her old friend Willa Herring
(Miss Porter's, '28), she walked with new intention and kept her
left hand carefully pointed outward for all to see.

"What a way to get engaged!" Willa exclaimed, as she laid her gloves in the empty chair beside her. "Everyone is talking about it. They all want to know how you will redo Dogwood, now that you are the mistress of the place."

"But there was hardly anything to the engagement! I just said yes and moved in." Astrid replied with uncharacteristic modesty. "Anyway, it's Charlie's house. I can hardly tell him which shirt to wear, much less how to decorate Dogwood."

"Don't be daft, darling! You downright make him." Willa's healthy auburn hair, wavy and bobbed, as well as her straight, white teeth, were her birthright as a member of the De Bord family of Madison Avenue and Rosetree Walk, White Cove, although her full, chic prettiness had not peaked until her acquisition of an even finer surname. That happy event occurred last November, when she was married, in magnificent style, to Sherman Herring, the shipping heir. "I can't wait till you're a real married lady. Then you and I can grow very competitive about our parties and homes and who we manage to bag as guest of honor, and then *Leisure & Play* magazine can write about the rival hostesses Mrs. Grey and Mrs. Herring, and they will do those wonderful little cartoon illustrations of us, in which we will both look so exquisitely skinny, and we can pretend to hate each other, and they'll just eat it up!"

"Of course, *you* will have to be the grand dame, and *I* will have to be the upstart," Astrid replied, casually batting a blond lock away from her eyes. She was wearing white naval-style pants (a gift from Billie, who had come by them at a speakeasy that somehow or other attracted both Barnard girls and sailors); her blouse was simple and white. She had thought it best that she let Charlie's gift speak for itself. "That's the way they'll write it, you know—because I am to be the wife of a bootlegger!"

They both broke into cascades of laughter and signaled for iced tea. "Even better," Willa said as she adjusted the low scarf neckline of her sleeveless white chiffon dress. "You were always interesting, my dear, but you are about to become so obviously doubly more so."

When the waiter returned with their iced tea, Willa ordered crab salad for both girls, and slouched rakishly into the fan-backed wicker chair. Astrid smiled deferentially at her, but of course she knew in her heart that she'd always had a unique kind of flair, even when they were just girls in school uniforms, crossing the quads in identical garb. But Astrid had woken up in a blissful mood, and the sun was shining, and she felt perfectly at ease letting Willa play the older and more experienced girl. After all, she had been married for nearly eight months now, so she did probably know a thing or two, and her wedding—right here in the club, on a crisp autumn day that had proved perfect for the bountiful yardage of lace that she had worn—was one of the most successful and talked of in recent memory.

"Now," said Willa, widening her eyes, "tell me everything."

"Oh, there's just so much to decide! I don't even know where we'll have it yet, and of course that will determine everything—what sort of flavor the thing has." Astrid took a gulp of iced tea. "Dogwood would be ideal, for it has so many delightful spots . . . but that means a much smaller guest list, because they won't want to let just *anybody* in the place. You should have seen how Charlie's man Jones reacted a few days ago when Max Darby landed on our lawn in order to say hello to Cordelia! He threatened to shoot him."

"No!" Willa's glossy lower lip dropped.

"*Yes.*" Astrid closed her eyes and waved away the wisp of gossip. "Then there's Trinity on Main, but that doesn't really seem like my and Charlie's style, and perhaps they won't want criminals like us anyway? In which case, *we* certainly don't want Trinity."

"What about Marsh Hall?" Willa took a ladylike pull on her straw.

"Available," Astrid said with a glitch in her voice and a roll of her eyes. "But *nooooo*—on account of Mother. And of course the country club is out, because you already had the perfect wedding here, and how could I ever follow that?"

Both girls sipped their tea and avoided the real reason Astrid and Charlie would never be married at the country club, which was that it was owned by Duluth Hale's in-laws. Instead, Astrid paused and sighed heavily, as though to say, "This is all so exhausting," and Willa responded by sitting up straight and giving her the understanding look of an older sister. It occurred to Astrid, as she observed the slightly patronizing downturn of Willa's painted red mouth, that being a bride was not a new land that she had personally discovered, and suddenly some of the fun went out of it.

"I suppose you ought to have it at the Yacht Club then," Willa replied, her eyes crinkling at the corners.

The waiter appeared and put down a spare, prettily garnished plate before each girl. By the time he had absented himself, Astrid had realized that Willa was exactly right. You could not have a bootlegger's wedding at a church, and Charlie wouldn't set foot at the country club—the Yacht Club, however, was situated right on the sound, had always been open to those who could afford its membership, and was the sort of place that attracted the well-heeled but was also not averse to a rowdy party. The ceremony would be held at sunset, reflected spectacularly in the waters that spread out from beneath the wide deck, which would be strung with electric lights and paper lanterns and a great variety of floral arrangements. She could picture it so clearly that it was almost as though it had already happened.

"That's perfect!" she exclaimed.

"You see," Willa crowed, clapping her hands together, "I *told* you I would help you get all this wedding nonsense in order."

After that, Astrid let Willa do the talking. There was plenty to discuss—the mortifying details, the near tragedies, and the ultimate triumphs of her own wedding day.

"It was a lifetime ago," Willa sighed, before launching into her reminiscences. "I was so hopelessly naive and without taste, it seems to me when I look back. But of course I've grown up fast since."

The more she went on and on, the less and less Astrid listened, and not just because Astrid felt sure that, in the end, she would do things her own way. Of course it had originally been her idea to have lunch with Willa; Willa, she knew, would inaugurate her into the world of married women—stately, cool women who knew how to decorate a house and please a young husband. But now as Willa covered precisely these topics, Astrid began to fear that none of them was quite so interesting as she had imagined they would be.

"Of course you must be careful about reducing," Willa went on, as Astrid put a full forkful of crab salad in her mouth. "I did it rather *too* effectively with the unpleasant effect that I had to have emergency alterations to my dress on my wedding day!"

"Oh, dear," Astrid replied blandly.

"Yes, I know! It was terrible! Almost fifteen pounds! But really it was all because of my mother-in-law, the old bird. There's nothing worse than some dowager dripping jewels and watching every bite you eat—that's what they're like in the old families, you know. Although I suppose you won't have that problem—for I am to be the grand dame, and you are to be the upstart!"

Although this had originally been Astrid's little joke, it stung now to hear it out of Willa's lips. It wasn't that Astrid felt that her fiancé was in any way inferior to Willa's husband—she knew perfectly well that the Herring wealth was only a few generations removed from slave-trading money, and that plenty of fortunes gained in far more deplorable ways than bootlegging came to seem august and respectable quickly enough. And it wasn't even that she really wanted to be a grand dame. She was hopelessly girlish, and many lifetimes away from seeming anything of the kind. But she heartily disliked the idea of closing even a single door on herself.

"Can you imagine?" Willa went on, oblivious to the slight, or perhaps merely content to let it hang in the air. "There I was, *minutes* before walking down the aisle, or I don't know, probably late already—and meanwhile, the dressmaker is still pricking me with pins, and I was sure I would faint . . ."

Astrid drummed her fingers against the white tablecloth to the right of her half-eaten crab salad and glanced away from the large, shiny jewel on her left hand, which suddenly seemed to her like a very low price for her body and soul for all eternity.

For several minutes Willa continued in this vein, gushing

on, until a new topic came to her and she suddenly clapped her hands. "But of course we must talk about the wedding night!" She leaned back in her chair again and lifted a manicured eyebrow that was sharp with naughty implication.

"The wedding night?" Astrid repeated hesitantly.

"Yes—*you* know what I mean." Willa made her face very long and serious. "It's dreadful, of course, and as soon as Sherman went back to his own bedroom, I cried and cried."

This change of conversational direction caused a wave of seasickness to pass over Astrid, and for a brief moment she tasted crab salad at the back of her throat. The idea of doing something so grown-up and permanent made her recoil. *Surely Charlie won't be like that*, she wanted to say. Instead she made a little moue of her mouth and said, "Did it hurt bad?"

"Oh, *Lord*, you have no idea. It's grotesque, really, how they poke at you, and then afterward naturally they're not the least bit amorous anymore . . . but you must go along with it. It's your duty as a *wife*. And you do get used to it eventually, and if Charlie is nice like Sherman, he will try to do it quickly so that you can have it over with. Try to think of something pretty that you want to buy and keep your eyes on the ceiling and you'll hardly feel a thing."

Astrid had to look away from this unpleasant sermon. With her soft pink cheek rested on her other fist, she let her eyes drift across the emerald field, where people dressed in white were going about their various sporty activities. Eventually they settled on the figure of a man she knew but had not thought of in some time. His name was Luke; he was a horse trainer there, and he had been her mother's plaything a month or so ago. He was now leading the horse of some other wealthy lady, his slender figure moving confidently as he whispered to his charge, his dark hair flopping over his pretty eyes.

"Oh, dear, I've made you nervous now, haven't I?" Willa said.

"No, it's not that . . ." Astrid replied vaguely. In fact, the sight of Luke had made her stomach turn again, this time in agony, and she thought of how sweetly pink his face used to get when she winked at him. He did not look capable of poking and prodding at her or turning away coldly when he'd done his business. Every gesture he'd ever made toward her was gentle and adoring. Suddenly she was longing for the simplicity of that kind of flirtation, when all is suggestion and nothing very much has happened yet.

Of course, she'd been at least half interested in Luke only because it allowed her to do her mother an unkind turn. Really he was nothing more than a handsome, humble boy, and there was nothing she wanted from him now. But for one brief moment, gazing at him at a distance, she couldn't stop herself from feeling the teensiest bit irritated by Charlie's proposal—which, after all, she could hardly have refused when it followed so quickly after his father's horrific death—and how it would prevent her from ever again having that wonderful, novel sensation a girl gets just before she is about to share a first kiss. Not to mention how it would keep her from ever being able to walk into a hotel bar and pretend she was somebody else, or fall in love with somebody older and wiser, or be called a society grand dame. Charlie would expect to have her every night, and she would never again be allowed to float in that wonderful, romantic place of mere possibility.

"You know," Willa said, changing the subject awkwardly, "it looks very much like rain."

The air *was* particularly dense, Astrid noticed, and a cloud had been dimming the sun; perhaps that was the only reason that gloomy thoughts had crept into her afternoon. "Oh, don't feel bad, darling—I'm very grateful for the warning. But I know it won't be like that with Charlie," Astrid announced, returning to her usual blithe form.

Willa's eyebrow rose again, this time a touch skeptically. "They're all the same, dear. But let's not dwell. What is Charlie going to wear for the ceremony?" she went on, reaching for her glass of iced tea, so that her engagement ring fell against her wedding band, creating a faint clicking sound.

In the next moment the little cloud passed, and the light came down stronger than before on the two girls sitting near the edge of the open-air luncheon room. It caught in Astrid's ring, lighting it up. For a moment a blaze of diamond was all she saw. She glanced out across the green, but Luke was gone, and good riddance. A boy like Luke would never give her jewelry or host lavish picnics with her, would never inspire *Leisure & Play* stories, or anything else.

She didn't have to be a bride the way Willa had been a bride, or a wife the way Willa was a wife, with a retinue of servants and a husband who was usually off playing golf. She and Charlie would make a name for themselves as a very new kind of young marrieds—they would be always together and have small, simple evenings that were notable for the conversation that was had rather than the jewels that were worn. And when they did the thing that husbands and wives did together it would be very lovely and delicate and not at all the horrible way Willa had described it.

"Have you been listening to a word I've said? Charlie's his own man, I can't tell him what to wear," Astrid replied gaily, signaling the waiter for the dessert menu as she determined to banish those troublesome emotions she couldn't fully understand. "Let's talk about what *I'm* going to wear!"

9

"MISS, ARE YOU WAITING FOR SOMEONE? I CAN SURELY fetch you when they arrive. There's no need for you to go on standing there."

Letty—who had been leaning in the open doorway trying to enjoy the shade of the foyer while also keeping an eye on Dogwood's big front gates—turned at the sound of the slightly frantic voice. It was Milly, Cordelia's English maid, descending the main stairs with a basket of laundry in her slender arms and a particularly beleaguered quality to her uneven eyes. She must have been the only soul working that day. A humid languor hung over Dogwood; the boys were swatting flies in their undershirts, and ice cubes were in short supply because everyone had been melting them on their foreheads last night trying to get to sleep.

"Oh, no, Milly, thank you, that's all right." Letty shook her head and returned her attention to the sloping hill, the two rows of lindens that lined the drive down to the main road, where any minute Grady should be arriving. She could not possibly explain to Milly why she felt the need to wait for the only person she had ever personally invited to Dogwood, instead of loitering casually upstairs as Cordelia or Astrid would have done. He wasn't as fancy as the other people who dropped by for iced tea or highballs, she might have said, but wouldn't that sound cruel to a girl who had traveled across a vast ocean just to zip up other girls' evening dresses? But then Milly was gone and an old black roadster appeared, motoring up the hill. Letty's stomach whirred.

When the car slowed to a stop and he opened the driver-side door, she suddenly realized that she had no idea how a girl was supposed to act around a boy who was taking her to the movies. Panic gripped her thoughts—would he expect a kiss on the lips? She should have asked Cordelia earlier, before it was too late. Would he think she was pretty enough to go to all the trouble?

Quickly she turned to the hall mirror for confirmation that she didn't look awful. She was wearing a pleated white skirt and a light brown blazer that had once belonged to Astrid; it was a bit too large for her, and so made her petite body appear even smaller. On her head she wore a soft brown beret, pushed back, which gave her a continental air. She had trimmed her own bangs to make the plucked arcs of her eyebrows visible, and then used some of Astrid's rose-scented oil to give her dark hair extra gloss.

"Hello, beautiful!"

"Oh!" she gasped. In her distraction she had not heard Grady come in. She glanced over her shoulder to see if anyone was behind her. "Me?"

He laughed and kissed her lightly on the hand. "I forgot how funny you are." Then, offering her his arm, he said, "Come on, or we'll be late for the picture."

As they motored toward the city, she decided that she liked the rather literary way he dressed, in the tweed pants of a knickerbocker suit and with the sleeves of his white shirt rolled to the elbows. In the days since she had seen him her memory of the way he looked had faded and now she saw that the reality was better than the picture in her mind. At first this worsened her shyness, but by the time the skyline of Manhattan was coming into view over the low, dirty suburbs of Queens County, she had relaxed into the forward motion of Grady's old roadster, and all her apprehension had been transmogrified to excitement.

"I haven't been to the movies in ages!" Letty said, as

the skyscrapers on the horizon grew taller and the distance between them and White Cove increased. "Not since I got to New York."

"Well, that's just criminal." Grady cast his eyes toward her and smiled. "No young men have thought to take you?"

She blushed slightly, but the speed of the car and the wind in her face were conspiring to make her bold. "I suppose I was waiting for the right fellow to ask me," she replied in her most twinkling and girlish voice.

For a minute Grady did not reply. His eyes were on the road and his cheeks looked suddenly ruddy. Perhaps her flirtation was too bold after all, because he made no response to it and only asked, "Did you go often back home?"

"Oh, yes, all the time!" Letty gushed, spilling words to cover up her awkwardness. "Whenever I could. Cordelia was the only one who'd always go with me no matter what— the theater was in the next town over, and we had to walk a long ways, but I didn't mind." For a moment she was Letitia Haubstadt again, who used to run the mile to the theater in anticipation, and who felt weightless all the way back home, for the glamour of moving pictures had never failed to transport her. "Sometimes that was the best part of my whole week."

Grady smiled when he saw that she was smiling. "Which were your favorites?"

"Oh, anything with Ruby Carlyle in it." Letty turned her

eyes to the sky and began to play with a strand of dark hair. "I adored *The Lady of Havana* and *The Knights of Calizar* and *Little Mab*. And of course, the ones with Valentine O'Dell in them!"

"Why in hell," Grady blurted, his voice getting suddenly low and gravelly as he gave the steering wheel a slap, "do the girls so love that damn Valentine O'Dell?"

Letty's heart sputtered and she turned in the seat to gaze at him with enlarged eyes. She had never seen him angry before, and had never heard him curse. She hadn't meant any harm with the Valentine O'Dell comment—but then again, the world of dating was new to her, and perhaps she'd stumbled upon a rule she was ignorant of; perhaps, once you'd agreed to a date with one man, you were obligated never to find another handsome, ever. "But you mustn't think—"

"Miss Larkspur," Grady interrupted, making his voice very deep and mock-serious, and slowly turning his face in her direction. "I was only making fun. And, to prove it," he went on lightly, "to show you that I am not in the least jealous of Mr. O'Dell, no matter how handsome he may be, and no matter how the ladies do swoon over him, I am going to take you to one of his pictures this afternoon!"

Letty giggled in relief, settling deeper into the passenger seat of Grady's car. "Oh, thank you!" she gasped and clapped her hands.

"I'm cleverer than most, you know. I can't compete with the Valentine O'Dells of the world with my good looks alone." He paused, and clownishly pumped his eyebrows as though he were a heartthrob of the big screen. "So I must use the Valentine O'Dells to my advantage."

"You know," Letty mused coyly, "I'm not truthfully sure Mr. O'Dell is even my *favorite* leading man . . ."

"Oh, no? Who do you prefer? I must keep informed of any new competition."

"Well, if you insist, I will tell you that I thought Willard Dory was quite romantic in *One Night in London*. And of course no one can dance like Burt Perry. . . ." She closed her eyes and leaned back into her seat and tried to think of all the other stars whose mystical, sorrowful, gleaming eyes she'd felt boring into hers from the blackness of the little theater in Defiance, Ohio.

For a long time she had avoided memories of that theater, as well as anything else to do with her upbringing. This was partly because she lived in fear of betraying her backwardness to the privileged young people of White Cove, and also because she didn't like to think how her younger siblings must worry about their runaway sister. But for some reason, with Grady, it didn't feel so bad to talk about where she was from.

Their conversation continued in this easy manner. He was just as courtly as always, but she sensed something new in his posture toward her. There was an almost protective quality in the way he spoke to her, now that she was a passenger in his car. As they rolled into the city, the blare of signs and the sounds of cars and people everywhere—the yelling of housewives leaning from second-story windows, fanning themselves, smoking cigarettes, watching the activity down below—stole their attention. By then Letty had begun to feel that she was just like a girl in a movie, taking a long drive on a summer day with a young man who is too poor to impress her family, but who shows much promise, and who in any event is very good at filling a simple afternoon with wonder.

When they stepped out of the afternoon heat and into the large building on Fiftieth Street, she saw that the movie houses of New York were not at all like the little storefront in Defiance that used to stoke her imagination. Her vision began to adjust, and then seats upholstered in red velvet appeared out of the darkness, and instead of one old church organ, dozens of musicians were assembled in the orchestra pit down in front. They were playing a song that sounded like the breezes of a summer night. There were two levels of seats, like at the opera, and the high ceilings were painted in gold and turquoise and decorated as ornately as a pharaoh's tomb. Around them young people on dates, and children aimless on a summer afternoon, and tough-talking men, and fancily attired women who removed their hats arranged themselves in the long rows.

"I think there might be as many people in this room as

ANNA GODBERSEN

lived in all of Union," Letty whispered as they lingered at the top of a carpeted aisle that sloped down toward the tapestry that covered the big movie screen. There was a real stage, and she already felt giddy in anticipation of seeing the projections of giant actors moving across it in black and white.

"You may be right." Grady took her arm, and guided her to a seat in the middle of a row. "They say this theater was built for fifteen hundred."

Marveling at the idea that she was surrounded by a town's worth of souls, Letty closed her eyes. She took a breath. There was some alchemy in the mingling everyday odors of perfume and popcorn and cigarettes; to her it smelled like heaven. The orchestra stopped playing briefly, and she listened to the hushed voices and the hurried footfalls as latecomers settled themselves. For a moment she thought she felt Grady's fingers brush against her hand. But when she opened her eyes to glance at him, she saw that he had just been removing his hat, which was now perched on his knee. She was already giddy, knowing the movie was soon to start, and couldn't be sure if the sudden quickening in her belly had anything to do with his touch.

The orchestra began again. A soft tide of strings lifted the curtain slowly up, and with it all of Letty's inner spirit became elevated, too. There were a few coming attractions and other short films at the beginning, and then big scriptlike lettering

122

announced the Valentine O'Dell picture, and everyone around her became very quiet—almost ceased to exist, at least as far as Letty's consciousness was concerned, so complete was her absorption.

The story began to unfold: A Chicago heiress named Alexandra Barrington was being pressured to marry a young man of her own social class whom her parents deemed a proper match, but she—a modern girl and a free spirit—had refused. Alexandra was played by Sophia Ray, whose lovely face Letty was familiar with from many other films; she had been a child star in vaudeville and married her stage partner Valentine O'Dell when they were both sixteen, and nowadays she played opposite him in most of his films. Although Letty had known about Sophia Ray and Valentine O'Dell's romance since as long as she could remember, she never tired of reading it again whenever it was covered in any of the movie magazines. Others around Letty laughed at the foppishness of the Barringtons and their society, who were indeed played rather clownishly—but Letty was most moved by Alexandra's great, welling eyes as she faced the horrors of being shackled to a man she didn't love for all eternity. Eventually she snuck out into the world dressed as a boy and a great many adventures ensued.

Soon thereafter Valentine O'Dell made his entrance, wearing rags and playing a guitar, his strong jaw somewhat obscured by five o'clock shadow. But Letty could tell by the twinkling in his eyes that this character would be as dashing and romantic as Valentine O'Dell characters always were. At first it seemed that Alexandra and the hobo would despise each other, but eventually the musicians at the front of the theater took up a gay, manic tune, and the characters on the screen continued on their adventures together. For a while everything was either very funny or very sweet—the heiress and the hobo were falling in love!—until it all began to go terribly wrong. It seemed that the hobo might die, and that Alexandra might return to her foppish fiancé, and Letty found herself praying to God that she would not be so foolish as to marry him, even if he was rich and handsome, because it would be a betrayal of her true love.

"Oh!" she even cried out loud, when things were looking especially bad. That was when she felt Grady's hand again, this time most definitely reaching for hers, and she took it and pressed it with the force of her hopes for Alexandra and the hobo. But in the end the fiancé proved to be a cad, and the hobo survived, and it came out that all along he had been a successful songwriter who was only out in the wilderness seeking inspiration for his new stage show, and the story ended with a lovely wedding.

As soon as the lights came on in the theater, a racket of seats folding back and bodies moving toward the entrances and loud voices talking about what they had seen rose up around Letty. But she wasn't ready to move and break the spell just yet—she felt as though she had traveled a long way in the course of an hour and a half, and that she was as tired and spent as though she'd gone to the moon and back. Tears streaked both her cheeks. Grady, beside her, waited patiently until she was ready to leave. Most of the audience had fled, and ushers had moved in to sweep spilled popcorn, when she realized they were still holding hands.

"Oh," she said awkwardly, as she removed hers so that they could stand up.

Grady looked away and carefully placed his hat back on his head.

The world outside had undergone a change. Night had fallen and the smells of the city—of gasoline and garbage and fried food—had been washed away. Something almost sweet lingered in the air now. It had rained, and the streets were slick from the downpour, so that the streetlamps were reflected on the wet pavement and the puddles that spread out from the curb. They meandered in the general direction of the car, but when they reached it, neither seemed to notice particularly, and without discussion they kept on walking.

To Letty, the neon signs and the storefronts appeared unworldly bright as they glided by. Grady bought sugar-dusted donuts from an almost empty shop, and then they kept moving on down Broadway, where the lights became even more glaring, and the sights wilder.

"Do you think someday *we'll* be famous?" she asked, as they passed a theater where the names of the principal actors were illuminated from a huge, glowing marquee.

"I don't doubt it for a second. You will be a famous actress, and I will be a famous writer, and when they adapt my stories into films, I will write the screenplays, and I will make sure you get all the best lines. . . ."

Grady winked at her as he took the last bite of his donut and discarded the white paper, and they continued on, through streams of theatergoers and peanut-hawkers and pickpockets. Everything they passed appeared illuminated, but they themselves were apart from it, sailing just slightly above the crowd. They had gone somewhere together in the darkness of the theater, and the world seemed almost novel now. It was so vivid and so full of possibilities—but that was a secret between the two of them.

"I've missed the city," she whispered, wide-eyed.

"You mean you don't like it out on White Cove?" he asked.

"No, no," Letty replied quickly, for that wasn't quite what she meant. "It's very luxurious there."

"It's very luxurious, but"—he paused to give her a piercing look as they walked, their feet falling in mysterious tandem—"you prefer the hustle and bright lights of the city?"

"It's silly, I guess." Letty turned her head on its side and recalled the two-bedroom basement apartment—which she'd shared with three other girls and was, in the end, forced to leave in ignominy—and tried to pinpoint exactly what it was she missed. "When I lived here I spent most of my time at Seventh Heaven and never went to a single audition. My thrilling nights and incredible breaks were all in my head."

"Maybe they are just in your future."

Letty smiled at Grady, whose eyes seemed to gleam equally with the vision of the city and the vision of her. Manhattan was there for her—she could see it reflected on his face—and in a few weeks she would be here every night, singing in one of its clubs, making a name for herself at last.

She so liked what Grady had just said that she wanted him to say it again, in a different way, so that she could be sure that he meant it.

"Do you really think I have a big future?" She turned suddenly and found that he was closer than she had realized.

"Yes." His gaze held hers, and she forgot about the city's many stages and all the showgirls striving to get on them. His mouth wasn't far from hers; it would have only taken either one of them leaning slightly forward to produce a kiss, and for a long moment neither moved or took a breath.

When awkwardness began to creep in, she broke the silence with, "Thank you for taking me to the movies." But she spoke too formally and her voice carried strangely over the urban din.

His lips parted with the intention of a reply. But he didn't reply. Instead he stepped forward and put his lips against hers. When he drew back he did so only slightly, and she heard his breath becoming rapid. Faintly, she sensed his heartbeat. She had almost forgotten about all the other parts of her body when she felt his palm against her palm, just before he pressed his lips to hers again.

Often, when they were sitting by the pool or driving through the surrounding farms, Cordelia and Astrid would talk about kissing, and from their stories, Letty knew that they had done a good deal of it. She herself had only been kissed once, by Amory Glenn, under hateful and frightening circumstances. It did not occur to her until later that this was only her second kiss, so natural did it feel to be standing there on Broadway with Grady holding both her hands and pausing now and then to meet her gaze, as though he wanted to be careful not to offend her modesty, or else didn't quite believe that he was actually kissing a girl he'd thought of for so long.

The reality of the sidewalk, and the city spreading out around it in blocks by the hundreds, came rushing back to her when she heard the applause. She turned her dark head left and right and saw that all around them, passersby were gawking and whistling and clapping.

"Look at those two young lovers!" called an old man in the

ticket booth of a nearby theater. "They can't keep their hands off each other."

All of Letty's upbringing told her that she ought to feel shame at this moment. That being caught kissing in public would lead to months of judgments and recriminations from everyone she knew. But the faces of the people in the street, rosy with the light of the marquee and good cheer, didn't *look* judgmental. And the touch of Grady's hand in hers was too gentle and strong and wonderful-feeling to be bad. She smiled and gave a little bow, which heightened the applause around them, and then Grady took her under his arm and they walked on together.

From now on she would remember this kiss as her first, she decided. And when she was famous she could tell the tale of how significant it was that she had been kissed for the first time on Broadway.

10

CORDELIA WAS STANDING ON THE VERANDAH OF THE
Calla Lily Suite, trying not to smoke, when she spotted Danny
emerging from the allée of lindens and holding a yellow square
of paper that looked very much like a telegram. Immediately
she turned and hurried downstairs.

"What's got you so jittery?" he asked, having handed the
yellow paper over to her on the front steps. She gave him a
piercing look and decided not to explain that her long face was
because the telegram was addressed to Letty, and not to her.
It had been five days since Max Darby had taken her up in his
airplane, and every day that passed without a word from him
made her feel curiously earthbound and dull. Summer storms

had kept her indoors yesterday and the day before. Another five days like this would make her mad with cabin fever.

"Nothing, just the heat," she lied. In fact the rain yesterday had cooled the air, however slightly. "It's getting to all of us."

"Maybe." Danny grinned. "But you sure got down here awful quick even if it is so hot."

"Danny, go back to your post," she replied blandly. She was wearing a tank-sleeved dress of midnight blue that exposed her knees, flattered her long, tanned limbs, and brought out the warm hues in her brown eyes. If he had thought about it at all, it would have been easy for him to see that she was trying to look pretty for someone.

"As you like, Miss Grey," he replied with a courtly flourish of his hand, and then trotted back down toward the big black gates that marked the entrance of Dogwood. As soon as he was out of sight, she stepped into the humid afternoon and scanned the gray skies and the horizon line of treetops hopefully. But there was no sign of any bothersome intruders, so she turned around and padded toward the ballroom, where she found Letty standing in front of a mirror and earnestly singing one of the old campfire tunes, and Astrid listening from the bench of the white baby grand piano as she attempted to crochet something.

"Telegram for you," Cordelia announced as she sat down next to Astrid.

Letty stopped singing but did not immediately come

to see what the missive was about. She paused long enough to straighten the angled black line of her short hair and playfully bounce her shoulders up and down before skipping over, swinging her slender arms, which were draped in loose, bell-shaped white lace sleeves that lent her an especially nymphlike air. As she approached the piano she went up on her toes and twirled several times like a ballerina, then bowed deeply and dramatically for her two friends, who clapped.

"Well, who is it from?" Astrid demanded, sighing as the excitement died down.

Cordelia handed the telegram over to Letty, picked up Astrid's crochet, and began to idly undo her last few uneven stitches.

Letty ripped open the telegram and read it over quickly, and by the time her eyes had scanned to the bottom, she was smiling and biting her lower lip. "He wants me to meet his family this Saturday," she gasped.

"Who does?" Astrid asked, folding herself forward over her crossed knees and resting her chin on her hand.

"That nice fellow who took her to the movies." Cordelia looked up from the crochet work and gave Letty a wink. "Grady."

"Have I met him? I can never remember anybody, darling," Astrid explained apologetically. "Is he very handsome?"

Letty turned her head to the side and placed a contemplative finger over her lips. In a girlish, musing way she replied, "He *is* handsome. I didn't see it at first. But there is something so nice about his eyes . . . and he dresses . . . I don't know how to describe it, except to say that he looks cosmopolitan, intelligent, like he knows all kinds of people and places."

"Who are his parents, I wonder?" Astrid said. She had rested her head on Cordelia's shoulder to watch the way her fingers quickly worked the hook over the white yarn. "Not that it matters," she added.

"Oh, I don't know . . . I suppose his mother owns some little restaurant in the village and that his father writes for one of the socialist papers. It doesn't matter to me. He said he thinks we're both going to be famous, and that someday he'll write screenplays for pictures that I'll star in!"

Cordelia's mouth formed a lopsided smile. "Wouldn't that be something?"

"Anyway, can I invite him when the club opens, Cordelia? I would almost say he's my first fan—besides you, of course. He always gave me such encouragement, and that night at Seventh Heaven when I jumped onstage—"

"When was that? You've never told me that story. You know you are supposed to tell me *all* your stories!" Astrid exclaimed.

"Can you believe I did that?" Stars sparkled in Letty's eyes at the memory. "I scarcely can. It was because Cordelia was there, and I couldn't stand the idea that she'd think I was just a cigarette girl, you know . . . Cordelia, do you remember?"

Indeed Cordelia did remember, and she was about to relate the story of the night Thom Hale took her to Seventh Heaven, how when she entered that vast hall of debauchery, she saw a vision of a chanteuse, dazzling and confident in front of the band, and only afterward realized that it was a girl she'd known since they were both sporting scraped knees. . . .

But before she could get a word out, the phone rang in the next room, and her thoughts scattered over the possibility that it was Max Darby, calling for her. Her heart fluttered and her thoughts got quiet.

"Cordelia, darling, where did you go?" Astrid, speaking briskly, took Cordelia's shoulder and shook it. "Come back, why don't you."

"Sorry, I—" In the next room, she could vaguely hear Jones on the telephone, and her heart sank realizing that it was not for her. Of course, she and Max had made no plans. He hadn't explicitly said that they would see each other again; she was only making herself crazy, wondering when she'd get the chance to go on another adventure with him. "I don't know where I went."

"She's lovesick!" Astrid gasped gaily.

The word *love* clanged in Cordelia's ears. She worked the

crochet hook faster and narrowed her eyes. "No—no. It can't be love, I hardly know him, I only went flying that once and—"

"Ah ha! So it is that flyboy. I *knew* it," Astrid went on. "What fun it will be when Cordelia is with her pilot and Letty with her writer and Charlie and I will be king and queen of our roost, and we'll host splendid parties—everyone will think I'm such a genius at inviting people, but really of course it's just that I keep such good company always. I can't *wait* for that. Tonight I think I am going to practice my hostess skills, have just an intimate dinner with Charlie and see how I do . . ."

Gently, Letty reached forward and took the hook and yarn out of Cordelia's hands, which had become rather frantic while Astrid fantasized. Cordelia sighed. "Well, I don't know that Max'll want to come to any parties with me anytime soon . . ."

"But you do like him?" Letty asked earnestly.

"Yes," Cordelia confessed. "He's proud and rigid, really, and he doesn't like any of the things I like. I don't know why I'm even thinking about him!"

"Oh, I know why." Astrid giggled and leaned back against the piano, so that the keys made a faint noise. "You like him because he flies so high."

That sounded too simple to Cordelia, and she tried to think of what it really was about Max Darby that made her so desperate to see him again—but then her mind fixated on his self-assured comportment, the piercing blue of his eyes, and the things he had said to her while they were aloft before. "I like him because . . ." she murmured. "I don't even know if I *like* him exactly, it's just that I want to see him again so badly."

"Well, then you should see him soon!" Letty exclaimed with the bright optimism of a girl in the first throes of a new crush.

"I suppose." Cordelia shifted on the piano bench. "But he doesn't seem very likely to come back around at the moment."

"Then you ought to go find *him*, darling," Astrid interjected. "Think of something fun to do and then go knock on his door and tell him he'll be doing it with you. That's what I would do if I . . ." She paused and giggled and waved her hand in the air as though she were waving away a naughty thought. "That's what I would do."

Cordelia turned her head to the side and considered this. She'd never chased after a boy—when John Field, who she'd left behind in Union, was courting her, she'd only glanced at him a few times in the right way, and then he had chased her for weeks until she agreed to be his sweetheart. And Thom had always seemed drawn to her as though by some strange magnetism. But her life had changed dramatically since then, twice, so why should she think that it would unfold as it had in the past? Letty had drifted back to the center of the waxed floor, where she was pirouetting dreamily and half watching her friend. "Why are you smiling so big?" she asked.

"No reason." Cordelia tried to make herself stop smiling, but the idea of what she was going to do was making her feel light with nervous excitement and almost powerless over her expressions. "Nothing."

"When will you be back?" Astrid asked.

"I don't know," Cordelia said, backing toward the door.

"Charlie won't like it." Astrid winked. "But I do."

"In that case, don't tell him!"

By then her blood was pumping and her feet could scarcely keep up with the demands of her busy brain, which was appreciating, more and more every second, how right Astrid was. Max Darby didn't like her because she sat around in a big stuffy house on summer days, alternating between the lunch table and the swimming pool. It was possible that he didn't even like her per se—but he did admire her. And he admired her because she had driven with a sure and steady hand on a night when they were both in danger. Well, she could drive yet more steadily today, and she had nothing else to do, and a car at her disposal, and surely he would be more impressed by her showing up wherever he was than by waiting around for him like some fragile indoor pet.

It took her only a few moments of rooting through the back corners of her closet to locate a pair of snakeskin T-strap heels and a white scarf, which she tied Indian style over her forehead and knotted in the back. Danny gave her another look at the gate, but she ignored him.

"Not sure Charlie would want you driving that car," he protested faintly, pushing his flopping red hair off his forehead.

"I'll have it back before dark."

"But where are you going?"

"It's none of your business where I'm going, and anyway, I told you I'd be back soon enough."

"Charlie won't like it," Danny repeated.

But the gate was standing open, and she had accelerated through it and down the lane before he could stop her.

When Max had taken her up in his airplane he'd shown her where he lived, and she supposed that she could find Mr. and Mrs. Hudson Laurel's estate easily enough. Her instincts told her he was at the airfield, however, and indeed she was right. He was up in a red biplane that looked especially dramatic against the gathering dark clouds as he rose high and then swooped low over the heads of the technicians who were gathered by the hangar. She'd seen him do this trick before, but this time it made her heart flutter to think of what would happen if he did it wrong. Of course he pulled back just in time—and Cordelia, wanting to seem as nonchalant as the men wearing goggles and grease-stained jumpsuits, fought the impulse to applaud.

When he did finally land, the men by the hangar rushed forward to help him down. She could see them pointing in her direction and knew that they were telling him there was a girl waiting. He took a white rag from one of the men and wiped his brow, and then he came walking toward her, his path straight but not at all hurried, and his gaze fixed on the ground. He was wearing his usual uniform, the white T-shirt tucked into cargo pants, and there were places where the T-shirt was darkened with sweat. Just as he came into earshot, he lifted his eyes and smiled. After that she stopped wondering whether or not she should have come.

"I hope I'm not interrupting you," she called.

"No." He paused and appraised her, a few feet of humid air between them. For some reason, she stepped forward and offered him her hand to shake, as though they were business associates or men who have just discovered they'd attended the same college. "It's no weather for flying."

"Good! Then you will have no reason to refuse when I ask you to go for a drive with me."

He paused and his eyes went from her hand, as he let it go, to her face. "All right," he said simply. Then he turned and waved in the direction of the other airmen, who were pushing the shiny red plane into the hangar.

"I hope you don't mind if I drive," she said, turning and opening the car door.

"Miss Grey, I have no interest in telling you what to do or not to do." He closed the passenger-side door behind him and watched her as she started up the car.

"Really? It's funny—I've been trying not to smoke all day because I got the notion you didn't fancy it."

"I don't fancy it," he replied as they sped toward the main road. "But I admit I'd be disappointed if I thought you were changing your behavior to please me."

"That's very interesting." She tried to hide the happy upturn of her lips and kept the car straight.

For a while they drove in silence. The sun broke through the heavy clouds far out over the water, and to the east, showers chased them across peach farms. They kept the top up and the windows down. The car jostled her, but she liked it, as she liked the exhilaration of the wind in her hair, whipping sun-streaked tendrils across her cheeks.

"Did you drive a lot where you're from?" he asked presently.

"Only in emergencies, or to do an errand for my aunt. Not this kind of driving. Driving for the sake of driving, with nowhere in particular to go." She turned to him and met his eyes. "I like this kind of driving."

"You must miss her."

"No." Cordelia shook her head firmly. In the next moment, she began to worry that might sound too hard. "My ma died when I was little. I can't even remember her. My aunt thought it was her duty to care for me, but she didn't want me any more than I wanted her . . . but you must understand, aren't you an orphan?"

"I don't think of myself as one," he said, and then seemed not to want to say any more.

Before she could think of another topic of conversation, they came around the bend and saw a filling station, and she pulled over for gas. She climbed out and walked around the hood toward the pump, but Max was there with his his hand on the nozzle before she could reach for it.

"And all this time I thought you admired me for being such a modern girl," she exclaimed in amusement.

"I'm sure you are." He gave her a serious look and then let his eyes drift down over her figure. "But I'll not have you ruining a pretty dress like that just to prove you don't need me. I suspect we're both too practical for that."

"Are you sure it's practicality?" She leaned back against the car, crossing her arms over her chest and watching him pump gas with a playful light in her eyes. The air had that sweet, dusty smell that always comes just before it rains—she could tell rain was coming on, but it hadn't started yet. "But of course I wouldn't want to offend your sensibilities by accusing you of anything as pitiable as chivalry."

He laughed—one long, flat laugh—and said: "I'll show you chivalry if you let me, Miss Grey."

Her heart turned over at the way he went on watching her, even after he was done speaking, and she hoped she didn't blush. There was a way he had, of saying something and then being silent and still, that she found unnerving. When the tank was full, he went into the station to pay, and returned with two bottles of cola, which they drank as they continued to drive idly through the suburbs of Long Island, the fizzy sweetness teasing their tongues and settling their stomachs. It was not until they saw the filigree and turrets of the first tower of the Queensboro Bridge looming before them, its trusses silver against the black clouds, that she realized how long they'd been away, and that the wonderfully dizzy feeling she was experiencing might have as much to do with the fact that she hadn't eaten anything all day as with Max's company.

"I'm starving, aren't you?"

He murmured in reply—later she would wonder if that noise hadn't been intended to signal assent exactly, but already she knew where they should go. They sailed over the bridge and down into a city thick with men carrying their jackets laid over the crooks of their arms and women who had forgone the modesty of panty hose. Boys on the streets barked about fans, and policemen's horses swatted flies with their tails. Under a mauve sky that was heady with precipitation but as yet had declined to pour, Cordelia stopped the car. As she stepped out she handed the keys to one of the Plaza's liveried doormen.

She recognized the boy from the nights she and Charlie and Charlie's gang had been there, and she smiled her most winning smile as she told him, "Park her somewhere safe, will you?"

When she looked back at Max, she saw he was staring ahead blankly. For a moment she was afraid that he wasn't going to get out of the car. But then the bellhop jumped into the driver's seat, and he had no choice.

"Come on, then." She laughed, and led the way up the big steps. A newspaper photographer was loitering there, and he lifted his big, black camera, and before Cordelia could think she'd turned her face toward him and smiled. The flash went off, blinding them both. In the next moment they had passed through the revolving doors, off the dirty street and into the plush red-and-gold lobby with its quiet aura of opulent tranquility.

"I'm sorry if this isn't exactly your style, Mr. Darby, but my family—my brother and I—we like to come here from time to time and get a private dining room. I promise not to push any juleps on you, if you will only indulge me in having a sandwich before we head back home . . ."

The concierge recognized her then, and with a flourish ushered them to the little room with hammered leather panels on the walls and potted ferns that Charlie always requested.

"Oh, dear, you hate it here, even without the juleps," she

said, once the waiter had taken their order for hamburgers and colas.

"No, I'm plenty comfortable in these kinds of places, on account of Mr. and Mrs. Laurel." Holding her gaze, he lifted the napkin from the delicate china plate it sat upon, unfolded it ostentatiously, and lay it over the lap of his well-worn work pants. "I come here every night."

She blinked, wondering if she'd insulted him by implying that he was somehow less fine than she.

"I'm kidding you," he said after a pause, and grinned.

"I don't think I've ever heard you tell a joke before!" she replied, laughing. Then she mimicked him, shaking out her napkin self-importantly. "It scared me almost."

Every interaction they'd had up till then had been characterized by speed and movement, and now that they were sitting quietly, with no one around and no chance of acceleration, she began to feel intimidated by him again. It was not in Cordelia's nature to be easily intimidated; she had learned at a young age to protect herself from her aunt's demands and slights by always holding her head high and keeping a private tally of her own strengths that she could call upon when she was told to stand in the darkened closet for hours in punishment or scrub all the floors. But Max's steadiness upset her own.

"I'm still not entirely convinced that this teetotaling of yours is sincere," she offered with an arched eyebrow. "The arrangement you have with the Laurels certainly seems like a plum one, and I wouldn't hold it against you if you pretended to agree with their politics just to further the relationship," she teased lightly.

"I don't lie about anything," he replied sternly, but not unkindly. "Do you?"

"No . . ." Cordelia's breath was taken away by his directness. She felt as though she had been seen into, for though she was not exactly a moral girl, she had always been allergic to untruths. "I only meant, I wouldn't think badly of you, if that was the thing you had to do."

Max nodded, taking this in. "That's kind of you." His eyes rolled to the door as a tuxedoed waiter entered, carrying a silver tray aloft, and he did not speak again until the waiter had completed the elaborate process of laying out their lunch on the white tablecloth. "But I'm not just going along with Mrs. Laurel's belief in temperance. I've seen the evils that come from drink, and I'd rather stay far from it myself."

While he spoke he loaded his burger with ketchup and mayonnaise, and when he was finished he cut it in half and ate one half in three hungry bites, as though he hadn't eaten in a long time.

"It's not because I don't like a good time," he went on, wiping his hands on the napkin and then leaving it in a heap amongst the pompous table settings. "But my father was an airman in the Great War, and he came back from Europe with a ruined body and a mean spirit. He used to drink all day long and give my mama hell."

"Oh." Cordelia had taken one bite from her hamburger, and she set it down now and watched Max sympathetically. He didn't seem to be asking for sympathy, exactly—the way he told the story of his father was matter-of-fact. But she could see that the memory was awful. "That's terrible."

"He's dead now."

"I'm sorry."

"I'm not." Max picked up the other half of his hamburger, and began to eat again, though more slowly this time. "He did it to himself. I don't mean he was a suicide, but the way he drank in the end, it amounted to the same thing."

"Well, he couldn't have been all bad, or you wouldn't have followed in his footsteps." Cordelia took a sip of lemonade, and hoped he wouldn't recoil at the suggestion that he had something in common with his drunk of a father. "I'm sorry, I only meant—"

"No, don't say you're sorry." He laughed ruefully. "You'll think I'm stupid, but I never quite thought of it that way. I guess you're right, though." He met her eyes for a minute, and then cast his gaze back on the gleaming knives and forks, the flower arrangement on the embroidered white tablecloth, the gold salt-and-pepper shakers, and paused to work his jaw. "It's you who should forgive me. I'm not in the habit of talking to people familiarly, and I don't suppose I really know how to do it. But I like talking to you."

This was perhaps the closest to a sweet thing that Max had yet said to her, and she softened all over at the sound of it. "I like talking to you, too," she said, and then they moved on to other topics—the view of New York from above versus the view from below, the beauty of its lights pulsating at night, the strangeness of wanting hamburgers on a hot day, and on. They did not return to their childhoods, but there seemed to be no need—Cordelia felt that she knew where he had come from, and suspected that he had a similar understanding of her.

It seemed peculiar that, having traveled so far and with such desperate conviction to be part of a cosmopolitan milieu, she should find herself drawn to someone almost as plainspoken as John Field. But Max was not really anything like John, who in any event had been the only boy in Union to pay her attention. Once she'd caught his eye he became almost slavish to her.

"You're more interesting than the radio, I could listen to you for hours," he'd told her, one freezing night back in February, after dinner at Dr. and Mrs. Field's table, as he walked her back toward her aunt Ida's through the snow white streets. And though she'd loved that he'd said that at the time, she now saw that she wanted a boy to do more than follow her in blind devotion. She wanted a boy to challenge her, to tell her about things she'd never thought of, to show her new points of view.

She and Max talked a while longer, even after their empty plates had been cleared, and when they walked back into the lobby, he took her arm, seeming more at ease with her company and with the lavish surroundings. The rain had begun by then—it was a light rain, turning the streets sleek and the sky yellow, just enough to clear the sidewalks and keep people's heads down minding their own business, but not enough to make the roads unsafe. No one cared who they were as they made their way out, and when the bellhop brought the Marmon around, Max jumped forward and opened the passenger-side door for her.

"I hope you don't mind," he said.

This made her glad that she had fixed her lipstick before leaving the hotel, and she gave him a broad red smile before stepping down from the last step and shielding her hair as she moved from the shelter of the overhang and into the car.

"I'll not get in the way of your chivalry, Mr. Darby," she said as he started up the engine and turned the wheels in the direction of White Cove.

11

DOGWOOD'S LAWN WAS FRAGRANT WITH THE RAIN THAT had driven the boys indoors. Mosquitoes swarmed in the light that pooled from the high windows, and the cicadas sang their summer songs. Everyone was inside the big house, but Astrid had found that on this occasion she didn't mind so much. It was festive, the boys playing pool on the second floor, breaking into the old stores of bourbon, hanging their soaked shirts from makeshift laundry lines in the hall. The sultry weather had infused everything, even her skin, and she felt incandescent with the notion that tonight she was going to do something that she had never done before.

She had decided, that morning, when she woke up in a blissful mood and realized that she couldn't wait for the wedding to prove that Willa was wrong about what it meant to be man and wife. If Charlie and she were such a different kind of couple, why should they not be allowed to do everything at a more modern speed? The notion frightened her, but the fear created a tingling in her fingers and toes that was not entirely unpleasant. She would make a romantic dinner for Charlie all by herself and serve it in the formal dining room, without even Milly's help, and Charlie would be very impressed with her, as well as himself, for choosing such an incomparable girl to marry. Later, when the dishes were cleared, she would lean over and whisper in his ear, telling him what final surprise was in store for him.

All day her expectations for the evening had grown, and her good mood had bloomed along with her visions of domestic triumph. She'd sent Danny out with a shopping list and turned the oven on and then dressed in a bias cut evening gown of raw black silk that dangled from her soft pink shoulders on delicate spaghetti straps and swayed down, loose and sleek, against her slender calves. When Charlie came upon her in the hall he'd looked her up and down with a carnal light in his eyes. He had been on his way out to do some quick business, and had kissed her hungrily and promised to return home soon.

Once the roast was in the oven, she went into the enclosed porch on the west side of the house and lay down for a quick catnap.

It was the smell that woke her. Astrid was not used to

having to remember things—there was always a nanny or a servant or a social secretary to remind her that it was time to start getting dressed, and timetables had never been of any particular interest to her. She gasped and reached for her milky throat and a panic set in over the lost hours.

Night had come since she lay her head down.

"Damn!" she exclaimed for emphasis, before pushing herself off the couch and rushing from the library. The hall was already redolent with the strong odor of burned meat. The smell was stronger in the kitchen—but not strong enough, she was irritated to realize, to wake Len the cook, who was asleep on a chair, his real leg and peg leg splayed forward, his head tipped back, his several chins quivering with each snore.

"Oh!" she cried in frustration, as she pulled down the oven door and her soft skin was met with a blast of heat. She coughed, and then her heart sank at the sight of what was supposed to have been a very special dinner.

Len came lurchingly to. "What is it?"

"My roast! My roast!" Astrid reached forward to grab it.

"Careful." Len came hobbling over and elbowed her aside. He pulled the pan out, using—Astrid couldn't help but notice, even at the height of her frenzy—an old and probably dirty white undershirt. "That'll burn you bad."

"Well, why didn't you warn me it needed to be taken out?" she half wailed, half admonished.

Len chuckled, which only worsened her irritation. Otherwise he made no answer.

"Oh, it's ruined!" She balled her fists and stamped her foot like a child.

"No, no—it's not ruined," he replied, still with more amusement in his voice than she thought necessary. He inclined his weight forward over the roast, and with a large knife began to scrape at the charred bits. Astrid watched him skeptically, hands on hips, but as the seconds passed, she saw he was right—the meat came to look merely browned soon enough, and even its odors began to seem more appetizing than otherwise.

"I'm sorry," she said, with some difficulty, twisting her engagement ring on her finger. By the second utterance, she found it easier to say. "I'm *so* sorry," she gushed, "this is new to me, you know, cooking roasts and all, and I really should have asked for your help in the first place!"

"Oh, that's all right," Len said in a slow, amiable way, grinning wide to reveal an incomplete set of teeth. "My first piece of advice," he continued, turning and hobbling toward a small closet, "is that you put this on."

When he returned he was holding a long white cotton apron, which he put over her head. Astrid, smiling gratefully, tied the strings behind her back.

"Now, what else had you planned?"

"Baked potatoes and a salad of romaine hearts with

Russian dressing." Her voice had been proud until she saw his frown. "Is that bad?"

"No, no. The salad will be easy. It's only—baked potatoes take an hour maybe. You haven't started them yet, have you?"

She shook her head, and for some silly reason found herself wishing that a fat old man with a leg and several teeth missing would not look so terribly disappointed in her.

"I tell you what we do. I'll show you how to cut them real thin, and then we'll fry them—they'll be ready before you know it, and Charlie'll think they taste better, too."

"Thank you!" She beamed and followed him to the big butcher block under the window. After a minute, her gratitude waned slightly—she found that potatoes, when she sliced them, oozed strangely and slipped under her inexperienced fingers, and that she had a difficult time cutting them as thinly as Len was cutting his. After a moment she stepped aside and let her imagination drift to her tall, handsome man, his big, impressive features, and what a nice thing it was to be his little woman, waiting for him at home. . . . It was all very well for Cordelia to be running around opening speakeasies and Letty to be preparing herself for a life onstage. Evenings spent in the crook of Charlie's arm seemed like just exactly enough for her.

Before she knew it, Len's pudgy hands had turned a bag of potatoes into a high pile of pale slivers. "I'm sorry! Now you've done everything."

"I don't mind, ma'am."

"I know, but you see, I was utterly convinced that I would show you I'm not just a spoiled girl who can't do anything for herself, and now I've just gone and proven it to you!"

"I think you're perfect just as you are, ma'am."

"Keep saying things like that," she said, leaning forward and breathing in the thick air that rises up from anything being fried, "and you'll have to contend with me in your kitchen every night."

"Here," he said, handing her the frying pan's handle and showing her how to thrust it forward so that the potatoes sailed into the air and then landed, miraculously, just as they had been, except flipped to the other side. Gamely she tried it, although a few potatoes were lost in the process, and none of them landed quite so neatly. "There, see, you ain't so bad a cook. You keep an eye on that, I'll make your Russian dressing. No need to flip again—just make sure they don't stick to the bottom, all right?"

"All right."

As he moved across the kitchen and began taking things out of the icebox, she bent again and watched in amazement how quickly the potatoes had become pretty and golden. Only a few minutes ago they were just pasty unappetizing things, but already she had made them look so crunchy and delicious. It pleased her to think that soon they would be on one of the elegant china plates she had borrowed from Marsh Hall, and that Charlie would be eating them and marveling at what a tasty supper she had made him—he would be proud of her, and she would be proud of him, and they would drink champagne and waste away the evening in their favorite company. Perhaps she would have a little too much to drink so that he would have to carry her upstairs, and then . . . a shudder went up her spine at the thought.

Smiling daffily to herself, she reached into the pan, grasped a hot sliver, and popped it in her mouth. But the bite burned her tongue, and it didn't taste as good as she'd hoped. She reached for the saltshaker that rested on the back of the oven, and tipped it over the frying pan.

"Oh!" She drew in her breath when the top came off entirely and a white pile fell over the potatoes.

"What is it?" Len called from across the kitchen.

"Nothing!" She moved so that her body hid her mistake. She recapped the salt and shook the pan the way he had shown her. To her relief, the salt quickly mixed in, adding only a rough, glistening surface to the golden circles.

When she heard the sound of car wheels against gravel, she smiled involuntarily at the notion that Charlie was nearby, and she looked over her shoulder toward the hall, her fluffy blond hair brushing against her jawbone in expectation. The naked skin of her shoulders became alert. She wiped her hands on a damp cloth that was hanging from a nail on the wall and stepped away from the stove.

"I'll be right back," she announced, and passed out of the kitchen without looking back. Her eyes were focused on the front door and her sense that she was about to see Charlie was so strong that she did not at first notice how unhurried and light, how unlike Charlie's, were the footsteps outside.

"Oh, Charlie, there you are!" she said happily as the door opened. But it wasn't Charlie. It was the new man, the one with the long, dark lashes, and his features were not as relaxed as usual. His name was Victor—she had not wanted to know it, but he had rudely insisted on telling her that day he drove her back to Marsh Hall.

"Something's happened." He looked away from her and shook his head as though he were disappointed.

"But where's Charlie? I'm making him dinner," she said indignantly. Her lips trembled and her brow knitted up, but she went on with conviction: "A roast!"

"Something's happened," he repeated.

"What?" she shrieked. "What's happened?!"

"I'm sorry." He gave her a smile that was wavering but warm. "He told me not to leave your side tonight. *I'll* have dinner with you."

She took a few small steps toward the door as though she might see Charlie out there and be able to harangue him into staying with her. When she thought of what she had planned to give him, the humiliation began to build inside her. All of her fear and anticipation fizzled with the realization that her gift wasn't even going to be acknowledged, much less appreciated. "What about my roast?" she wanted to demand of him again, but she knew that would sound childish.

Victor lingered on the threshold another moment as the last car left the property at breakneck speed and the tall iron gates were sealed shut. "Damn," he muttered.

"Well, I don't much like it either!" Astrid crossed her arms over her chest and pressed her lips together in a pout. The dress was silky against her bare arms, which only reminded her what a special evening it was to have been, and of which she was now deprived.

He turned slowly, lingering in the doorway, his blue work shirt tucked into denim pants, and assessed her with his shrouded eyes. The face he wore seemed to indicate that something had been taken from him, rather than from her, and for a moment she forgot to be mad at Charlie and was mad instead at the man he'd left to babysit her. She let out a small growl of frustration and twirled round and stomped back into the kitchen.

"Everything is ruined, we'll have to—" She broke off when she realized that Len was not in the kitchen. Behind her she heard the door swing open, and knew that Victor had followed her. The muscles of her shoulders tightened in fury, and she paused, waiting for him to say something so that she could throw it back. He was silent, however—she couldn't even hear him breathing. After a few seconds she began to doubt that he was there at all. But her pride would not allow her to turn and look, so instead she strode forward, across the well-worn planks of the kitchen, and into the formal dining room that was to have been the setting for her last evening as a virgin.

"Len!" she gasped in surprise when she saw the one-legged man in the dining room, grinning over the table setting. Two china plates piled with handsome cuts of roast and beautifully browned potatoes sat with a bowl of green salad and a silver gravy boat between them. The candles she had earlier placed in silver candelabras had been lit, and the flowers that she'd sent Danny out for that morning were still in the white ceramic vases, just as she'd arranged them. It was a gorgeous table—just as pretty as her hopes—and this made her sense of abandonment that much more acute.

"It's all ruined." Her tone had transformed from anger to defeat.

Len's grin faded and his voice got grave when he said, "Something's happened?"

"Oh!" she screamed in frustration. "Why does everyone keep saying that?"

Victor came in behind her, and this time she knew for sure because he collided with her—gently, but nonetheless knocking her off kilter when he met her shoulder. This only worsened her humiliation.

"What's happened?" Len asked him.

"What's happened is that the young lady has lost her dinner date." Victor's manner had changed since that low curse on the threshold of Dogwood a few minutes before—he sounded ingratiating now, almost ready to laugh.

Len, sensing Victor's intentions, smiled again, and said: "Well, there is a fine meal here, and two young people to enjoy it. Should I get you kids some champagne?"

In fact, Astrid would have liked a glass of champagne at that particular moment, but she was no dumbbell, and she could tell when she was being pandered to. They were both eager to keep Charlie's girl happy, to keep her in line so that the boss could go on doing whatever it was he did, and this knowledge infuriated her even more. She would rather not have made a scene, but more than anything she wanted not to shed tears in front of Charlie's toughs—particularly not in front of the grizzled old cook—and the vision of all her labors and the knowledge that they would go to waste were conspiring to choke up her throat.

"Champagne!" she cried in outrage. "Who can think of drinking champagne when *something has happened*?" she went on with a desperate irony, stalking toward the windows, fixing her arms over her chest with her back to the men. "I wanted to

spend the evening with my fiancé, not with either of you bastards, so leave me be."

"Miss Donal," Victor went on in that cloying tone, as
though he hadn't even heard her insult.

"Leave me alone!" she shrieked. Her cheeks were hot,
and she knew shameful tears were on their way if either man
persisted even once more. But something in her tone must
have been enough, because she heard the floorboards creak as
they drew away, and then the door close behind them. A silence
followed in which she imagined she could hear the wicks of the
candles burning down and the wax melting away. She blinked
hard and forced her face to hold its expression. There would be
no crying—that was for children, and she was now the fiancée
of a man who did dangerous and exciting things late at night.
She could not act a child. But oh, how it stabbed at her, to be
left like this. To have been prepared to give herself completely
and to be rejected.

When she couldn't stand the silence anymore, she
dragged one of the lugubrious old formal dining chairs across
the floor so that the floorboards groaned beneath it and sat
down by the bay window, propping her elbow up against the
dramatic curve of the chair's back. No doubt the Grey siblings
were out there somewhere, going about their important business. It was almost half a day since Cordelia had left in pursuit
of Max Darby, and though it was Astrid who had first suggested

this course of action, now she felt jealous, and wished that she could go off chasing something shiny and new. But of course she couldn't—what but a boy was there to pursue?

In fact Cordelia had just left Max by the gate of the Hudson Laurels' place. He had not needed to say, and she had not needed to be told, that it would have been an awkward scene if she had gone with him as far as the front door. They had shaken hands by the side of the road as night fell, and then he had closed the driver's door behind her. Had she hoped there would be a kiss? Even without one she was smiling to herself when she started up the engine, and went on smiling until she came around a bend and realized that she was being followed by a Ford with its headlights off.

The skin at the nape of her neck went cold. She had noticed a brown Ford several times on the drive back from the city, but she hadn't thought anything of it when Max was driving. Now that she was alone and the darkness was near complete, the car's presence seemed ominous. Of course it was possible that the driver had simply forgotten to turn his headlights on, and there were lots of brown Fords. Perhaps the car had nothing to do with her. But she accelerated as she came around the next bend anyway.

She was going almost forty miles an hour—the Marmon was smaller and faster than the Ford, she felt sure—and for a while she thought that she had lost the other car. But then the road straightened out and she saw, in her rearview mirror, that the Ford was still behind her. The driver flashed his lights twice before turning them off again.

Cordelia swallowed and pressed her foot on the accelerator. The line of her shoulders had gone rigid, and she gripped the wheel as she sped down the country road. But the Ford matched her pace. She could almost make out the faces of the two men in the front seat now. She had kept the Marmon's speed up, and she was driving faster than anyone usually did on this stretch of road, but the car behind her went on steadily gaining. She stepped hard on the gas, and threw her gaze over her shoulder, looking back in the vain hope that the other car's proximity was some trick of the mirror.

That was when she heard the blare of horn, sudden and loud, from up ahead. Her head swiveled in time to see headlights coming from the opposite direction, fast, and she felt a presentiment of impact. Her foot softened on the pedal but she was too terrified of what was behind her to brake. The car coming from the other direction was a green roadster, and it missed her by so narrow a margin that both cars rocked violently and she was able to meet the other driver's eyes.

"Charlie!" she shouted as he passed.

In the rearview mirror she could see that the men pursuing her had swerved right to avoid a collision. She pulled left suddenly, stopping short just long enough to throw the car into reverse. The Ford sailed by—maybe the driver was distracted by the oncoming car, and was momentarily unable to match her every move, but she knew she didn't have long until they turned around. She drove backward as fast as she could, her arm thrown over the seat and her eyes focused frantically behind her. When she saw Charlie's car coming back her face relaxed, but the rest of her remained rigid until she had pulled her car alongside his.

"How many of them are there?" Charlie demanded. He had three men in the car with him, and they were all leaning toward her, their breathing heavy and the whites of their eyes big.

"Two, I think," she said, and put her hands over her face.

"Stay here," he yelled—at her, she assumed—and then she heard car doors slamming.

"Charlie, don't be stupid, get back here, you'll make yourself a target," one of the other men called in a tense whisper.

But Charlie didn't listen. Two shots tore into the country night, and when she opened her eyes, she saw her brother standing in the middle of the road, his suspenders forming a black X on his back, his arm extended in the air, holding a six-shooter from which smoke wafted. He fired two more shots as the other three men moved more cautiously along the side of the road, in the shadows, guns drawn. Several seconds passed and quiet descended again. She could hear everything—insects, leaves, owls, the winking of stars. Then she heard the sound of an engine starting up. Her heart thudded and kept on thudding, even when the sound grew fainter, and she knew that the Ford had retreated.

Charlie stood there a few seconds longer, his broad back lit up by the headlights of the Marmon, his shoulders rising and falling almost as though he were panting. Eventually he lowered his gun and slowly turned around. It was stupid, what he had done—she could see that. If the men had come back they could have killed Charlie easily, illuminated as he was and entirely exposed. But he did not have the look of someone who had just done something stupid. He was grinning wide and there was a manic light in his eyes as he sauntered toward her.

"Yellow bastards," he said when he reached Cordelia and opened the driver's-side door.

She stepped out and found that her legs were unsteady from nerves. "You sure they're not coming back?" she asked.

"They ain't coming back," he said and shook his head as though to say *This is what I live for*. "But what did I tell you about going out alone?"

There was no real reproach in his voice, however, and she managed to smile a little in reply. "I'm sorry, Charlie. How could I know I'd be followed?"

"Never mind that. I'm only glad I found you. I've been

driving around White Cove like crazy, trying to spot a speeding Marmon. Just don't do it again." He threw his arm around her, and made a hooting sound. "If I may say so myself, I put those boys in their place. What do you say we go celebrate with a drink?"

Meanwhile, Astrid's tears had dried. She was hungry, but she disliked the idea of ingesting any of the meal that she had slaved over only for it to be rejected and was almost ready to go upstairs and lay down on her bed, when she was startled by a loud popping.

"Oh!" She turned and saw Victor over her shoulder. "I didn't hear you come in."

He smiled at the compressed air wafting over a just-opened bottle of champagne.

"I don't want any," she said pathetically as she turned her head away.

"Come now, yes, you do." He stepped toward her, and when she wouldn't return his smile, he picked up the chair with her in it and placed it at the head of the table. She felt like a doll when he did this, and might have protested again, except that her lonely time spent gazing out the window had only made her feel worse, and she was privately glad for the attention. Once she was situated, he sat down in the chair that had been intended for Charlie, and poured a glass of champagne for each of them. "There's a fine meal here," he said in a fatherly way, "and it won't go to waste."

"I don't much feel like talking," she warned.

"I figured you might say something like that." There was a twinkle in his eye as he reached into his chest pocket. "That's why I brought these," he went on, showing her the pack of playing cards before shuffling them. She watched, not sure what to do, until he winked at her and said, "Go on, have a sip and I'll deal. Do you know gin rummy?"

"Know it?" The wink warmed her, and when she spoke again her voice grew playful despite the degradations of the evening. "It was all Mother and I did when we lived in Europe! We were always in a train or a hotel or a boat, and there was never anything to do."

"Good." His hands moved quickly over the pliant deck, doling out red rectangles, and before she knew what she was doing, she'd picked up the hand and begun to arrange her cards. "Not so fast," he said, winking again and lifting his glass.

"Ah, I've been very rude!" She was regaining her charm, and it felt good to smile now in her plush confident way, showing that she was not really such a baby, and lift her glass to his. "Cheers. You must forgive me for making a scene earlier, it's only that I worked so hard . . ."

"You did work hard, but now we shall enjoy the fruit of your labors. To this meal."

They clinked glasses and drank. Astrid closed her eyes, enjoying the fizzy sweetness on her tongue, and when she opened them again she was pleased to see a pair of aces and a slew of numbered clubs. From the deck, she picked up a card she could use, discarded one she couldn't, and raised her big eyes to watch Victor put a piece of roast in his mouth. He gave no obvious signs of pleasure, only put his fist over his mouth as he swallowed. Then he sipped from his champagne glass. Without saying anything, he took his turn, and afterward put a forkful of potatoes in his mouth. Again she fixed her gaze on him, not breathing or blinking, waiting for some indication that he enjoyed the food. He chewed twice and paused, looking at the ground as though he was considering spitting the bite out. But he didn't. He only chewed twice more and turned his eyes to meet hers as a lump went down his throat.

"Oh, dear." Astrid's lips parted. "It's terrible, isn't it?"

Light passed over his dark eyes, as it always does when people are considering whether or not to tell the truth. One last tear broke free and ran down the side of her nose, along the nostril, and into her mouth. She knew that he was thinking she would break down again, and she wished that she could pull the thought right out of his brain. The tear was just a random left-over tear that she couldn't explain. Her cooking was atrocious, she could see that clearly now, but somehow the realization that the meal she had made was terrible didn't make her sad.

It cleared the decks of all her misery; everything that had been so tragic a moment ago now seemed funny. Without breaking his gaze, she put a few potatoes in her mouth—but the saltiness stung her taste buds and made her wince, and she couldn't turn the bite over in her mouth even once before spitting it back on the plate.

"You were brave to have gotten that down," she laughed, once she'd managed a gulp of champagne.

"Aw, they weren't so bad," he said, picking up his cards.

"Don't start lying to me now, Vincent—Victor—whatever your name is."

"All right—they were pretty bad." He grinned at her and refilled their glasses. "But I never had much of an appetite—champagne is dinner enough for me."

"Don't go easy on me, fellow," she shot back. "And don't think by buttering me up you'll get me to put in a good word with your boss, either."

"I've eaten some bad meals in my time." He paused for effect, and more or less subdued the smile he'd been wearing since she'd begun to act carefree again. "This may possibly be the most inedible plate of food I have ever been served in my many long years of eating."

"You bastard!" she hooted. "The worst? You're in trouble now, my friend—earlier I was going to go easy on you when it came to our little game, but now I shall show you no mercy."

"Ah, it's on, then?" he replied with a wise smile.

"Indeed it is, mister." She sat up straight in her chair and focused on her hand.

Victor poured more champagne, and by the time Astrid had won the first hand, another bottle had to be opened. By the third hand, she felt sure that he was letting her win, but she didn't mind much about anything anymore. The petulant girl who had cried over Charlie's absence was gone, and Astrid had returned to a more sensible self. It was a good thing that Charlie had missed her first culinary efforts, she had begun to see, since the meal was such a disaster, and nice of Victor to let her practice on him. And she did enjoy his company, even though he was just the newest man, lowest on the totem pole, and had none of her Charlie's swaggering importance. She liked the card game, too—it was irreverent and not at all stuffy, and she thought maybe that once she mastered a dish worthy of her fiancé, she would try the same thing on him. That would be the night she slept in the same bed as Charlie—by then she would have everything just perfect, and be truly ready to act like a wife in every way.

The hours peeled away, and before she knew it, her lids were getting heavy and her body slumped, pleasantly weary, in her chair. Cooking, when mixed with emotion, really fatigued a girl. "How can it be . . ." she murmured, resting her head against the back of the chair. The room had grown blurry and purple and everything seemed to have a nice golden edging. "How is it that you handle the cards with such agility, and yet play so poorly?"

She expected him to admit to letting her win, but instead he said: "On account of how I grew up, which was with my older brothers, in a saloon on the West Side. Rough place on the waterfront. A lot of money changed hands at the poker table in the back room, and one or two men lost their lives over it, including the best card dealer that ever was. My older brother, Barry, he ran it, and he figured that if it was a kid doling out the cards, the fellows would be less likely to come to blows. He was partially right"—Victor paused and pointed to a small scar, near the corner of his left eye—"but that was later, when I was old enough to fight back."

"Sounds like a mean place."

"No—it was the best. Kind of joint where everyone checked their worries at the door. The beer was cold, the jokes came easy, we could smell the ocean, and everyone was always happy to be there. Everyone who hadn't lost money, that is. But *we* never lost money—no one ever loses money selling liquor, as I guess you know by now."

"Is it still there?" By then Astrid's voice had gotten so soft and mumbly with oncoming sleep she wasn't even sure he'd understand her, and her eyes were closed, so she couldn't tell whether he was looking at her or far away.

"Yeah, though my brother's gone. Gone in the war. But the place is just the same. One of my brother's war buddies' widow bought it—she gave me a nice price for it, too, even though I was too young to bargain with her. And she always sees that I'm well taken care of when I go there now. Didn't change the name neither—place is still called Barry's Tavern, and it's operated just the same, as though Prohibition never happened. It's its own country down there, I guess—too lawless for the Prohibition agents to touch. You'd like it—the toughs would want to play cards with you, and you'd never have to pay for a drink. Maybe I'll take you there someday."

Later, she could not be certain if he really was so bold as to say that last bit, because by then she was well into dreamland. She slept solidly and for a long time and when she awoke, alone in her own bed on the third floor, she sighed and turned over in the soft, clean sheets. She had dreamed of a place with warped, wide plank floors and a scratchy old phonograph, where everyone laughed and forgot their woes and no one cared if your name had ever appeared in *Leisure & Play*, and where you could faintly smell the sea.

12

THE OTHER TWO GIRLS WHO MADE THEIR HOMES AT Dogwood were still in bed when Letty closed the ballroom doors, took a deep breath, and threw herself into a task that she had been going about for several days now. She warmed up her voice and stretched her legs. She looked into the mirror and smiled with all the brilliant confidence she hoped to one day possess and glowered with the smoky detachment of a woman twice her age and mugged like a comedienne. She sang one song and then sang it again—with different intonation and different faces, as though she were performing it in a different persona. Once she had gone over every number she knew too many times to count, so that she became fearful of scratching her voice, she began to dance—dances that she had seen in movies, as though she were moving across the room with an invisible partner, dances that she imagined chorus girls doing in the big revues, and then a dance that expressed nothing but herself and the shimmering future she was always reaching out for. It wasn't until twilight had begun to cast shadows across the waxed floor that she ceased her movement and collapsed.

She had not intended to be melodramatic; it was only that she felt so suddenly and wonderfully drained. Astrid and Cordelia were hardly conscious when she began, and the hours had passed in a fever that made her forget everyone else, except perhaps Grady, and the way his eyes had seemed to confirm her suspicion that she would one day be a star. But her swoon had caught someone's attention, apparently, because in the next moment she heard a worried cry and footsteps pattering toward her.

"Oh, miss! Are you all right?"

Letty sat up, brushing dark stands of hair away from her eyes, and saw Milly, the maid, standing over her, gazing down with those lopsided eyes. "I'm sorry," she said sheepishly. "I didn't know anyone was here."

"No, no, *I'm* sorry, Miss Larkspur." Milly reached out with both big hands and pulled Letty to her feet. "I only heard you when I was passing on my way to the kitchen and your singing sounded so lovely and I wanted to hear some more, so I thought I'd listen from the doorway and not disturb anyone."

"Well, that's all right." Letty arranged the black skirt she wore over black tights and a black camisole and tried not to look as pleased as she was to have an audience. That someone, anyone, no matter how humble, actually wanted to listen to her brought a healthy color to her face. "I was only practicing."

"For Miss Cordelia's club? You must be awfully brave. My knees would shake, I'd be so nervous having to get up in front of people like that."

"Oh, believe me, I'll be nervous." Letty could see that the other girl was impressed, and she smiled involuntarily at the notion that she had earned another admirer. Then her thoughts jumped to the club when it was finally open and the stage being built and herself upon it, bedecked in sequins and feathers, just like a real singer. "How did you know about that, anyway?"

Milly shrugged. "I hear things. I didn't mean to pry. But you see, I came here thinking I'd go to the movies all the time and ride the streetcars and meet my friends in coffee shops. They pay me well enough, but I don't get so many kicks. So it's nice to at least hear the gossip." She had been fidgeting in her apron, and now produced a cigarette, almost without noticing she had done so. "And nice to hear some music," she added shyly.

"That's awfully kind of you," Letty replied in a warm, majestic tone that she hoped would make her seem adequate to the girl's desire for story and melody. "Were you going to smoke that?"

"Oh, no." Milly hurriedly, and rather ridiculously, tried to hide the cigarette in her palm. "Sorry, miss, I—"

"Oh, don't apologize on my account." Letty nodded, smiling, to show her it wasn't anything to feel bad about. "I was only going to ask if you wanted to sit on the porch with me for a minute? My legs are sore from the dancing, to be honest, and I could use some fresh air."

Once they were situated on the imposing stone steps outside, gazing into the cool darkness, Milly turned to her and in a barely audible voice said, "Don't tell them, all right?"

"Oh, they don't care. Cordelia is always smoking these days, anyway, so why should they mind?"

"I suppose it's not the smoking I'm ashamed of so much as taking so long a break." Milly exhaled into the dense black night. For a while she smoked quietly and neither said anything. Stubbing out her cigarette, she switched to a less apologetic tone. "Now that Miss Donal is here, I'm doing the job of three girls, and I haven't a moment to myself."

Letty sighed and rested her head on her own shoulder. She remembered that tone—it was the tone of her older sister's voice on laundry day, or during canning season, and really almost every day since their mother passed away and Louisa was forced to become the woman of the house. "Sounds like you're run off your feet," she said sympathetically.

Milly produced another cigarette and might have lit it, too, had they not been startled by the creaking of the hall door. Both turned around with guilty faces to see Cordelia advancing across the floor of the ballroom arm in arm with Astrid's stepsister, Billie. Cordelia was a loose and gleaming column of aubergine, her summer hair pinned back so that a few tendrils whispered against sharp cheeks. Even on the arm of Billie, she looked sophisticated and citified, and Billie was wearing flared brown men's trousers, which was a mode of dress that would have caused a girl to be looked at askance for another twenty years if she'd gone about that way in Union.

"We're going to Manhattan," Cordelia announced.

"To see what all the newest speakeasies are about," Billie seconded.

"When I went into town last night, I saw how little I know about speakeasies, and Billie has promised to be my tour guide, and it will be much better if there are lots of us!"

It hadn't occurred to Letty that Cordelia was so friendly with Astrid's stepsister, but now they looked as thick as thieves—like two people who had spent the afternoon together drinking too much coffee and obsessively plotting something extravagant. For a brief moment Letty felt jealous of this closeness, but then Cordelia gave a sly smile and said, "Are you going to come with us?"

The question was addressed to only one of the two girls sitting on the steps of the verandah, and in an instant the spell of camaraderie with the maid dissipated. Letty glanced awkwardly at Milly, who had averted her eyes and made her cigarette disappear. She needn't have tried to make herself so invisible, however; Letty could see that Cordelia's mind was elsewhere. Her eyes were bright with excitement for the evening that was about to unfurl, and already her thoughts were ahead of her body, out in the world somewhere.

"Wear the black beaded thing you have," Cordelia pressed. "Please, Letty?"

When Letty stood up, she could not bring herself to glance at Milly again. It did tug at her conscience that the English girl would probably have liked to come into the city with them and see what the young people did there behind unmarked doors at night. But Letty had spent plenty of time looking in from the outside herself. No longer was she just the middle Haubstadt sister. Suddenly she felt very lucky to have friends who were antsy to do something gay—to be going along with them, one of the bright young things.

"Hurry, though," Billie said as Letty passed her on the way to put on the beaded black dress. "I want to leave before Charlie gets home and insists Cordelia have a chaperone."

* * *

With the onset of dusk, boats owned by Hales and Greys had moved stealthily away from run-down piers and out onto the sound. Bigger ships, lingering some miles off in the Atlantic, carried cases of liquid gold beneath false bottoms and would soon be boarded by buyers and good-time girls and perhaps, if it was an unlucky night, a government agent in disguise. Deliveries would be made through back-alley doorways to speakeasy proprietors, some of them grateful customers, and some who'd been made customers through coercion. All over the city and her suburbs, preparations were being made for a busy night. The crowds were coming—the kinds of girls who flit toward nightclubs in their colorful getups and the boys who want to talk to them, everyone shouting out to the bartenders that they'll have one more.

Oblivious to all this maneuvering was Astrid, who sat alone in the third-floor turret room that had once been occupied by Grey the bootlegger himself, admiring her reflection in the mirror. She wore a silvery evening dress that Charlie had given her in another season, her hair was slicked straight back from her forehead, and she had painted her lips a devastating shade of red. She'd spent much of the day lazing in bed, until Charlie came and woke her with a hundred apologies and kisses on the tender skin of her arms, and promised to make last night up to her tonight. After that she had eaten a little and taken a long time to dress. It hardly surprised her, and did not bother her in the least, that she had not left her room for the entire day. There were windows on three of the four sides of the room and she had experienced all the grand fluctuations in weather from this pleasant, private aerie.

"Aren't you coming with us?"

Astrid looked up and saw Letty in the doorway, wearing a beaded black dress that transformed her from a shy girl to a lady who might plausibly sing hot music in a speakeasy. "Oh, how I'd love to, darling," she replied, smiling to see her new friend like this, "but Charlie is planning something special for me. Have lots of fun for me though, won't you?"

"Are you sure?" Letty's blue eyes were as big as a cartoon's. She seemed to be hoping that Astrid would change her mind. And for a moment, Astrid did waver—that imploring face Letty was wearing made her want to say yes to anything, and the notion that she might be left out of a fun evening made her feel a little sore. But Charlie had neglected her, and he had promised to make it right, and she didn't want to budge until he had done so. Something special was what he had promised, and she was holding out for nothing less.

"Yes, doll, but wink at all the boys for me!"

When Letty was gone, she returned to carefully shaping her brows, dusting her cheekbones a tawny blush, and making her eyelashes very black. The light was dim, and her pupils were big and mysterious, and she was glad that she was so lovely tonight. Surely Charlie would take one look at her and vow never to leave her lonely again. She had been lost in this reverie for some minutes when she realized the phone was ringing. Its ghostly repetition echoed up the main stairwell of Dogwood to her remote corner, and she became conscious of it in the way that one suddenly notices the detail in a painting which has always been there, and knew that it must have been ringing a long time.

"Oh, bother," she said and pushed away from the vanity. "Telephone!" she called from the doorway of her room, but the ringing continued, and she heard no one moving to answer it. In a huff she descended the stairs.

"Hello?" she demanded, once she had reached the library and picked up the receiver. Hearing her voice out loud in the quiet dark room made her suddenly cognizant of the fact that if no one had come for the phone, then she must be alone in the house.

"Where's Cordelia?" Charlie demanded without pausing for the nicety of a greeting.

"She and Billie and Letty left for the city," Astrid replied matter-of-factly. As it happened the stillness had just ceased to seem pleasant, and a chill ran up her back, and she did not feel matter-of-fact at all.

Charlie cursed. "We gotta find her. It's dangerous tonight," he said. "Don't leave Dogwood. Victor will be there any minute."

"But, Charlie, tonight is the night we're going to . . ."

"I know. I'm sorry, baby, tomorrow, I promise. Something has happened."

"Oh," she said acidly. "Like last night?"

"No," he replied, ignoring or perhaps not noticing her sarcasm. "Much worse. I'll explain later when . . ."

There was more—she could still hear his voice as she lowered the receiver down and smashed it against the cradle—but she was no longer interested. Every word of Charlie's excuse stung, and she did not wish to be stung. She was looking painfully lovely and she only wanted to be admired and cared for and touched. She scowled at her reflection in the black window and let her blood grow hot. Spinning on her heel, she strode back toward the hall, pushing hard on the door. When she saw the man on the other side she almost screamed in fright.

"Victor!" she gulped.

This time he did not seem so sorry to be her companion for the evening. "I guess you're stuck with me again," he said with a grin.

"Yes." She pointed her nose in the air and declined to smile back. "Get the car warmed up while I get my wrap. We're going into the city."

His face went pale and serious. "I can't do that."

"Fine." Astrid's eyes narrowed and her lips constricted furiously. "I will just have to drive myself."

She could still hear the phone ringing in the empty house as she stalked across the lawn to the place where Victor had left his car. He followed just behind her and when she reached the car he put a hand on her shoulder to stop her. But she turned around with such rage that he stepped back, knocked off balance. Their eyes met and they both knew that she had called his bluff.

"You wouldn't resort to brute strength to keep me here, would you?" she asked, though she spoke in so intense a voice that there was no mistaking it for a question. She held his gaze another minute, letting her eyes simmer so that she was sure he fully understood what lengths she was willing to go to in order to leave the property. Then she went around to the passenger side and slammed the door behind her.

"Drive fast," she instructed Charlie's man, once he was situated, and drive fast he did. They caught up with the other girls a long time before the Queensboro, and proceeded into the city like an outlaw caravan.

13

THE LAND OF NIGHT IS FULL OF FAMILIAR FACES, WHICH
is why young people, the girls in particular, are paid such lavish attention, given the best tables, and shepherded in past
hungry crowds. They are new, which is solid currency after the
sun goes down and the streets fill up with lost souls seeking
whimsy and distraction. And so it was no wonder the way eyes
followed Cordelia Grey. Astrid was very proud to have recognized a star the instant she appeared in her midst, and was
happy to be slightly blinded by her wattage as they walked, a
brash foursome, past the fleets of limousines on Park Avenue
and down the steps into the ground floor of a brick townhouse
that appeared staid enough from the outside, except for the

windowpanes, which were rattled by an uncommon amount of noise rising from beneath the parlor level.

"Ooooo!" Astrid squealed when she saw the mattresses piled high in the big back room and covered with several layers of gauzy white coverlets. She always admired a clever trick, and though she was sure this décor hadn't cost a thing, it looked almost fancy with the murals on the walls, which depicted a sylvan scene framed by diaphanous trompe l'oeil window treatments. The light from the ceiling fixture was muted with a silk parachute that drooped lazily over the tightly packed guests. She hadn't been to a place like this since Charlie took over the business. "What is it," she crowed, "a speak or a bordello?"

"They call it The Bedroom," Billie said, surveying the scene. There were men with no-good faces leaning against the walls in the low light and girls wearing old-fashioned Edwardian nightgowns circulating with trays full of drinks. They weren't showing much skin, of course, but it was just the right amount of naughtiness, having waitresses dressed in their intimates, and Astrid's eyes shone to be out again among people who did thrilling, roguish things. Once she'd been reunited with her girlfriends, she had more or less forgotten her anger. She was satisfied by the notion that if Charlie wasn't going to appreciate the way the silver dress hugged her figure, someone here would.

Victor had spoken barely a word since they left Dogwood.

His eyes twitched nervously, and he insisted on accompanying the girls inside instead of waiting in the car. "You are going to get me in a world of trouble, Miss Astrid," he said tensely as Billie whispered to the doorman.

Once inside, he refused to act like a normal customer and stationed himself by the door, watching the four girls at a distance. Astrid gave him a dirty look and then decided to ignore him, sinking into one of the mattresses, patting it so that Letty would drop down beside her, and demanding that Billie get them some champagne. Billie gave her a wry smile, but she enjoyed obliging in these situations; shortly thereafter she returned with a bottle.

From behind wide-brimmed champagne glasses, the girls observed the room. There were men wearing tiny spectacles who looked like they spent their daylight hours in libraries, and debs in silks like Astrid and her friends, and musicians with holes in the elbows of their coats, and men with gold watch chains who flashed their billfolds and insisted on buying drinks for everyone else.

Just when she was growing tired of watching other people dance, a pack of college boys came in and fixed their attention on the four girls from White Cove. One of them—a tall, fair-haired boy with a weak chin and V-neck sweater—gave Astrid a wink, but she turned her profile to him and smiled instead at Letty. A vision of what they must look like materialized in her mind—Cordelia regal in her column of aubergine, the beads of Letty's dress twinkling in the low light, Billie rakish in her trousers, Astrid's whole self as soft and layered as a rose, their slender arms draped over one another's shoulders, their knees inclining toward each other—and she wished that there had been a photographer present so that she could have that picture of her friends in buoyant bloom preserved forever.

"I don't know that those fellows are up to our standards, do you?" she whispered to Letty, who was sitting beside her.

The corners of Letty's mouth curled up in nervous excitement. "How can you tell?"

"Well . . ." Both girls turned to assess the five boys who stood a few feet away, shooting glances in their direction. "They aren't *real* men, of course. But they might do to pass the time awhile."

"Come on, will you dance?" the boy with the fair hair and weak chin called out to Astrid.

She regarded him with a patient, discriminating air, before twisting herself around again and flashing her eyes at her elfin friend. "What do you say, darling? I'm not going to dance unless you do."

Letty's eyes glittered and her white shoulders rose and fell. "I do like that fellow Grady . . ." she said seriously. "But I suppose a dance doesn't really mean anything, does it?"

"Hmmmm . . ." Astrid lengthened her neck and pretended

to be considering their suitors. "Very well, we'll dance, but we don't come cheap, you know!" she announced with a note of challenge in her voice.

The fair-haired boy's face lit up and he put his hand out to pull her to her feet. One of his friends came forward to draw Letty onto the dance floor, and a third reached for Cordelia.

"Aren't you coming?" Astrid called over her shoulder to Billie, as the fair-haired boy draped an arm at the small of her back and grasped her hand in his.

"No, thank you." Billie was leaning against the wall, her legs long in front of her, her ankles crossed nonchalantly. "I know those boys from Columbia, and I've danced with them all before. You go on ahead."

If there was something a tad dismissive in what her stepsister said, Astrid didn't let it bother her. The fair-haired boy looked terribly pleased to be partnered with her, and he moved her around in a theatrical waltz that no doubt raised the eyebrows of Charlie's man, but which made her feel alive and girlish and as though nothing in the world mattered very much. In the silver frock she looked like a waterfall spilling between the men dressed in dark clothes, and she could see Cordelia in the deep purple being twirled around by one of the college boy's friends, and thought that there was nothing wrong with what she was doing so long as Cordelia was doing the same thing, too.

Just when Astrid was beginning to grow bored with her fellow, she found herself passed to the brown-haired one in the blue blazer who had been Cordelia's first partner.

"I'm Dickie," he told her, as he danced them deeper into the room.

"What a silly name," Astrid rejoined, softening the comment with her smile.

"You're not thinking of leaving yet?" His big mouth hung open even after he was done speaking, like a child's, so that she could see his fleshy tongue.

"Whatever gave you that idea?"

"You were looking at the door."

"Well, I'm here now, aren't I?"

He grinned and steered her on through the crowd. She was just beginning to grow bored with him, too, when she saw Peachy Whitburn coming through the door, her strawberry blond hair recently marcelled and her sporty, upper-crust mien obscured somewhat by the heaps of black jet she wore.

"Peachy!" Astrid squealed, abandoning her partner and throwing her arms around the other girl's neck.

"Darling."

They blew kisses at opposite cheeks, and Astrid pulled her toward the mattress where Billie was holding court. Letty had just landed for a respite, but she was otherwise occupied: Two of the Columbia boys had managed to ensnare her in conversation. They flanked her on either side and were making her blush with their questions.

"Such a treat to see you, darling, what are you doing here?" Astrid asked, handing the newcomer a glass of champagne.

"Well, it's the place of the moment, isn't it?" Peachy paused to sip—cautiously, as her position made it a bit challenging.

"Indeed, it is," Billie interjected, before returning to her previous conversation, which was about horse racing. "For now, anyway."

"But what are *you* doing here? I haven't seen you out in ages. Everyone says you've gone domestic."

"Oh, yes." Astrid dropped her head back and let a wave of fluffy blond hair fall away from her face. "I have, and it's divine. But Cordelia and Charlie are opening a club, don't you know? It's a lot of work, but they need to be out on the town, seeing and being seen, learning what drinks are being served and what music played in all the other speaks, you know. I'm just along for the ride—I'd do anything to help my family, of course. The opening will be soon, you must come, let me just ask Cordelia when . . ." She trailed off and turned her head toward the thicket of young people filling up the main space of the room, squealing and throwing their arms up in the air and shimmying their whole bodies. Though her eyes scanned the faces carefully, she could not seem to find Cordelia among them.

At first this seemed funny: "Oh, you know Cord, she's always running away," she brushed it off to Peachy. But then it began to seem strange.

"Hold this a moment, would you?" she asked Peachy. Once she was unburdened of her champagne she extended her hand to Dickie, who was loitering nearby. He obliged in lifting her up and appeared only a little perturbed when she walked away without thanking him. She went straight to Victor and whispered in his ear, demanding to know, if he really *were* keeping such a careful eye on things, where her friend had gone off to?

As it happened, Cordelia had not gone far. She had only disliked the familiar way the fair-haired boy had swayed her on the dance floor and had felt hot with all those other people crowded into the small space. The ladies' lounge was on the second floor and she'd had to make her way through a warren of rooms to find it. Once there, she didn't immediately want to leave its tranquil, red velvet environs. She splashed water on her face and repinned her hair back, so that it framed her face in loose, sun-streaked waves.

Once she had collected herself, she turned away from the mirror, and came face-to-face with a well-kept woman with green eyes. Aside from a few lines, her skin had a youthful tautness; she had the gaze of experience, but she was dressed in such an au courant way that it was impossible to place her age exactly. Her dark hair was cut the way girls of twenty wore it, short and full around her face.

"Enjoying yourself?" she asked.

"Yes, thank you," Cordelia replied, hoping that she did not seem intimidated. "Do I know you?"

"Not exactly." The woman extended a ring-bedecked hand. "My name is Mona Alexander—perhaps you've heard of me?"

"Yes," was all Cordelia could manage to reply. Charlie had told her about a Mona Alexander who used to be their father's lady friend.

"Your father was very special to me, and I was very special to him. He set me up as a singer, you know, when I had nothing. And now I am almost as famous as he used to be."

"Oh." Cordelia swallowed, unsure how to reply to such a comment.

"I'm sorry he's gone, kid. I cried for three days when I heard. What a miserable blow that must have been for you." Mona didn't look like the type to dispense sympathy, but her lips did flatten out in what was perhaps her closest approximation of a sympathetic expression. "Anyway, I'm not the kind to go in for any mothering malarkey—but I've read a little about you, and I have a soft spot in my black heart for girls like us."

"Like us?"

"Girls who come from nothing, but are not nothing themselves."

"Oh." It wasn't easy, but Cordelia managed to hold her gaze when she said: "Thank you."

"Don't take any bull, hear me? And you can always call on me if you need any advice. I'd do anything for Darius Grey, and anything for you, too." The woman produced a card from some invisible pocket and gave it to Cordelia. "Now go enjoy your evening, dear."

"Thank you." Cordelia fought the urge to curtsy, and went out into the hall. She continued on past the wood-paneled walls of what had once been a swank private house, down a stairway, toward the room with the mattresses and murals. Encountering the woman her father used to keep company with had unnerved her, but it felt good to be recognized for what she was, and there was something charismatic about Mona Alexander that reminded her how exciting it was to be out in the world.

When she came down into the small room with the bar in it, she heard her full name, "Cordelia Grey," pronounced in a suave, intentional tone. A cold current went down her spine. She had not seen Thom Hale since that day at the Beaumonts', and he had not become less handsome in the intervening weeks. He was dressed in a tailored suit that was either black or navy—she couldn't tell in the light—and his pale brown collared shirt was only a shade darker than his lightly tanned skin.

"Cordelia, I'm glad I ran into you."

He was the same as always—neat copper hair parted on the side, his clothes fitting him rakishly. In one hand he held a half-full drink, an amber liquid with a dark cherry in it, and in the other a recently lit cigarette. His manner—calm, urbane, never inconvenienced—struck her as especially deplorable. If she'd known how to slap a man, she might have slapped Thom now.

"I'm glad because—" He broke off and looked around him. "Would you like a drink?"

She shook her head.

"All right." He dragged on his cigarette. "I'm glad because I wanted to tell you that you must be careful."

Having nothing in particular to say to him, she raised her eyebrows and waited for his elaboration.

"Careful because—because it would be terrible if anything happened to you."

Cordelia stepped toward Thom. "Are you threatening me?"

"No!" he said and took a quick sip of his drink. "But it gets more dangerous every day. I don't know how much your brother tells you—but he burned down one of our warehouses yesterday. You don't think my father would let a thing like that go by without retribution, do you?"

Realization sharpened Cordelia's features. "You sent those men to follow me, didn't you?"

"What men?" Thom looked startled, but she couldn't be certain whether he was faking or not. "Did you see their faces? What did they look like?"

"You know them, then."

"No, no—I don't know what you're talking about. I'm just warning you to be careful."

For a long moment she held his gaze. Then she plucked the wafting cigarette from his fingertips, dragged from it, and, with her eyes steady on his, dropped what was left into his glass. His eyes went briefly to the ruined drink and then back to her.

"That's very kind, Mr. Hale," she said flatly, exhaling. "But I wouldn't take your advice if you were the last man on Earth."

With that, Cordelia turned and walked—shoulders back and head high, mindful not to trip on her perilous heels—into the room where her friends, and everyone else, were loudly going about their evening. She took a deep breath so as not to be overwhelmed by the stimulation there, the vivid colors, the red smiles of the girls and the white teeth of the boys, the music on the phonograph and the general din of glee.

"Where's Astrid?" she asked Victor, when she reached him.

"Over where you left her."

Cordelia's eyes darted to the mattress where Letty and Astrid and Billie were surrounded by those ridiculous college boys, all in their blazers and pastel sweaters, jockeying for position to romance the girls. "Go get them, Victor. I'll wait in the car. It's not safe to stay—Thom Hale is here."

He nodded gravely and went to do as she had instructed. It was possible that Thom came into the door frame and watched her swift departure, but she had no way of knowing, because her head was down until she reached the Daimler. Slumped in the backseat alone, she began to wonder if Thom had really meant to threaten her, or if some part of what he had said was sincere. Then she decided that either way it didn't matter. The whole night was ahead of her, and she didn't want anything from him.

Astrid was giggling when she spilled through the car door and into the backseat after Letty. "Whatever could have happened to excuse us leaving so dramatically?"

"Oh, just Thom Hale."

"Really?" said Billie, squeezing in behind Astrid. "That's not good."

"No, it's nothing," Cordelia said carelessly. "Only I want to have a good time tonight, and it would be impossible with him there."

"Right you are," Astrid went on, as the car peeled away from the curb. "And it was clever leaving like that, with everyone wondering where you'd gone off to. Leave them wanting more, as Mummy always says."

"To hell with men, anyway," Cordelia replied.

"Amen," Astrid seconded, throwing her head back and hooting with her hand over her lips like an Indian princess.

Letty gave Cordelia a private smile and reached out to squeeze her hand, and Billie leaned forward and instructed Victor where to go next.

After that, they never stayed in one place very long. They went up and down stairs, to tiny places with two tables, or vast halls filled with palm trees. Drinks came to them in chipped coffee cups or, at the places profitable enough to afford protection, fine silver-rimmed highballs. They went back to Seventh Heaven, where so much had already happened to Letty and Cordelia, and Letty's eyes scanned the bar hopefully. But her beau wasn't there, and neither was anyone else of particular interest, so they rolled on.

Later, at the bar of a hotel that was all black iron curlicues, Victor struck up a conversation with Cordelia—the topic of which is lost to history—and she momentarily forgot her friends. Letty was looking drowsy, and had rested her head on the bar as soon as they arrived. When Cordelia turned away from Victor, she saw Billie leaning forward to take Astrid's heart-shaped face in her hands and kiss her big, soft lips. By then everything seemed perfectly hilarious and inconsequential, so Cordelia laughed and turned to the bartender and ordered another round, and when she looked back she saw that they were still kissing. It was only when the drinks were served that their mouths parted and Billie took her hands off Astrid's waist. Then Billie raised her glass and toasted, "To hell with men!"

The girls' careless spree continued on through the veins of Manhattan a while longer, but Cordelia could not be sure how long, because by the next morning she could not remember the drive home. She only remembered putting her head down against the soft satin sheets and feeling dizzy and wishing that Max Darby liked dancing in nightclubs. But then a conviction came over her that the evening had been perfect just as it was, with Astrid and Letty and Billie at her side, and that there would be plenty of time for the pilot in her future. . . .

On the other side of the house, in the turret bedroom, sleep was not to be so easily had, even after dawn began making herself known in the pink margins of the sky. It was around then that Charlie burst into Astrid's room. At that hour even the rowdiest Manhattanites were in bed, and Astrid had changed into her nightgown and put her hair up in curlers.

"Hey! What do you think you're doing?" she cried out. At this point she was still feeling delightfully drunk and silly, and she went on in a good-natured voice: "We're not married yet, mister. If my mother knew you came to my bedroom late at night like this, she'd sic our private detectives on you, I'm sure."

"Damn right we're not married yet."

He was standing at the end of her bed, and he seemed at that moment much taller and blockier than he had before. His shirtsleeves were rolled to his elbows so that she could see his forearms, which made her excited and angry at once. The silliness drained from Astrid's face once she'd read his posture, and she pushed herself up against the pillows and squared her shoulders for what was coming.

"What do you mean by that?" she demanded in a decidedly colder voice.

"I told you to stay put."

"If you have to, tell me to stay put on a night when nothing is happening. Not on a night when my friends are all going out to have some fun. It's been such a long time since I've had any fun." Here she paused pointedly, and gazed up into his angry brown eyes. Before speaking again, she focused on her cuticles and affected a careless tone. "Anyway, I can't see *why* it matters so much to you what I was doing tonight."

Charlie sighed and put his hands on the base of the bed frame, leaning his whole weight against it and hanging his head. "I run a business. The situation changes every day, every minute. I'm sorry if I haven't been as sweet with you as you like . . ." He trailed off and stepped back from the bed and turned toward the window. It was perverse, Astrid knew, but she never wanted him to kiss her so much as in these moments, when his back was to her and he seemed almost exhausted by the roller-coaster ride they took each other on. The muscles of her face relaxed, and she raised her arms toward him. He never saw this gesture, however. He spoke before she did, turning his face slightly—she could see his slab nose in profile, but his eyes didn't go as far as to reach her. "Maybe it was a dumb idea, you moving in here so quick."

The air went out of Astrid's lungs, and her arms fell onto the silken coverlet like a slap. "Maybe," she replied venomously.

Charlie heard the change in tone and matched it. "What did you think you were doing out there? Cordelia was so tight she had to be carried to her room. Have fun, if you want. Don't go to every joint in town and dance with every fellow there. Don't kiss your sister."

A little gasp escaped Astrid's lips, and she had to cover her mouth with her hand to disguise the giggle that followed, because she had forgotten the part of the evening when Billie kissed her. The kiss hadn't been *real*, of course—it hadn't meant anything, the way it meant something when Charlie kissed her. It was only that they were having such a perfectly wild night and everyone was watching them, and when a girl gets watched like that, she begins to feel that she is the prettiest sight around, and wants nothing so much as to put her lips to her own reflection. "Oh, Charlie, don't get so sinister, you are so unappealing when you are sinister like that! Anyway, Billie is my *step*sister."

"Victor told me—" His voice was filling up with rage, and he had to break off, as though he couldn't bear what he was about to say. He paced in an angry circle at the foot of her bed. "Never mind. You know what you did, and it's not how I want any wife of mine acting in public. Do you hear me?"

Astrid narrowed her eyes and iced her words. "Yes, Charlie, I hear you."

"You do?" He stopped pacing and his face became briefly pliant and patient. But it was too late for Astrid—she had passed over the border into the land of fury, and would not be coming back no matter what he went on to say. "Good," was what came out of his mouth, though she was barely listening anymore. "Because I got a lot on my mind and I don't have the time to keep you in line at night. The Hales, they're throwing all they got at us. Tonight they vandalized the club. Luckily I had some boys there, working, they had only taken a break for dinner, they got back before too much damage was done. But the message is clear enough. I don't know what comes next, though I know it's something, and that I'm not going to like it. Anyway, I'm sorry if I've ignored you, but you know I'll make it up to you."

"Oh, that's all right." Astrid crossed her arms hard over her chest. "I wouldn't want you to put yourself out."

"No, but I—" Before he could finish his sentence, Charlie caught on. His eyes blazed as he realized Astrid wasn't going to come back around to sweetness. "Oh, damn you."

"Damn me? Damn *you*! If you think it was all too hurried, me coming to live with *you*, perhaps it was all too hurried us getting engaged!"

"You think so?" he spit back.

"Yes!" The scream that followed was instinctual and loud enough to hurt both their ears and probably to be heard in the far reaches of the house. Charlie stepped back and assessed her. He seemed to be wondering if she was serious or not. In fact, she had no idea whether she was serious, but she held his gaze, and lifted her chin, and did her best impression of a girl who wasn't going to back down.

Was she angry with Charlie because he'd ignored her for days, or because he was spoiling the end of a perfectly frothy evening? Was it because she had been ready to do something frighteningly grown-up with him, and he had been too dumb to know? All the emotions she'd experienced since moving into Dogwood—that nasty sensation of being left behind, the boredom, the wanting—flooded her insides, clamoring at her that she should hold her ground.

"All right," he replied darkly. "Well, all right."

She pulled her engagement ring off her finger—this hurt, and not just because the knuckle was slightly swollen. She thought sorrowfully of the night he'd given it to her, and how proud she'd been to wear it. But he was already halfway to the door, and she didn't flinch when she said, "I'll take my things back to Marsh Hall tomorrow."

By the time the door sounded behind him, she had turned on her side and buried her golden head in the pillow in a vain attempt to sleep.

14

CORDELIA WOKE UP LATE WITH A DULL ACHE IN HER forehead and a scratchy throat. Letty must have already risen, or at any rate there was no sign of her in the Calla Lily Suite. If the two girls had spoken before falling asleep the night before, Cordelia couldn't remember it. She couldn't remember falling asleep at all. When she rose and went to the vanity in the dressing room, she saw the kind of girl she'd always hoped to one day meet in New York City: a bit gaunt in the face, but with a bright loveliness in the eyes that suggested that the mind behind them contained all manner of stories. And however weather-beaten she was from the late night, there was a great contentedness springing from deep inside her. That was Max, she thought. She had seen him in her dreams, and they had been orbiting each other like two celestial bodies. Outside, the storms had broken and sunshine had returned to White Cove, and she stood in front of the mirror in her slip, and shivered at the memory of the way she felt when he turned his gaze on her.

"Len, I'll have breakfast on the verandah," she said as she breezed through the kitchen. She had scrubbed her face clean and pulled the black tunic that she liked to wear by the pool on over her slip, but otherwise she was in the exact state she'd been in when she awoke. Her hair still smelled faintly of smoke. She liked the idea that the experiences of the night before were still on her skin and in her hair, that every tiny inch of her was being formed by the places she'd been. That she couldn't quite remember those places—at least the last one—did not trouble her. Billie could remind her, she supposed, or maybe the newspaperman who had been buying her old-fashioneds would oblige her with a record of events in his column.

Music came from all the trees—a symphony of birds and insects—and someone was splashing in the pool.

"There you are, miss." She turned and saw Len, carrying a glass of juice and a plate of fried eggs on a lunch tray.

"Thank you, Len."

"Might want to read the papers, Miss," he said, and placed a folded gray broadsheet beside her breakfast.

"Thank you," she replied, although she did not immediately

do as he'd advised and open the paper, and instead nibbled at a piece of bacon thoughtfully and listened to the sounds of the afternoon and wondered when she would next see Max, and under what circumstances, and what great fun it would be to show him off. Perhaps he would be her date for her own club's first big night.

With a lazy stretch, she spread open the newspaper. Her eyes were drawn straightaway to the words *Max* and *Darby*. A subtle electric charge passed through her body when she saw in print the name that she had been thinking to herself over and over again, and she sat up straight in her chair, the better to read some news of him. The story above it was run in a larger font—it concerned an investigation into a fire in Rye Haven two days ago—but nothing held any interest for her besides the small column in the bottom left-hand corner. Then she realized what it was about, and her heart went silent.

THE WILD NIGHTS OF A BOOTLEGGER'S DAUGHTER was the headline, but below that, in lettering that was only slightly smaller, it said MAX DARBY SHOOTS DOWN RUMORS, DENIES KNOWING MISS GREY, and below that, in quotation marks, "SHE WAS JUST A GIRL I HELD THE DOOR OPEN FOR."

Cordelia's face fell as her eyes moved feverishly over the following paragraphs. There was no real story, of course. A few anecdotes from last night filled the first paragraphs, all of which came from the newspaperman who had bought her drinks. He made it sound like every one of her nights was like that. It was not until she turned to page eight that she found anything about Max. Apparently there had been rumors of a romance, based on the sighting at the Plaza, and the newspaper ran the photographic evidence alongside a more thorough denial from Mr. Darby of their having anything to do with one another. *"I never read the papers, so of course I didn't recognize the young lady, but I was raised to open the door for a woman when I can. . . ."*

"Oh, you idiot," she said out loud, as mortification engulfed her.

She folded up the newspaper with two decisive gestures and put it back on the table as though that could make the whole thing go away. In a matter of seconds she had gone from feeling very tall and impressive to very small indeed; humiliation and hurt warred within her for prominence of place. Briefly, she tried to convince herself that maybe the situation wasn't as bad as it seemed. Maybe he had simply panicked upon being called for comment, and maybe he wouldn't read the column and find out that she'd been running with flappers all night. Maybe in a little while the phone would ring, and he would apologize, and they would go dancing, someplace where they were sure not to be photographed.

Foolish as Cordelia felt right then, however, she was not fool enough to really believe that. She had seen enough of Max to know that everything he did was full of intention. If he had told a newspaper that he had no idea who she was, and had merely opened a door for her, then he meant not to see her again. Cordelia wrapped her arms around herself and gazed out on the soft expanse of lawn, the dogs of loneliness gnawing at her heels.

"Cord!" her brother called from inside the house. She twisted in her chair, a hint of a smile emerging on her face through the sadness. Her brother was here, as he always would be. So she had gone chasing after a boy who flew shiny airplanes—that was a mistake, but she was still here, among people who cared for her. Among a strange kind of family that happened to be the only people she could trust.

"Out here!"

"Cord!" His feet clapped against the floor of the ballroom, echoing against its empty walls. He came through the double glass doors and onto the verandah with an intensity that surprised her. When he stopped, it was with a fist against his hip and a seething in his eyes. She blinked at him, unsure what he was about, but hardly getting the reassurance she had been expecting. "How do you feel?"

"Like hell," she replied weakly.

"Gin will do that." He was tapping his foot and his eyes were boring into her expectantly.

Cordelia pushed herself up in the chair, suddenly

self-conscious of the rather sloppy way she'd put herself together, of her smoky hair and the shadows under her eyes.

"You were a wreck last night." He exhaled hard through his nostrils. "Do you even remember coming home? Do you have any idea how much manpower I lost last night trying to find you?"

She blinked again and tried to make her brain work, so that she could know why he had been so keen to find her last night. "Well, I was at all the places one might expect!" she said with a brassy smile. "You see even the gossip columnists found me," she added, waving her hand in the direction of the odious newspaper.

"That's not funny." His face was so stony that for a moment she couldn't help but find it just a touch amusing. She knew better than to laugh, however. "I needed all my men last night. More than that, I needed not to worry that it was *you* they were after."

"Who?"

"Who do you think?"

It did now occur to Cordelia that she might have been more careful after being followed the other day, but Charlie himself had taken her out drinking right afterward. And Billie had been so enthusiastic yesterday—there would've been no saying no to her. Going into the city hadn't seemed so foolish at the time, but her head hurt too much to explain. All she could manage to do was stare back at him blankly.

"The Hales, of course." He threw up his hand in exasperation.

"What happened last night?"

He let out a long, raspy sigh and cast his eyes out toward the trees as though he wasn't sure he could trust her with the story.

Cordelia's palm rose to cover her mouth and her chest tightened in anger. "Does this have something to do with your burning their warehouse?"

"How did you know—?" He broke off and brought his fist down hard on the metal table, which shook, the fork clattering against the plate, the yolks of the eggs quivering in their whites. She was relieved he didn't push her to answer that, but a wave of shame passed over her nonetheless. She knew how it would sound if she said that she had been told about the warehouse by Thom Hale. "Yes, probably. It happened earlier the night you were followed."

"The Hales retaliated, then? How did you know it was them?"

He shook his head. "They didn't try to keep it a secret. Anyway, I knew something was coming, what with the damage we've done to their business. But don't forget—it was them that declared war, not us."

Cordelia nodded gravely. The happy cloudiness she'd woken up to had been cut away now, and her mind was racing with the several dark turns of the afternoon. "What can I do?" she asked, making her brown eyes wide and serious.

"You?" He snorted and stepped back from the table. The way he fixed his eyes on her was new, critical, almost the way Aunt Ida might have looked at her. "You can start waking up before noon, for one thing. You can take your one assignment seriously. I want to open the club as soon as possible, this weekend if we can manage it, and you haven't done a single thing. Jones and I have been doing everything for you."

This bruised her and she crossed her arms over her torso again, trying to think how to respond.

"You've been spending all your time with that damn hotdog pilot. Lot of good that will do us—you being seen around with a teetotaler."

"Well, I won't be seeing him anymore."

"That's something," he said, but the news only made him look angrier. It seemed to remind him of a whole other category of sins. "Where's your head been, Cord? I thought you wanted to be part of the family."

"I do!" With his last breath, her father had declared her an equal heir to the family business, and now she wanted nothing more than to make good on his edict. "I was only out last night to learn about speakeasies, to be seen, to get attention for our place." Charlie gave a slight nod, acknowledging that this might be partially true. Emboldened, she straightened and continued: "I *did* bring in the musical act for the first night."

"What?" Charlie narrowed his eyes, almost as though she'd called him a bad name.

"The musical act. For opening night." His expression did not change, so she added, more tentatively this time, "Letty?"

There was a long minute when he didn't do anything. Then his lip drew back on one side and he moved his head so that he was staring down at her from a skeptical angle. "I'm fighting a war here, Cord. The Hales want to take everything Dad worked for. They want to knock us out. I've got men injured—men who followed me even though they're old enough to be my dad. Meanwhile, you got this one simple thing to do. And you tell me—what? That you're going to bring people into a new night-club with some little girl from Ohio who has never been on the stage in her life?"

"But she's good! You said it yourself."

"Cord." Charlie shook his head and turned his eyes toward the ground. He laughed mirthlessly and said, "Maybe I had the wrong idea with you and this club."

The elegant table, the expansive verandah, the strong sunlight on the rolling lawns, all appeared soft and a bit pathetic to her in the wake of this comment. She knew what she looked like, lazing about as morning turned to afternoon, and she despised herself for it. From somewhere in the recesses of Cordelia's mind a memory emerged—her father, looking at her with such pleasure and pride, and telling her that she was like him, that she was clear-eyed and unsentimental, that she knew when to let go of dead weight. They had been standing in the hallway, and they had both been happy, and she had believed him for no other reason than that he said things with such authority that they stamped out doubt.

"No—no . . . you didn't have the wrong idea at all."

"No?"

She sat up straight. "Charlie, I can do this. Just give me one more chance."

A panting briefly interrupted their conversation, and she turned to see Letty's dog Good Egg loping up the hill. Behind her, wrapped in a white robe, was Letty. Cordelia's shoulders tightened, and she swallowed hard. "I'm the girl for this, Charlie," she said, meeting his gaze and holding it.

Charlie wagged his index finger at her, as though he were her parent and not her sibling. "One more chance. No more running around with flyboys, all right? And if you go out to do family business, fine—but two bodyguards go with you at all times."

Without smiling, he turned on his heel and went into the house. Cordelia closed her eyes, tipped her head against the chair's back, and groaned, quietly, so that no one else would hear. The sun was very bright—it warmed her bare calves as she waited for Letty to make it up the hill—and strong enough that it was difficult to see.

As Letty came up the hill she saw Charlie standing on the verandah in shirtsleeves and seersucker trousers, and while his presence might once have made her shy, or persuaded her to take the long way around to avoid him, today she didn't mind him being there. Charlie was now not so much a frightening figure to her as he was the boy who had first suggested she sing at his club. And after last night, she felt even more at home at Dogwood.

It had been her intention to wake early and rehearse again but she had been up so late last night with the girls, and they had drunk so much gin. Her thoughts were scattered and a low throb emanated from her forehead. The swimming had helped, but she still didn't see how she was going to remember the words to any of the songs. But going out had been worth it. They had been to so many places and were treated like very interesting people at every one of them, and she had never felt so much a part of Cordelia's gang, or like Billie and Astrid were her true friends, as she had during their carousing.

"Come on, Good Egg," she encouraged happily, and her dog went bounding ahead of her toward the house.

By the time she'd made her way up the stone steps to the wrought-iron table, Charlie was gone, but she saw that

Cordelia was there, her eyes shaded from the sun with a flattened hand.

"Good morning," Cordelia said, in a voice that Letty, despite their many years of friendship, did not recognize. It was deep, hoarse with something, which Letty supposed was the smoking she seemed to be doing so much of recently.

"You didn't finish your breakfast," Letty said, once she could see that this was the case. In fact, the plate of eggs was barely touched.

"No, I don't have much appetite this morning."

Letty pressed her lips together and took a long look at her friend. Cordelia's hair was limp, and the skin under her eyes had a faint green tinge. "What's the matter?"

"I've got to tell you something, Letty." Cordelia reached forward across the table, her long fingers fumbling for a cigarette. "I know you're excited about the club's opening—"

"Oh, I am! I've been practicing all my songs and the dances that'll go along with them. But don't think I'm not open to suggestion. I am, of course. I only want to be prepared, but I'll sing any songs you want me to."

"That's just it." Cordelia had managed to get a cigarette lit, and her eyes drifted toward the grounds. She shifted her jaw back and forth—a bad habit she used to have when she was younger and anxious, before John came along. "You can't open the club."

"What?" The earth below Letty's feet seemed to fall away. She waited for the punch line, to wake up from the dream, or at the very least for some small act of grace that would fix this, that would make it not so bad as it had initially sounded. "But I thought Charlie said—"

"We all think you'd be a fine act for the club, Letty. But the opening, that's a big night for us. A big night in a big city, and I'm afraid for the Greys' speakeasy, what we need is a star." She exhaled in a hurry, and added, as though this would somehow soften the blow: "A real star."

"Oh," Letty managed. She tightened the robe around her and turned her face away from Cordelia toward the big stone tiles of the porch. Now she was the one who couldn't make eye contact. The joy drained from her small frame. All her frenzied rehearsing yesterday suddenly seemed embarrassing, like the foolish leaping and yodeling of a girl who didn't know her place in the world. "Oh," she repeated, in an even fainter voice.

"Lets, I'm sorry." For some reason Cordelia was talking louder now and at a rapider clip. "I know you were excited. But this is a serious business, and I'm afraid—well, it's just what I have to do. That's all. You understand, don't you?"

Letty nodded, perhaps too enthusiastically, to overcompensate for the fact that she couldn't bring herself to look at Cordelia. If she did, or if she attempted to speak, she knew she would begin to cry. Still nodding, she passed into the house, through the ballroom where earlier she had sashayed and pliéd and done the Charleston, back when she'd still labored under the delusion that someday soon she'd be a nightclub singer. What a pitiful creature that girl seemed now. She trudged into the main hallway, so lost in her own thoughts that she didn't at first notice Astrid coming down the stairs.

"Oh, darling! There's a telegram for you," she said as Letty reached the second step.

"I'm not sure I could read right now." Letty had still not regained her voice—she sounded, even to herself, like she was speaking from beneath the staircase.

"Might cheer you up." Astrid paused as Letty passed her on the way up.

"I'll read it later."

Letty's shoulders remained slumped as she moved slowly, determinedly toward the Calla Lily Suite—the room that she'd slept in for many weeks now, but which was still decidedly Cordelia's—where she landed facedown on the white bed-spread and finally let out the low moaning sob that had been building inside her since she'd stood on the verandah and listened meekly while she was told that everything she had been living for was a lie.

Downstairs, in the library that nobody used anymore, Cordelia sat alone, feeling shattered by the night before and all the things that she had done. She wanted very badly to hear the voice of someone she had known for a long time. The slow, country voice of John Field saying her name as though it was the prettiest word he knew.

She did go as far as having the operator connect her to Union, Ohio, and requesting Dr. Field's line, which was one of the few private house lines in town. "Is it an emergency?" the operator asked, and Cordelia told her that it was. But then she felt ashamed of herself. What did she have to feel shattered by, besides the misbegotten attentions of a very questionable fellow, and her only half reciprocated interest in another, and the grave wrongs that she herself had done to her family and to her oldest friend? Why would the boy she had married only to leave behind want to know anything about that? In the harsh light of midday she wasn't sure why anyone would ever want to hear from her again, so she put down the phone and walked out of the house.

15

FOR A LONG WHILE AFTER THE CROSS-COUNTRY WIRES
had ceased to crackle with remorse, Letty remained upstairs,
prostrate on the bed. Nobody came to disturb her, which was
a sure sign that Cordelia was giving her a wide berth. Letty
felt blue and emptied out, and she longed, however idiotically,
for a friend as old and close as Cordelia upon whom she could
unburden her miseries.

It was only one of the many injustices of that afternoon
that the only person who might sympathize with her sad and
sorry situation was also the person who had taken from her the
thing she'd been most looking forward to. Singing at the nightclub had been more than that, even—it had been the event

her every second was building toward. The sense of belonging she'd felt that morning had evaporated in seconds, and the dull pain that follows drinking had returned to her forehead. Once she had managed to stop crying she went into the dressing room and situated herself in front of the vanity, but she no longer liked what she saw in the mirror.

The brightness had been sapped from her eyes by the previous night and it was impossible for her to smile, much less mug. She knew she would feel better if she danced and practiced—but what good was that anymore? What good was anything? She had probably been a fool to believe that she could be somebody. None of the people who occupied the rooms below could understand what it was she'd dreamed of, or what Cordelia had cost her by taking away the gig.

But of course she did know a person who understood, and she laughed out loud to think that it had taken this long for her mind to come back around to him. Her view had grown so desperately narrow—she had been so broken up over losing her chance to perform at the club, drowning in that lousy, worthless feeling, that she had forgotten the world outside Dogwood. Grady would listen to her. He was the one who had encouraged her in the first place, and he would surely encourage her now, at this nadir of suffering.

Letty was still a little teary when she boarded a subway car for the Village. But she managed to hold her head up by clinging to the memory of the way Grady had made her feel, like a girl in the pictures, a girl who was at the very beginning of something wonderful; and as she came around the corner onto Barrow Street, she almost managed to smile with the notion that everything was about to be made all right.

Then she did see him, and broke out into a run. "Grady!" she cried. "Oh, Grady, I'm so glad to see you!"

It was not until she reached him that she realized he was wearing a tuxedo, and that his hair was pomaded with extra care into two high, fair ridges over his brow. An older gentleman, also wearing a tuxedo, and a woman draped with an embroidered and tasseled wrap, lingered just behind him as though he were escorting them somewhere. Though ordinarily Letty would have been stunned into a shy silence by the presence of such well-dressed people, at this particular moment she could not help but rush straight to him, already spilling her tale of woe.

"Oh, Grady, the most terrible thing has happened. Cordelia told me this morning that I can't be the singer at their club. I'm back to having nothing again, and I feel so alone out there at Dogwood . . ." She would have gone on—indeed, she still wanted desperately to catalog all the indignities of the day—but she had noticed that neither Grady nor the two people behind him seemed in the least moved by her story.

"Letty Larkspur," Grady said finally, in a stiff and formal

manner that indicated a great distance had opened up between them, "these are my parents, Lewis and Roberta Lodge."

"Oh, well," Letty stuttered, "I'm awfully—I mean *very* pleased to meet you!" She tried to put aside her misery for a moment to give them a pleasant impression of her, but she could see that everything had already gone terribly awry. No one budged to shake her hand—his mother only glared at her from the other end of a long, pointed nose and made a disapproving sound from the back of her throat before turning away. Her husband followed quickly behind her. Grady's brow crumpled over his gray eyes and he looked at the sidewalk and then back at Letty as though wishing she would do something different. What that thing would have been she couldn't imagine. Her mouth opened, but before she could think of what to say, he went to follow his parents. He reached the car before they did and opened the door so that they could climb inside.

"I'll be right back," she heard him say, and then the car door slammed.

"I've been awful somehow, haven't I?" she asked when he returned to her.

"Didn't you get any of my telegrams? Didn't they tell you that I'd called?"

"Your telegrams?" she said, but by then realization was upon her. The dot of her mouth quivered and her eyes got big. "We were supposed to have dinner."

"Yes. Tonight. We were supposed to have dinner tonight. My parents loathe this part of the city, but they came tonight because I told them how important it was to me, what a special girl you were. My place is filled with twenty dollars' worth of flowers. I kept calling you to see if I could pick you up, but there was no answer. I tried to tell myself it was only that you were getting yourself ready for tonight." He shook his head, and put his hand in the pocket of his jacket, as though he was rummaging for something. "What an idiot I am. When you didn't show, Mother and Father kept saying that we ought to forget about it and just go have dinner, but I made them wait two hours, insisting you were on your way and worth every minute, even though it meant missing our reservation at the Colony."

There were many things that Letty wanted to say, but somehow, "Oh, no," was the only thing she could manage to give breath to. The setbacks of the afternoon seemed another lifetime away already.

"It's my fault, I suppose, for wanting to make it all happen so quickly—" Grady began to say, but he was interrupted by his mother. She had rolled down the window of her limousine and was staring out at the boy and girl standing awkwardly on the walk.

"Young lady, you have already ruined my dinner. Would you kindly allow me to enjoy the rest of my evening?"

"I ought to be going." Grady sighed and put both hands in his pockets and rocked back and forth. "Mother is awfully upset, and now she'll be very scandalized by the knowledge that the first girl I've wanted them to meet since prep school is not only very rude, but also the kind to sing in nightclubs."

"I'm so sorry, I can explain everything that happened!" She opened her palms up to him hopefully. Had she meant to grab his collar, touch his face? In any event, he stepped back, and she had no choice but to lower them, slowly and pathetically, to her sides. "I'm sorry," she repeated in a smaller and more chastened voice.

"At times, you and I have seemed to be the perfect company." Grady's gaze went to the treetops, and then to the pavement—but never to a place where he might accidentally see the sorrow in her face. "And other times you seem not to care about seeing me at all. That's fine, I suppose, only—only I don't much like the way it makes me feel."

"I'm sorry, I—"

Now his eyes did meet hers, and she found that being looked at in such a situation is infinitely worse than not being looked at. "In fact, I'm rather sick of the game, and I don't know that I care to see you anymore."

"Oh, Grady, please don't say that," she whispered. Too quickly he was in the car, and the car had sped down the street, and she was alone in the hot, still night.

Or not completely alone, for as soon as she'd scrunched up her eyes—as though that might take the sting away—she heard footsteps on the stoop behind her and a low whistle. She kept her eyes tight and her hands balled up with fistfuls of skirt and hoped this unwanted presence would dissolve back into the city. But no such luck.

"Those Lodges sure do travel in style."

It was a male voice, neither young nor old. She prayed that he was talking to someone else, but apparently he was alone, because when he went on, he addressed her.

"You look classy enough, but not of their ilk. The sort to drive around in limousines, lunching at the Ritz, flying down to Florida whenever the weather round here gets so they don't like it. Must be a nice way to live, don't you think?" When she didn't say anything, he repeated himself. "Don't you think it would be nice?"

"I think it would be nice." Her voice sounded hollowed out.

"Me, too. That's why I can't figure the Grady fellow. Wants to be a writer, wants to make his own way in the world. If I was born with a silver spoon in my mouth, I wouldn't care if I knew how to read. I'd have daiquiris by the pool and pay someone to read to me. Takes a strange man to work when he doesn't have to, and stranger yet to turn down money that could be his for nothing."

"The Lodges are pretty fine, are they?" Her shoulders

went slack. Suddenly she felt sore and fatigued from her practicing the day before.

The man whistled again. "They are pretty fine. Haven't you ever heard of Dorian Dog Food? That's where her money came from, piles of it, and he's from one of those nice old families that send their sons away to school. I'd say they are pretty fine."

Another car passed on the street, but it was not Grady coming back to see if she was going to be all right.

Turning, she tried to smile, but it was a weak attempt. "Everything that goes down must come up, right?" She had once heard a girl say this in a radio play, and it had sounded irreverent and brave in her lyrical radio voice. But the words were like lead when Letty heard them coming out of her own mouth.

The man, who had a five o'clock shadow but otherwise didn't look much older than Grady, put his cigarette to his lips, considering what she'd said. "I think it's the other way around," he replied after a while.

This, for some reason, was the thing she finally could not bear. She covered her face and hurried down the street, hoping that she could make it around the corner before the tears started and she embarrassed herself again.

"Don't go." Cordelia sprawled across Astrid's bed and watched her friend imploringly. She'd spent most of the afternoon walking the grounds and brooding, and had come indoors just in time to see Letty advancing toward the gates, a tiny figure clad in white amid a field of green. Angry at herself, she'd pulled her sweat-dampened tunic over her head and thrown it across the room. Even after she knew Letty was gone, her guilt had thrummed on unabated, and for a while she stewed in her suite, wondering how everything in her life had turned to rot so quickly. She continued in a similar state of mind until she heard an unusual amount of traffic on the main stairs, and had drifted into Astrid's room. "Please, don't go."

"Can't be helped, darling." Astrid bent over the chair of the vanity, turning her face this way and that to best assess whether or not the wide-brimmed black hat she was wearing should come with her or not. "I might have to murder your handsome brother if I stay, and prison garb simply won't do justice to my figure."

"But couldn't you talk again in the light of day?" asked Cordelia, for whom a dramatic departure had always signaled an intention not to return. "Maybe you were both just over-heated last night."

Astrid straightened and caught Cordelia's eye in the mirror. "There's been plenty of time this morning for him to apologize, if indeed he was merely 'overheated.'" With nimble fingers, she removed the hat, and then walked across the floor and handed it to Milly, who was struggling with one of the several pieces of luggage that had reappeared in the hallway that morning. "But he has more important things to see to, I suppose, and it won't be *me* groveling to *him* saying *I'm* sorry."

"Why not?"

"Because I'm *not* sorry."

The strap of Cordelia's slip fell away from her shoulder and she put it back in place. "He didn't really say that he has more important things to see to than you, did he?"

"Oh, yes. He said it was a dumb idea, my coming to live here, and that he couldn't really think about me, what with the business and the Hales and how the situation with them changes every minute."

"Every minute? That's a bit much, isn't it?"

"I don't know." Astrid waved her hands in the air dismissively. As though this reminded her of something, she went over to the nightstand and picked up her engagement ring. "Something about the Hales vandalizing the club."

Cordelia had been lounging before but now she bolted upright. "My club?"

Astrid blinked at her. "Yes, I suppose."

Was that what Thom was threatening last night? Had he left The Bedroom and gone to the Greys' place to oversee the damage himself? Cordelia's jaw got tight and her teeth clenched together. Only when Astrid's green eyes sailed from Cordelia's face to her hands did she realize how overwhelmed with fury she was.

"I'm sorry," Cordelia whispered.

"Don't be sorry, darling. I know you want to talk to Charlie about what's happened." A fragile smile played on her face. "Well, go!"

Cordelia went to Astrid and put her arms around her neck. "Come back soon, all right?"

"All right." Astrid winked sadly and released Cordelia from her embrace. "Don't think I'd miss your club opening for anything in the world."

"I'll ring you."

She found Charlie in the poolroom on the second floor, playing billiards in a worn undershirt and tailored slacks. He was with Danny and some of the other boys, and when she came in, he glanced up from the table but did not speak. He seemed reluctant to acknowledge her at all, but after a moment of glancing from her slip to her face, he handed her the collared shirt he had been wearing earlier. With a faint nod of understanding she pulled it on and rolled the sleeves up. Once she was more covered he bent to take his shot.

"Astrid's leaving," she said in a soft voice.

"I know," he replied.

The ceiling fan went on whirring, and the boys in the corner stopped staring at her. "What happened to the club last night?" she asked when it was obvious he didn't want to talk about Astrid anymore.

"Not much. It's not the damage that they did—it was just a message."

"We can still open as planned?"

Charlie regarded her. "Yes, we can still open."

"What does the message mean?"

He shrugged. "Means something worse is coming. Maybe on opening night. There wasn't a lot of subtlety to the message."

"What did they do?"

"It was too disgusting to tell a lady."

Over his shoulder, she saw the boys trying not to laugh, and this made her angry, and wish that she wasn't wearing a slip and that her hair wasn't undone. "Well, can't we hit them back first?"

"With what? Already took most of their speakeasy customers in the city. The country club won't budge for obvious reasons. Hard to know who they supply privately. I'd like to hit them the way they hit us, but Jones keeps saying we're a business, and we can't waste resources on violence, except when necessary. Wish he were wrong, but—he's usually right."

Outside, the sun was shining, and Cordelia went to the window seat and sat down. It would have been a good day to be by the pool, but she had no desire to swim. "I had so many ideas last night, Charlie. I watched and figured out what makes all these different places special, and I know just what we'll use for our place and what we won't."

Charlie sunk the eight ball and handed off the pool cue. "Yeah? Good," he said, sitting down next to her.

"I'm sorry," she said.

"I know."

She closed her eyes and wished that from the first moment she'd walked into the bank, she had thought of nothing but how to open a speakeasy. That she had stayed at Charlie's side and learned everything there was to learn and personally chosen every chair and glass and uniform. That she had not grown weak and distracted by matters of the heart, which were in any event fleeting. Her mind went to Max, with his fancy airplane, how he looked down on a miniature landscape, acting so superior, as though he knew anything about life and the choices people had to make. She felt disgusted, remembering how impressed she was by him, how godlike he had acted as he piloted over the heads of little people everywhere.

She might have tried to say all this, but Charlie didn't seem to need to hear it, and by then her mind had moved onto something else. "Charlie," she began. Her mouth had gone dry and her brain began to tick. "Did you know that the Hales have a submarine?"

"What?" His brows drew together.

"I saw it when Max took me up in the airplane. Apparently Duluth Hale got it in the Great War. They use it for deliveries."

"How?"

"I don't know, but Max says he's seen it leave every day at dawn. It was later in the day when I saw it—a great big thing rising out of the water."

Charlie shook his head and looked over his shoulder at the other boys, who were going about their business, focused on the pool game or involved in low conversation. When he turned back to Cordelia there was a burning light in his eyes. "Hot damn!" He jumped up and slapped his hands together, loudly enough to catch the attention of everyone else in the room. "Well, hot damn."

"Did I do right finally?" she couldn't help but ask.

"You did right, sister." He slapped his hands together again. "God damn, it's going to be a good day."

Grabbing both her hands, he pulled her to her feet. Cordelia beamed at him and he beamed back. "Come on, Cord," he said, throwing his arm over her shoulder and steering her toward the door. "We got some work to do."

"We?" She was so pleased to be back in Charlie's good graces, and she wanted to bring attention to it, just once.

"Yeah, and I'll tell you what we're going to do. I have this friend in the Coast Guard—not a friend exactly, more like someone who I pay to act friendly. What do you say we call him up and tell him a story?"

16

BY THE FOLLOWING THURSDAY, THE CYCLE OF HUMID
rain and heat had broken. The sun was strong and the air was
warm wherever it shone, but cool pockets hid in the shadows.
People who had wasted days fanning themselves on porches
or in the shadier corners of the house went back to work. At
Marsh Hall, where the tropical fluctuations of the weather had
interfered with the social agenda of the lady of the house for
some days, an uncharacteristic serenity ruled, and Astrid, if not
exactly happy to be back, couldn't help but feel that she had
emerged from a period of confusion and madness into more
tranquil waters.

The day was just beginning and she didn't see the point

in rushing to repair a dress she might not wear again; it was just as well to spend an afternoon by the pool thinking about the clothes that she would order for the fall. Perhaps she would go back to school that fall, in which case she would need different things—but that decision was a long time away. She wanted to soak up the beauty of the day through her pores and later go out again, refreshed and lovely as ever, so Charlie would hate himself for being so mean. Tonight she wanted to have twice as much fun, to make up for all the fun he'd deprived her of.

"Miss Donal?"

She opened her eyes and turned her face up toward the maid. "Brenda, how clever of you, I was just getting thirsty—would you bring me some lemonade?"

"Shall I bring two? You have a guest."

Astrid twisted in the white chaise and saw, between the row of thin cypress that lined the pool deck, a small figure in a petal pink jumper walking across the lawn. "Yes, thank you."

Till then, no part of Astrid had wanted to be back at Dogwood. It was a nuisance, of course, the way her mother's face kept silently telling her "I told you so," and irksome that even Billie seemed unsurprised by the turn of events. But the sight of Letty did make Astrid miss living in that big, lawless house with her best friends.

"Letty, what a perfect sight you are, how did you ever get here?" Astrid called, her arms opening wide for an embrace.

"I walked," she said in that guileless way she had, as though this was a perfectly natural thing to do.

"That's such a long walk, dear, you could ruin your shoes! There's a new invention called the telephone, you know."

Letty's face flushed. "Yes," she said, in a way that implied that wherever she was from, she hadn't used a telephone very often.

"Oh, never mind. Sit, please, and tell me everything there is to know. Unless it has to do with Charlie—I cannot stand his name, and don't want to know what's happened to him. Unless it's very bad, of course, and he's suffering mightily."

"Oh—I haven't seen much of Charlie." Letty glanced away and made a show of arranging herself on the chair next to Astrid's with her legs folded up under herself and her chin rested in her palm.

"Never mind, darling, better not to talk of him. Now tell me—did you come all this way just to see me?"

"Well, yes," Letty said, but the darting of the pure blue disks of her eyes said otherwise. "Actually, I was wondering if you knew where Cordelia was."

"Cordelia? Surely you've seen her at Dogwood?"

"She hasn't been around much. I think she might be avoiding me."

"That doesn't seem very likely." Astrid turned her face to the side, trying to recall in what order everything had happened that week. "I talked to her a few days ago, and she told me she was too busy for a visit, on account of they're opening their speakeasy this weekend, and there's so much to be done. Sounded obsessed, that one. Why? Are you all right? You look a bit peaked."

"Oh," Letty sighed, as though she were releasing the weight of the whole world. "I'm fine."

"Really, darling, you don't sound the least bit convincing."

Letty shifted uncomfortably for a few moments, and then her body deflated against the lounge chair. "I'm just awful, to tell you the truth. I've been wanting to talk to someone, but usually I would talk to Cordelia about something like this, and she's so hard to find these days, and I don't even know that she's the right one to . . ." Letty trailed off dejectedly.

"Well, don't be a ninny, tell me what's happened!" Astrid turned on her side and took her sunglasses off and tried to appear attentive, even though the stucco bungalows that flanked the pool were unbearably white without them. "I can't stand being left out of things and not knowing what the latest is."

Letty pressed the red lips of her small mouth together, as though she were trying to keep a wave of emotion at bay. "I lost the gig," she managed, her voice cracking horrifically over the sentence.

"Which gig?"

"At the club, of course . . ." Letty averted her eyes and then Astrid remembered with a start that Letty was supposed to have opened Charlie and Cordelia's club. "Cordelia says they need a *real* star."

The maid came back with the lemonade then, and Letty kept her head down while Brenda set up the tray between them, and went on gazing at her hands until Astrid lifted her glass and waved it in Letty's direction. "Oh, applesauce. You *are* a real star," she said, taking a big, sweet sip of lemonade. "But oh, I *am* sorry, you dove, that wasn't very nice of them to do that."

"I probably didn't deserve it." Letty fidgeted with her skirt, and her voice wavered, and for a moment Astrid was panicked, thinking the other girl might cry. "But you see, it was everything to me. It's like this—you were born into the fancy world, and Cordelia always had a magical ticket to gain her entry, if she only knew where to turn it in. But me—all I've *got* is me. And I thought singing at that club was going to be the making of me."

"Well, *I* think you are just perfection." Astrid put her sunglasses back on and rolled onto her stomach so that she could get some sun on the backs of her thighs. "Really marvelous. And I have an eye, Miss Letty Larkspur, so don't think I'm saying this just because we are friends. This is nothing more than a temporary setback. Think how much better success will taste when you make it on your own! Work your way up to singing at a nightclub . . . preferably one that isn't backed by a big hothead like Charlie. Then you'll know it's not just luck."

Letty nodded vigorously and hiccupped.

"To hell with them, Letty. Really. You've got it all, and you must not waste that feeling sorry for yourself. Now smile a little, will you?"

The edges of Letty's mouth did struggle upward in an attempt at smiling, but in the end they collapsed back and a tiny wail escaped her throat.

"Come, really, is it so bad? Unless of course there's something else nagging you. Is there something else?"

Letty turned her face up to the sky, squinting. Her head bobbed twice. "Yes . . . there is. It's—it's that I've been such a wretch."

Here Astrid couldn't help it, her mouth buckled in a vain attempt not to laugh, for though Letty looked so entirely serious, she didn't seem the teensiest bit capable of being a wretch. "How? I don't believe you."

"Oh, no. I have been terrible. It's that fellow Grady."

Astrid stared back blankly. "Grady?"

"Grady Lodge. He was at the Beaumonts', remember? And he was courting me, I guess, and I was supposed to have dinner with his parents last weekend and I forgot entirely. Then I acted like a complete fool and went to his apartment, where I had already made them wait so long, and then I went on and on about how I had lost my chance at being a nightclub singer!"

"That doesn't sound so bad," Astrid replied. She had finished her lemonade, and put the glass aside on the concrete. "After all, it was very big news."

"You would think so, but it seems the Lodges are very fine people. They were certainly finer looking than I expected."

"*No.*" An idea had seized Astrid, and her eyes got big with it. "No!"

"Yes, I had just assumed they would be simple folks, like him, but—"

"Not *Grady Lodge*, of the *Lewis Lodges.*"

"Yes . . . I think his name was Lewis." One of Letty's pin-thin brows drew closer to the other quizzically.

"Oh, darling, I was so distracted that day! I just thought of him as your nice-seeming friend and then didn't think about him anymore. I only saw him at a distance, I believe, and anyway, I haven't seen Grady in years."

"But you can't *know* him . . . ?"

"Of course I know him." Astrid paused and covered her mouth as she experienced the rush of anticipation that comes whenever a really delicious story is about to unfold. "I've known him for years. But I haven't seen him since the summer he and Peachy . . . *well.*"

"Peachy Whitburn?"

"Yes, dear, everyone knows they were sweethearts of at least a year when he started at Columbia College—we all expected they'd marry. But before he could propose she went off to the Continent for some European finishing and got in a run of trouble there, because she was seduced by a married Frenchman."

"No!" Letty whispered.

"That's not the worst of it—she was terribly rotten and sent Grady letters detailing the whole affair, saying she would break it off, but all the while carrying on. Well, he dropped out of school after one semester, and none of us saw him anymore. The rumor was he wanted to be a writer, *Lord* knows why. That was two years ago now. I have seen a story of his here and there, they're quite good, though none of us can understand it. Why would he want to be a writer, when he's already a millionaire?"

A gasp of anguish escaped Letty's mouth and she turned her face away and buried it in the back of the chaise.

"Oh, who cares about millionaires!" Astrid's heart felt lighter with no Charlie tugging at it, and she was sure if Letty would just unbury her face she would feel the same. "Who cares about young men? You are going to be a singer or an actress or a chorus girl, and that's *so* much more exciting than bagging a beau who can buy you little nothings!"

Astrid reached over and brushed a few of Letty's bangs

away from her face; the dark-haired girl looked back and whimpered.

"Darling, don't be silly, your whole future is ahead of you. All you have to do is go out there and ask for a part—something small and reasonable just to start with. From there, no one can stop you. Don't feel bad about anything you've done, and for God's sake, have fun."

"You don't think I'm horrible?"

"Lord, no."

"And you really think it's going to be all right?" Letty straightened and a ray of hopefulness fell across her face.

"I know it is. You go into the city right now before your nerves get the better of you and find yourself a job. And have Brenda tell the chauffeur to take you to the station. You've got to start treating your shoes better."

Letty nodded determinedly, and she sat up and began to smooth her dress and hair as though she actually might go and do as Astrid had directed.

"There, you see? You don't need to marry a man with millions. You only need to be your exquisite self."

In her hands she held a copy of *The Weekly Stage*. It was days old—she had been fidgeting with it since she bought it, dog-earing pages and circling ads for open calls in pencil. Unlike when she was working at Seventh Heaven, dreaming of landing

a big role but not truly ready to put herself through the scru-
tiny of auditions, now she looked for notices that were seeking a number of girls—more than anything, she wanted to
be realistic this time—and she'd avoided the more plum and
pretentious parts that would earlier have caught her fancy. As
she rode the westbound train away from White Cove, she went
over those notices with a singleness of purpose that had eluded
her thus far.

When she disembarked, the smell of the city rushed
back to her, the same way it had on the first day she saw it,
and she became elated again with all the possibilities of that
first glimpse. By the time she climbed onto the stage at the
first casting call, she was able to go through the routine she
had practiced so many times in the Dogwood ballroom almost
without thinking about her movements. When she finished she
heard the clapping of perhaps a dozen people, and she bowed
and smiled and lingered for a moment in the glow of the spotlight.

"Thank you, Miss Larkspur, that was very good," a reed-
thin man in the front row said. His legs were crossed the way a
woman might cross her legs and he kept a pencil behind his ear.
As her eyes adjusted to the darkness of the theater, she decided
that there was nothing about him that she might be attracted
to, at least not in any romantic way, and this fact made her feel
instantly more at ease.

"Thank you."

"I like you. Are you available in the evenings?"

"Yes."

"Are you available for the rest of the afternoon?"

"Yes."

"Because I think I could use you, but I'll need to see some other girls first. Have a seat, please."

"Yes, of course," she replied. Even though this wasn't the resounding *yes* she'd always hoped for, at that particular moment it was enough to fill her with gratitude. "Thank you," she said again, bowing furtively to the man before making her way up the aisle.

She was moving carefully in the darkness when she heard someone hiss her name. "Letty, you were great!"

"Who is that?" she whispered back, putting a hand on one of the velvet-covered seats and sitting down beside the voice. But she knew before the reply came. "Paulette!" she gasped and put her arms around the girl who had taken her in when she was destitute and didn't know the city at all. "What are you doing here?"

"Same as you. I need a job." In the dim light of the theater, she could just make out the familiar shiny, wine-colored lips and the dark hair, ironed into big waves.

Down on the stage, another girl was performing. Her routine involved a parasol, and though her singing was slightly off-key, she had a flirtatious way of moving that Letty was sure would catch the attention of a theatrical producer—at least all the theatrical producers with whom she'd yet come into contact.

"How is Seventh Heaven these days?"

"Oh, the same in the bad ways. Mr. Cole is still a miserable sack of beans, and the customers still seem to think they've bought a ticket to a petting zoo. But now it's bad in new ways, too. No one goes there anymore except tourists watching their dime."

"But everyone always wanted to go there," Letty replied in disbelief.

"Nothing stays the same forever." Paulette shrugged.

"Are the same girls living with you in the apartment?"

"Yes, same girlies. Nothing's changed, except that I have less money."

"I'm sorry."

"So goes life. I was hoping this might be something for me, but from what I can tell he's only keeping you wee things around. I think he just asked me to stay as a courtesy. But I'm not worried. They can't say no to a face like this forever, right? I'm glad to see you—I was worried about you, what with the bad way you were in when you went off."

"I'm sorry—I should have somehow let you know that I was all right. Life has been swell really. I've been staying in White Cove."

"White Cove, Long Island?" Paulette exclaimed, loud

enough that the man with the pencil behind his ear turned and cleared his throat. "How'd you manage that?" she went on in a low whisper.

"My friend from Ohio, Cordelia, her father is—was—he has a place there."

"Cordelia Grey is your friend?" Paulette's voice got loud again, and the man in the front row stood up and asked that whoever was making noise be quiet or leave.

The girls exchanged conspiratorial looks but kept quiet through the next four auditions, after which the man in the front row stood up and announced: "Will Miss Bates, Miss Logan, Miss Appleton, Miss Larkspur, and Miss Preston please stay? As for the rest of you, I am grateful for your time."

"Oh, well, you see?" Paulette said. "My luck is down these days, and tall girls are out."

"That's too bad," Letty said. Everyone in the theater was talking now, and there was no need to whisper anymore, but she couldn't seem to get her voice to a normal decibel. Her happiness was all tangled up in blue.

"Oh, honey," Paulette went on in a softer tone. She must have noticed that Letty's small face was vacillating between a stricken expression and one of jubilation. "You deserve it. Don't waste any time feeling bad for me."

But Letty couldn't help feeling bad. "It's only that it would have been so nice to be in the same show."

"It would have, but it's not to be. Anyway, now that we've seen each other, you'll know not to act like a stranger."

Letty nodded sadly. Then her mind grasped onto something that might make it better. Though her heart shrank every time she thought of the nightclub that was supposed to have been her big break, she couldn't stand the idea of Paulette going off like this, especially since at one time she'd helped Letty so much. "Paulette, would you really rather work someplace else?"

Paulette laughed faintly. "Yesterday I thought about asking for a job mopping floors at some old ice-cream parlor I passed. I'd probably make more money, and at least I could count on a little sweetness."

"Because you see my friend Cordelia is opening a place. A nightclub. If you went there tomorrow and told her you know me I'm sure she'd give you a job. It's in an old bank, on West Fifty-third."

"Thanks, maybe I will." Paulette bent down and pulled Letty close to her for a hug. "It was good to see you," she said and went out.

The man with the pencil behind his ear called the five remaining girls down to the front row of seats. They all looked like her—petite and pale-skinned and dark-haired. The job he was offering wasn't glamorous, and he went to some lengths to impress upon the girls that they would have to start tomorrow night, no exceptions, that they would get no special treatment, that they would be required to be on hand six nights a week, indefinitely, and that the pay would be low. Apparently these grueling conditions were the reason that the revue was constantly in need of new chorus girls, and Letty supposed she should have felt mistreated by them, except that she was so euphoric with the miracle of having been given her first job as an actress that she almost couldn't stop smiling.

Mr. Archly—for that was the name of the man who had cast her—did not exaggerate. He kept them through the afternoon to learn their parts, and the choreographer, whose name was Miss Chastain, did not smile once as she corrected the placement of their feet and their musicality and the quality of their arm gestures. By the time the wardrobe man Mr. Singer came out to measure them, they had already lost one of the girls, but Mr. Archly said he knew that would happen, and that he really had only needed four. For the first time he smiled, and said that he'd thought the remaining four had been the strongest from the beginning. Then Mr. Singer went away and Miss Chastain clapped her hands and they were back to work.

By the time Letty and the other new chorus girls were dismissed, the actors and singers and comedians who were performing that night had begun to arrive, carrying shopping bags and waving cigarettes and laughing. Letty watched them shyly in the hallway as they passed, wondering what they had filled their daylight hours with, and what assignations they had to look forward to when the show was over. Out on the sidewalk, the light had faded enough to make the big sign proclaiming the Paris Revue glow against the plum dusk. Her whole self swooned with the bittersweetness of having secured a show business job and having no Grady to tell about it.

"Isn't that sign beautiful?" Letty asked Mary Preston, one of the other new girls, as they lingered in front of the theater while the after-work crowds streamed past. The streets were littered with wrappers and papers and other discarded items, but in the magic-hour light, even trash looked like treasure.

Mary grinned. "You know I came all the way from Alabama for a chance like this?" she said in her pretty lilting Southern way.

"I'm from Ohio," was all Letty could manage in return, but she was smiling so big that her actual words were insignificant. This seemed to her like the first real moment of her life.

"Well, I'll see you tomorrow?" Mary said.

Their heads bobbed in agreement, and then they parted, two small girls following their own paths into the wide city. If she hurried, she knew that she could make the 7:58 train back to White Cove, but she was in no mood for hurrying off. She wanted to walk slowly and smell the wafting perfumes of bouquets that men had bought for their sweethearts and watch couples holding each other tight as they dashed along the pavement on their way to or from something that made them grateful to be in each other's company. Going home felt the same as going to sleep, and she was too bouncing, too overcome with bliss, for that. She wished her mother could see her now, a New York girl who had just earned her first real job.

Her chest rose and fell with the thrill of her new life, and with the prospect of soon telling Cordelia everything. Of course she still felt a touch wounded by how harshly Cordelia had taken away the thing she'd promised, but Letty felt she understood what Cordelia had done better now that she herself had a vocation. They were not children anymore and fate was sure to throw them in the way of hard choices. Yet the many years when Letty and Cordelia had been each other's only sympathetic ear were a bond that would not be easily dissolved. And so it was natural that Letty should feel desperate to tell her old friend that she had finally gotten what she'd always wanted, the thing they had gushingly talked of on their long walks home from Defiance: a paid job at a real theater.

"Hey there, Miss Larkspur."

The sound of her own name—the name she'd given herself—startled Letty from her thoughts. She glanced up at the pretty windowless limestone facade and then to Danny, whose gentle eyes could barely hold hers.

"You found us," he said with a smile. The building was a bank; her feet had carried her to Cordelia's club.

She nodded her hello, and then he turned awkwardly and went down the street on some errand or other.

Other young men, most of whom she recognized from around Dogwood, were streaming in and out the big doorway, and curious passersby clotted the sidewalks, whispering to each other about what was being built there. That she had been recognized by one of these men made her look like a very important person, Letty sensed, and for a moment she felt quite fully like a chorus girl who is recognized by doormen everywhere and shepherded into whatever charmed room she desires to enter. She reached the entrance with her head high and an air of drama to her gait.

"Hey there!" were the brunt words that halted her parade. She had just stepped over the threshold, and a bear-sized man with a hat pulled down over his eyes appeared and blocked her way.

"Hello." She smiled up at him before trying to pass.

"Where do you think you're going?"

She peeked around his big frame at the frenzied activity of the room—small wrought iron tables were being arranged across a vast floor, and some sort of construction was being done behind the walls of teller windows that flanked the main space. "I'm Letty."

"Who?"

This bruised her confidence some, but then she

remembered what she had done today, and the thought put a smile of impenetrable confidence on her face. "Letty, Cordelia's friend. I'm here to see Cordelia. You can ask Danny, if you want."

"Nah, that's all right," the man said after a minute. "I remember you now. Sorry to give you any trouble, miss—but the Hales followed Miss Cordelia again last night, and we're all a little on edge that they'll try to nab her. Or worse."

"I understand. You were only doing your job."

"She's that way." The man pointed toward two big copper doors on the far side of the room. Letty curtsied and moved forward, slowly so that she could take the place in. Old murals covered the ceiling, which gave the whole place a celestial ambiance, and the mystical sunset light filtered down from high up on the walls. On the east wall of the building—Letty noticed with a tiny pang—several of the teller windows had been removed and a stage was being erected. It glistened for a moment before her like a mirage, and she had to close her eyes until the pang had passed and she had remembered how much better off she was forging her own path. No less an authority than Astrid Donal had assured her of this.

She was halfway across the mosaic floor when the room fell quiet. A saw stopped, and the various male voices shouting back and forth ceased. Letty herself paused and unconsciously stepped to the side. A woman in a white, drop-waist summer dress and pearls, her artfully made-up face shadowed by a wide-brimmed white hat, was gliding through the maze of tables toward the exit.

A slow, lone whistle cut through the silence. From a distance the woman's beauty had looked impeccable, but when she gusted by in a gardenia-scented cloud Letty could tell that she was at least thirty-five. The perfume was still lingering in the air when the woman stepped into the sliver of streetscape, and outside.

"That was Mona Alexander," one of the men working on the bar said, as activity resumed.

"Who?" his partner replied.

"Mona Alexander. When I was coming up, she was the hottest singer around. She's going to perform on opening night."

Letty had never seen a woman silence a room like that, and she felt almost ridiculous for having believed she was capable of doing what this woman was going to do—hold the attention of a big rowdy drinking audience and make them listen to her. But, perhaps someday she would—and with that happy thought Letty advanced through the copper doors that the man in the hat had indicated.

Cordelia's back was turned when Letty came in, and she held the telephone in her hand. She wore brown wide-legged trousers that Letty had never seen before and a pale pink blouse, and Letty almost didn't recognize her. She was nodding and listening to someone talk, and then she said, "Thanks, Roger," in the voice of a much older woman and hung up.

"Who was that?" Letty asked.

"Oh, Lets! I'm so glad you're here," Cordelia said, though she gave no sign of coming to greet Letty in the door frame where she was standing. The girls smiled at each other almost shyly, as though over the several days that had passed without seeing one another they had become strangers.

"Who is Roger?" Letty repeated the question since she couldn't think of anything else to say.

"My press agent." Cordelia lit a cigarette. "Isn't this place tops?"

Letty's mouth opened and framed the foreign phrase *press agent*.

"We're opening tomorrow night, and we're calling it The Vault, and Roger says everyone wants to come and his line is always engaged." Cordelia rested her hips against the desk, which was an imposing mahogany piece of furniture with massive, engraved legs, the kind the director of a bank might sit behind. "I found a whole box of rolls of amusement park tickets at a supply store down on Thirty-seventh Street that already had The Vault printed on them. Apparently there was a ride that went by that name at a park in Queens, but they had to close after an old lady had a heart attack and died. Anyway, how it will work is, the customers will walk in and buy tickets at the first teller window, and then they can use their tickets to buy drinks at other windows further in. Isn't that clever? I thought of that. And the drinks will come in Ball jars, won't that be pretty? And Mona Alexander, who was one of Dad's girls a long time ago, said she wanted to perform for no fee in Dad's honor, and—"

Cordelia seemed to have plenty more to say, and probably would have gone on, but the phone rang and she turned around and picked up the receiver. Letty had never heard Cordelia talk so much at once. In Union, she'd been the kind to say little and watch, and had always seemed more interested in Letty's fantasies of stardom and fame than in telling her own stories. Now she spoke a few rapid sentences into the receiver and glanced back over her shoulder as though checking to see if Letty were still there.

"I only wanted to tell you that I got a job," Letty said, as though to justify her continued presence. Though her voice was irritatingly meek when she had most definitely instructed it to be bold and careless, she went on: "A part. In a revue—"

"Isn't that something?" Cordelia's red lips sprang into a smile. Letty could hear the mechanical voice on the other end of the receiver, and in the next moment, Cordelia returned her attention there. "Sorry, what was that?"

Letty felt as though she had just dropped a precious heirloom down a long elevator shaft, and had to watch as the treasured object fell into the gloom and disappeared without a sound forever. It was perfectly obvious from Cordelia's posture, which was straight and full of newfound importance, that the telephone call was not going to be a short one, and Letty did not think she could withstand even another minute of lingering invisibly, half in and half out of the room. She was all the way in the hall by the time Cordelia noticed her departure.

"Tomorrow night is the opening!" she called after Letty. "Wear the red dress we got you that day we went to Bergdorf, all right? To match the tickets."

"I can't," Letty said, although the telephone conversation had started back up, and she was the only one to hear herself. "It's my first night at the Revue."

For a moment she watched Cordelia from the quiet of the dim hallway, her shoulders thrown back, her narrow waist obvious in the slim trousers. Cordelia's indifference shouldn't matter so much, Letty knew. She might even have come to expect it by now. She longed, a little bit, for the Cordelia she used to know, the one she sat with by the radio, listening to tales from faraway lands, imagining the future. But mostly she felt betrayed.

Charlie was coming in off the street with his hair of polished metal as she made her way to the entrance, but he didn't notice her, and she didn't bother to catch his eye. Of course it smarted to be leaving so soon, and with less celebration than she had hoped for. But she had spent all day learning the dances and expressions that would make a raucous audience follow her with their eyes, and she no longer needed her friends in order to be seen.

17

TWENTY-FOUR HOURS AHEAD OF THE EVENT, THE rumor that a club called The Vault would be opening Friday night was circulating among all those who cared about such things. The beat cops knew, and had been duly taken care of, and many of them had already converted this windfall into new presents for their long-suffering wives. A few federal agents had even caught wind of the place—but they were a beleaguered lot, and those who did have the resources to take on such a joint were stalled by the knowledge that it would only result in a few misdemeanors, instead of hitting at the heart of the Greys' operation. The gossip columnists had been tipped off, as had personalities worthy of appearing in gossip columns. Though revelers at speakeasies throughout the city craned their necks, hoping to catch a glimpse of the eighteen-year-old girl who was said to be in charge of this place, no one could say with any confidence that they had actually seen her.

In fact, on Thursday night, Cordelia had gone to bed early for the first time in a week, in one of three rooms her brother had rented in the St. Regis. She and Charlie had stayed there for several nights already. Every day had been full of preparations for their club, and mostly they had been in the city too late to go home to Dogwood. Over the course of the week, Cordelia had found herself summoning all of the inner mettle she had accumulated during her stern Ohio upbringing. The obsessive attention with which she had once scanned days-old newspapers for any mention of a magical land called New York and a long-lost father named Darius Grey served her well now, as did the self-reliance she'd stored up to survive Aunt Ida's withering comments and severe punishments. Not to mention the knowledge she'd acquired working in Uncle Jeb's hardware store. The boys building out the stage and finishing the bar blinked at her, surprised, when she pointed out their shortcuts and told them how she wanted the job done, but they did not try to cheat her again. More than once she summoned an old trick of hers: looking into the eyes of men twice her age without flinching, as though there was nothing they could tell her that she did not already know.

At times she seemed to be watching from outside herself as a far more assured young woman busily attended to a vast new world of responsibility. But on Friday morning, she woke up alone in the luxuriously anonymous hotel room and felt very much herself.

No alarm was necessary; her eyes were wide open and her mind came alive a while before the sun rose. Out on the street she could hear delivery trucks, and she lay for a moment in the darkness listening to her heartbeat and wondering how she had come here, to this extraordinary point of living. Then she thought of Astrid, who would not philosophize, who would simply issue a quip and saunter on in the same remarkable direction she was always heading. Cordelia had already made her preparations. She now had only to rise and see about the results.

So she left the bed and put on men's trousers—not fitted like the ones her brother had had sent over from Henri Bendel's earlier in the week, so that she could meet Roger Tinsley in style, but a well-worn pair that were loose on her, and which she rolled above the ankle—and tennis shoes and the pink chiffon blouse she'd worn the day before. In the wan electric light she applied lipstick. Then she wondered if lipstick was appropriate to her mission today, but Charlie knocked on her door before she could take it off, and after that she didn't think of it.

Even in the near darkness, she could see that her brother's eyes were shining. Neither Grey sibling said anything. They walked past the guard who stood outside Cordelia's room at all times and down the thickly carpeted hall.

At that hour there were few cars on the road, and they drove out of town in a silence that was dense with anticipation. It was the first time Cordelia had been without a bodyguard since the night the club was vandalized, and it was comforting to sit with her brother in the cool dawn, away from the noise, and know that she was safe. Later there would be plenty of noise, so she let herself be lulled by the jostling of country roads and enjoyed the quiet. In Rye Haven they stopped for gasoline, and Charlie bought them cups of hot coffee from the breakfast joint next to the filling station. After that, it wasn't far to the place where they left the car by the side of the road. It was a short walk through the woods to the water. There was a fisherman's shack there, and Charlie borrowed the absent man's rowboat, and they glided out across the still water as the first orange hue began to emerge along the horizon line.

The morning had not advanced enough, however, that a boat somewhat offshore would be visible if its lights were off; a few such vessels—she knew, even though she could not see them—were out there in the mists. She also knew an estate called Avalon was close by, where Thom Hale was probably sleeping the sound slumber of all slippery, unscrupulous boys.

Whenever she thought of the place, she thought of swaying in Thom's arms on the outdoor dance floor with a pistol in her garter, and what a seamless job Thom had done of appearing to care for her.

Presently she heard shouting at a nearby pier. She and Charlie both turned in that direction, as what looked like a whale's back breached the glassy surface. The shouting intensified, and they began to make out through the gloom the men who stood by many cases of contraband, waiting for the hatch to open. As soon as it did, a hurried transaction began—men strained to hand the cases down to outstretched arms. Cordelia sipped her coffee and breathed in the muggy, brackish air. It was a smell she would remember for the rest of her life.

"Wait for it," Charlie whispered.

Someone on the pier lit a cigarette, a tiny flair against the lightening sky, and the next thing Cordelia knew was that sirens were echoing off the water and several large vessels turned their big flood lights at the same time.

"This is the Coast Guard," a man announced with the majestic vibrating authority of a bullhorn. "All crew are to come up from below. Any weapons, leave them behind. We are seizing your ship under suspicion of rum-running. Any property destroyed at this point will be punishable by law."

"Is that your friend?" Cordelia whispered to Charlie, as the ripples from the speedboat reached their flimsy bark.

"Yeah, though I don't know if I'd call him a friend. More an ally. We're on the same side, I guess you'd say."

"Do you mean you paid him?" Cordelia asked.

"He'll get plenty of glory for this, just wait. And he didn't get any money from me today, but that's not to say I don't pay him lots of the time."

More of the Coast Guard fleet swarmed the pier, and Charlie and Cordelia went on watching from a distance as one by one, little figures emerged from below the surface with their hands raised. The grand house behind them remained silent, but Cordelia knew, with a burning satisfaction, that Thom and his father were up there watching in the dark, furious at the interruption of their business. No deliveries would be made from the Hales' stores today, and those speakeasy proprietors and bon vivants who had remained loyal to them even after Charlie's campaign would suffer tonight. The Hales would probably be able to pass off the proximity of the illicit alcohol seizure to their house as coincidental—but their supply routes would be interrupted on one very significant night, and probably for days to come.

"Revenge is ours," Charlie said, lifting his coffee cup toward Cordelia.

"Long live the house of Grey," Cordelia replied.

Several of the papers ran late editions with banner headlines proclaiming the presence of a German submarine in

Long Island Sound. The accompanying articles contained little information, although one described the location of the raid as "within spitting distance of the estate of Long Island business-man Duluth Hale." Much greater space was given to the photographs, which included shots of grinning Coast Guardsmen holding up seized liquor, several weapons that were taken from within the vessel, and views inside the submarine itself.

These editions weren't on newsstands until mid-morning, and didn't reach the doorsteps of suburban subscribers until around noon, where even the finest residences, because of the proximity of the raid, were eager to hear the story. Everyone at Marsh Hall had been warned that Astrid was uninterested in news regarding Charlie Grey or anything at all having to do with bootlegging, and so the late edition was thrown away without her seeing it, and it was not until her erstwhile fiancé called on the main house line that she heard of the early-morning doings less than a mile from her home.

"Astrid." Charlie spoke hurriedly and without the faintest hint of apology. Her breath shortened upon hearing his voice for the first time in a week, just as familiar to her now, as though nothing had happened. "Have you seen the paper?"

The butler had brought the telephone into her old bed-room, where she was getting dressed for what she knew would be a very full sort of night, crammed with detours and antics and beautiful, strange characters. It was going to be the kind of night you go on talking about forever. Of course, a girl always remembers what she wears on such occasions, which is why her favorite dresses were laid out on her bed, so that she would have time to make the proper selection.

"No, Charlie, those papers are trash," she replied distractedly as she rummaged through her makeup tray for a tin of gunmetal gray eye shadow, "which I certainly am not, which you would know if you ever paid any attention."

Testing the eye shadow on her full upper lid, she waited for Charlie's reply, but instead heard the muffled sound of a hand covering a receiver while something else was said nearby.

"Is that all you wanted to know?" she snapped, when she realized she was being ignored.

"That and why you left your engagement ring at Dogwood."

"Did I leave it?" she answered coolly. "I suppose it didn't suit me quite so well anymore."

"I'll get you another, then."

"Charlie, I—"

"Only I don't have time for that right now. Right now I need you to stay at Marsh Hall. I'd rather you were at Dogwood, but if you're going to be difficult, just stay where you are. It's for your own good, you hear?"

"Ooooo!" she growled, the sound originating from someplace deep in her belly and rising shrilly when it reached her tongue. Without thinking, she threw the eye shadow tin at the vanity mirror. Her honeyed reflection wobbled with the impact, the sharp points of her cheekbones and the dark centers of her eyes turning temporarily blurry. "You beast!"

"What did you say?" Charlie shot back.

"I called you a *beast*! How dare you—how dare you—" But she could not think of a way to ask him how he dared try and leave her out of the biggest night of the summer on some flimsy safety pretext. "How dare you try to cage me!"

"Oh, come off it," Charlie went on, "this ain't some old novel."

Astrid would have liked to hurl his words back at him, but before she could think of a rebuttal, the line got muffled again. "Charlie Grey, you'll not ignore me!"

"Just stay there!" Charlie yelled, taking his hand off the receiver. The sudden loudness of the voice, and the realization that others were with him, wherever he was, infuriated her more.

"Fine," she said and she put the phone down hard.

The impact shook the vanity, and her reflection blurred again. When the blurriness passed, she saw how the tension in her face—the crease between her brows, the tightness of her usually pliant lips—made her look older, and she hated Charlie for it. The club was Cordelia's club, really, and Cordelia was still her best friend even if Astrid couldn't stand the sight of her brother, and anyway she didn't need any justification to show up at a place where everyone was planning to be that night. Several phone calls had come in that morning already, from girls she'd gone to school with, and boys she'd once kissed at dances, regarding The Vault and whether or not she could get them in. She stared at her reflection a while longer, willing her forehead to soften and eyes to get moist and mysterious.

Once her blood had cooled, and she had begun to feel more like that fresh girl she knew she was at heart, she ran a brush over her fluffy yellow hair, gathered her diaphanous dressing gown around her slim body, and left her bedroom behind.

"Where's Billie?" she asked the butler after she told him that she was done with the phone.

"In the library, miss," he said. Astrid whisked by him in that direction, where she found her stepsister below twenty feet of bookshelves, surrounded by potted ferns, on a puckered leather chaise with her face covered by a copy of *Madame Bovary* in the original French.

"Billie, you're coming to the opening tonight, aren't you?"

Billie removed the book and regarded her sister. "Don't you know me at all?" she replied in her flat, amused way.

"Good." Astrid smiled, hovering over layers of Persian carpet. "What do you say we get dressed early and make a whole day of it?"

The corners of Billie's mouth flexed. "As you wish."

Astrid smiled back, and twirled around. "I'll be ready in an hour . . ." she called out as she strode back toward her room. "Tonight we're going wild!"

18

LETTY HAD KNOWN PLENTY OF MELANCHOLY IN HER
seventeen years, but melancholy had no hold on her when she
woke up at Dogwood on Friday morning, even after she realized
that another night had passed without her oldest friend bothering
to inform her of her whereabouts. *Tonight is my first night onstage*,
she thought with a smile. On her way into the city her sense of
wonder mounted, and by the time she disembarked the wound of
Cordelia had shrunk to almost nothing. Instead her attention was
grabbed by the whimsical angle of the hats on the women who were
filling the train, clusters of shopping bags in tow, for the return trip
to Long Island, and the sound of a solo violinist on a nearby platform, and the faint smell of car exhaust mixed with hot dogs.

The glowing sign at the theater that bombastically announced the Paris Revue greeted her like the warm expression of an old friend. As she went in through the side entrance, a heavy young man with a kind, soft face held the door for her.

"You one of the new chorus girls?" he asked.

She nodded and turned to smile at him as they advanced up the stairs.

"I'm Sal." He offered her his hand.

"Are you in the show?" Letty asked.

It was dark in the stairwell, which had been painted black a long time ago and was papered with well-worn posters and notices, but light enough that she could tell he was giving her a twitching sort of smile.

"What do you play?"

"I'm the fat man, of course!" he said. Letty drew her brows together and wanted to tell him that he wasn't really so fat as all that, but then she saw the lunatic light in his eye, and knew he didn't mind.

"Do you make them laugh?"

"Oh, I'm a dangerous sort." He gave a ghostly flourish of his stubby fingers and bulged his eyes. "Grown men have choked to death laughing over the things I do!"

"I'll watch myself around you, then," she replied with a giggle. They had arrived on the second floor, where a hall led to the women's dressing room on one end and the men's on the other.

"No, no, you need not worry about me! I'm made of jelly beans." He grasped his rotund middle in a goofy way that made her want to laugh again and leaned forward conspiratorially, as if to tell her a secret. "The one you need to worry about is Lulu."

"Lulu?" Letty whispered back, biting her lower lip. "Who's Lulu?"

"You haven't heard of Lulu yet? Don't let *that* on. Lulu's the diva who sings the big numbers, and she despises it when people don't know who she is."

"Is she very mean?" Letty returned his smile and opened her eyes wide with exaggerated innocence.

"She tortures all the new girls, so be warned!" It was possible, she thought fleetingly, that he was drunk, for he had a way like Union's town drunk, in whom any ordinary event could cause fits of laughter. But Letty knew that she herself was not drunk, and in Sal's presence she was finding everything funny, so perhaps it was just his way.

"Is she terribly vain and proud?" Letty went on, matching Sal's near hysterical tone.

"Is who terribly vain and proud?" A tall woman with white-blond hair was leaning in the door frame at the end of the hall, wearing a Chinese-style robe. Beyond her, Letty could see girls rolling down panty hose and taking curlers out of their hair.

Letty giggled again, and answered her. "Lulu!"

"Oh, Lulu." She cleared her throat and arched one of her thin brows. "Well, I guess you don't know yet that I'm Lulu."

"Oh, no no no! We must have been talking about some other Lulu!" Letty said quickly and absurdly, waving her hands as though that might clear the air of her gaffe. Her cheeks were red and her stomach had dropped, but Sal didn't seem the least embarrassed—he was snickering into his big, meaty hands.

"Get out of here!" Lulu barked at him, although it seemed possible that she herself was smiling. "Stop trying to get the kid in trouble."

Sal gave a low, courtly bow, and reached for Letty's hand, which he kissed once very properly, and then thrice more with a voraciousness that suggested he might soon begin to eat her fingers. It tickled, and she had to swallow another laugh as Lulu reached out, sweeping Letty under her wing, and bringing her into the women's dressing room. "Lesson number one, my dear, never trust funny men. They don't even know what *they* mean half the time, and even if they did, they'd say anything for a laugh."

"I'm sorry about that—you don't seem vain at all." Letty willed away the blush, but her stomach was still aflutter from her misstep. She had been so happy to have someone talk to her, and Sal had seemed so doughy and amusing, and then he'd set her up. "You seem awfully nice, really!"

"Don't be absurd, honey. I am *terribly* vain—proud, too. But *mean* I am not. No, I like to keep all the new girls in my good graces. 'The diva who is cruel to her underlings merely cultivates her own successor.' An Ital named Nicky Machiashtelli said that."

"So you don't hate me?"

"Not yet, honey." Lulu winked at her. "What did you say your name was?"

"Letty Larkspur."

"You're over there," she said and pointed Letty in the direction of one of the cubbies that lined the wall. "Better go get ready, call time is now."

The space of the dressing room was filled with girls who were chewing gum or talking or smoking or singing to themselves or gazing into hand mirrors. None seemed particularly interested in the new girl, and yet Letty couldn't help but brim with delight to think, *I am one of them.* The chorus girls were easy to identify—they were the young, sylphlike ones. There were older girls, too, and girls that weren't so conventionally pretty, who she supposed played types and made jokes or sang beautifully. They were all in various stages of undress but seemed blissfully unaware of their partial nudity, and they made a racket with their passing back and forth of makeup items and hair tonics and sweet-smelling things.

"Thank you," Letty said, turning toward Lulu. But Lulu

had already drifted away to her corner, which had its own vanity mirror and cushioned seat. Shyly, Letty went forward, through the mass of bodies, to her own cubbyhole. Here, her breath was stolen, and she fell in love for the first time.

Under the name LETTY LARKSPUR, in a worn wooden cubby, in the soft light of many bare Edison bulbs, hung a white costume covered with downy feathers. The neckline was a subtle sweetheart shape, and the waist was marked with ivory grosgrain ribbon. A feathered cap hung next to it on the hook, along with a pair of white hose. Letty caught her breath finally, and ran her fingers down the costume, and closed her eyes. The mingled smells of stale smoke and tuberose perfume filled her nose, and for a moment she thought she might cry, because she had never been so happy.

At evening time all manner of cars were passing through Manhattan, some looking for trouble, some with trouble already in their backseats. Many others had by then committed to their first stop of the evening. Cosmopolitan New Yorkers had been called upon by their personal bootleggers and were pouring drinks in the carpeted sunken living rooms of their apartments, or otherwise they had been led to a corner table at their favorite restaurant. And in one particular theater, the orchestra was launching into the resounding opening strands of its final number.

The chorus girls lined up in the wings, and Letty, sixth of eight, held her breath and waited for her turn to enter stage right at a theatrical prance. Like the other girls, she kept her hands at her waist and her elbows high and lively and she put her feet forward in such a way that her hips swiveled back and forth. Her mouth was open, wide and red and happy, and she looked into the audience as she went out. The stage lights were bright, but she could still see all the people in suits and dresses, inclined forward, animated by the dazzle of the show. As the chorus girls swirled onstage, Lulu was lowered, singing, on a golden swing, her twenty-foot-long feather boa dangling across her bosom and down to the floor.

The song was about the show itself and thanking the audience for lending their hearts to the endeavor, and as Lulu came closer and closer to the stage, the girls began to dance around her, their bodies rising and falling in a wave, their voices backing hers up. The girls were supposed to each make their own individual gestures—by turns goofy and graceful—and though earlier Letty had feared she would forget the timing of her parts, and had rehearsed them obsessively in her head, she didn't need to think now. She moved naturally with the other girls, as though everything she did really was spontaneous. When Lulu reached the stage floor, she stepped off her swing and advanced toward the audience, her arms raised toward the corners of the theater with an invincible smile.

Then the music was over suddenly and the audience stood and began to clap. The applause, when Letty heard it, seemed almost like a tangible thing, a great lumbering friendly animal coming toward her. Her chest was pumping, and though they had been instructed to wear giant gleeful smiles at that moment, she could not possibly have done otherwise. In front of her stood Lulu in her gauzy gown taking several sweeping bows before slinking off the stage. When she was gone, the chorus girls popped up and, holding hands, went forward to take their bows. They bowed twice, turned at the same time, and skipped off the stage in a line. The applause was still strong as Letty left the heat of the stage lights and passed through the slightly cooler darkness on the stage's margins, and it went on ringing in her ears and buoying her up as she hurried after the other girls toward the dressing room.

"I can't believe we did it," Mary said, putting her arm around Letty's waist. "That was better than I ever could have imagined."

"Yes," Letty said, because there was no word to describe the amazement she felt. "Yes, yes, yes!"

As they came into the dressing room, Letty saw Lulu sitting at her vanity. The blond hair was gone—or rather, it was perched on a nearby mannequin's head—and she was removing a hairnet from her short, mousey brown locks.

"Larkpsur," she said when she saw Letty. "You were good."

"Really?" Letty said, unable to hide the happiness this brought her.

Lulu shrugged. "Someone thinks so—there are flowers for you in your cubby."

"Oh."

Mary lifted her eyebrows at her and gave a squeal of excitement. A second wave of girls—the more experienced dancers, the ones who did the really ornate routines—were coming in from their bows now, wearing gold tap pants and black tops, and they flowed around Letty. Everyone was talking—someone's costume had broken mid-performance, and another girl was shouting that she was in a hurry to get to her date. The word *date* made Letty think of Grady, and then her heart skipped when she realized that perhaps he had been out among the audience, that he had seen her onstage her first night, and that he was going to forgive her.

This prospect set her aglow as she advanced toward the vase of two dozen red roses. Her hands floated up to cover her mouth when she got close to them, for she'd never seen buds so dark or so big.

"Who are they from?" Mary urged, as she bent to pull down her tights.

Though Letty was tempted to tell her the entire story of the millionaire who lived in a garret down in the Village, she just gave her new friend an excited shrug and plucked the card.

Her body slumped when she saw instead Cordelia's familiar handwriting, and the words:

Dear Letty,
Congratulations. How I wish I could see you tonight.
I'm sorry I haven't been a very good friend lately. I
hope you'll forgive me and that you'll come by The
Vault tonight and have some fun.
Love, Cord

"Ah, me," she said and sighed.

Mary glanced over at her, but didn't say anything, for which Letty was grateful, because it gave her a minute to straighten her spine and let the disappointment roll away. Once she had accepted the fact that Grady probably hadn't sent a limousine to pick her up after her show, and almost certainly wasn't going to whisk her off for an intimate dinner at the Plaza, she began to melt somewhat toward Cordelia. The person to whom she had first whispered her visions for a grand life still remembered her, still cared about those long-ago hopes. And she'd sent a gift that was making the other girls shoot Letty winks and good-naturedly envious glances. Plus, the flowers *were* very striking. They were good enough for a star.

"Some of the boys in the band invited me to a coffee shop down the street," Mary said as she pulled a brush through her hair. "Want to come?"

"Oh, that sounds fun!" Letty bent to roll down her tights, and knew that she needed Cordelia to see her like this, shimmering with the confidence of her performance. "But tonight I have something I just have to do."

"Well . . . maybe tomorrow?"

Letty unzipped her costume and returned Mary's smile. "Yes, I'd like that."

19

"WHERE TO?" THE MARSHES' DRIVER SAID AS THEY
came off the bridge into the city.

In the backseat lounged Astrid, her fire-engine red dress
spilling down over her slim torso and across the baby-soft
white leather upholstery. The silky dress skimmed her limbs
in a way that was just suggestive enough, and since it so flattered her actual form, she had decided that she needed no jewelry or ornament of any kind. Beside her sat Billie, wearing
wide-legged navy trousers, her eyes lined in kohl and her hair
shiny and pushed straight back. Both girls' legs were crossed,
and tipped toward each other, and a silver flask of whiskey
lay between them. They had already taken nips, which had

heightened Astrid's anticipation for the evening ahead and made her feel all golden inside.

"The Jungle, Girl Leslie's, the Kentucky Room?" Billie suggested. "Or we could keep it classy for once and just go straight to the Ritz."

"I think I'm class enough without the Ritz."

Billie gave her a sly smile. "That's fair enough."

Astrid closed her eyes and tried to imagine the place where she'd most like to go. Velvet curtains and potted palms and convex mirrors and cleverly attired cigarette girls were fine, but at that particular moment she felt she wanted something more. She imagined a simple room with rustic wood walls and beautifully carved chairs where the men were handsome in a seafaring way, and they all competed to talk to her.

"Darling." She leaned forward and gripped the front seat and tried not to make it obvious that she couldn't remember the driver's name. "Do you think you could find a place on the West Side called Barry's Tavern? I think it's near the waterfront somewhere, I'd guess maybe in the Fifties . . ."

The driver assessed her from under the black visor of his hat. "I suppose," he said reluctantly.

She liked the idea of going someplace that her mother's driver didn't want to take her, and she patted his shoulder and said, "I knew you were a good sort."

They drove up and down the streets as night began to

fall. The driver had to stop and ask someone. But they found it eventually—an old shack built right on the wharf, illuminated by a neon light that proclaimed BARRY'S TAVERN, and seemed clearly to be younger than every other aspect of the place by twenty years or more. The river was beyond the tavern—though you could barely see it for the giant ships themselves huddled on the water.

"Is that the joint?" Billie took a doubtful pull from the flask.

Astrid rolled down the window to smell the sea. It was not as lovely as she had imagined, and she wrinkled her nose. The salty, breezy air mingled with tar and something faintly like dying animal. But the picture that Victor had put in her mind that night when they were playing cards was still strong. Plus, by then she had fixated on the notion that it would become one of her discoveries, and soon all the young night creatures would go there, and marvel in her cleverness at finding it.

"I don't know," the driver said, his gloved hands clasping the wheel nervously. He had not yet cut the engine.

"Oh, don't be dull!" Astrid laughed and took a sip of the whiskey and jogged her shoulders irreverently. "It'll be *such* a gas."

As she stepped out of the car the skirt of her dress unfolded and swirled down around her legs, and the loose bodice, which was gathered below the waist, kissed her skin. The night was warm and twinkling, and she was happy that she wore no man's ring. Billie came around and they linked arms and walked forward with rocking hips, mindful not to put their elevating shoes into the cracks of the wharf.

"Oh, dear," Billie whispered as they stepped into the room.

The walls were covered in unfinished plywood, and though the floor was made of the same, it was painted a far darker shade by the many dirty boots that had trod it over the years, and had acquired a texture from the coins and lemon rinds and other detritus that had been ground into it. A decidedly sour smell emanated from somewhere, which might either have been beer or the men who occupied the place, of whom there were fewer than ten, arranged around three large tables. Half of them grinned like wolves to see the posh girls in their midst, and the other half glared suspiciously.

"Hello, you chaps!" Astrid sing-songed, and then strode to the bar, which was only large enough to accommodate four stools. Neither liquor bottles nor barkeep were in sight. Billie followed Astrid at a less eager pace, and perched on the stool beside her stepsister.

Slowly, one of the men at the tables stood and came around behind the bar. "We only have whiskey and beer."

"We'll have whiskey, then," Astrid replied brightly.

"If this is one of the 'experiences' your Charlie treated you to," Billie said as she lit up a cigarette, "you've done fine to move on."

"Don't be mean, they'll hear!" Astrid winked at one of

the smiling ones and accidentally let the strap of her dress slip. "Anyway, I think even Charlie would be a little nervy coming in here, so give credit where credit is due, darling. I found this one myself."

Meanwhile, the barkeep returned from the back room with two mismatched teacups that held a brown liquid in it.

"Lovely," Astrid said, looking into his eyes and putting her whole torso into her thanks.

Billie just exhaled and brought the teacup to her mouth. "Gah!" she exclaimed. Astrid turned in time to see her spit the brown liquid back into the cup. "Don't drink that," she told Astrid. "That will make you blind."

"Oh, hush," Astrid replied quickly.

"Believe me, some hicks down in Jersey made that in a dirty old barn." She coughed and pushed the teacup back toward the man behind the bar. "I hope you don't charge money for that stuff."

Over at the table by the door, one of the men who had been smiling was now frowning. "Wha's wrong with my whiskey?" he said. Either some harm had been done to his tongue or his teeth had been knocked crooked, because he didn't talk right.

"Nothing, sir," Billie replied blandly, brandishing her cigarette. "Except it ain't whiskey."

After that no one said anything, although it was clear

enough that he and the other two at his table had thoughts in their heads they weren't voicing. Astrid flashed decadent little smiles around the room, and then the awkwardness ended, because two new men—somewhat better dressed than the rest, but with a tough quality to their faces and their postures nonetheless—came through the door and sat down at an empty table. The barkeep went over to them and conferred in low tones and then he went to the back room.

"Say, I been wondering." It was not the man who made the whiskey, but one of the other men at his table, whose work shirt was rolled back to reveal faded ink markings on the skin of his forearm. "You, the dark-haired one. The not-as-pretty one."

"Ye-es?" Billie answered with perfect indifference.

"I been wondering—are you a boy or a girl?"

A cloud of smoke came out of Billie's mouth and obscured her expression. If this comment wounded her, she did not let on. Without a trace of hurry, she stood up and squished the cigarette out on the wood of the bar. "I've had enough," she said to Astrid. "I'll be in the car."

Astrid only nodded. Everyone in the room watched Billie as she walked to the door, her gait swaggering but untroubled. When the door swung shut behind her, Astrid took a breath and sat up straight in her chair. "Well, that wasn't very nice!" she said, attempting gaiety. "You may prefer one girl to another," she went on with a friendly wag of her forefinger, "but you should never express your preference when both girls are present!"

Chairs shifted against the floor, and sips of beer were taken across the room, but Astrid's comment appeared beyond the scope of these fellows. "Well, you are prettier," the whiskey maker grumbled eventually.

Astrid's posture softened and she turned her face to the side girlishly. "Thank you, really, but . . ." She reached for her cup and took a nervous sip. Nothing so bad had ever touched the inside of her mouth. She tried to smile at the whiskey maker, but the sip was burning her tongue, and she knew that if she didn't spit it out soon, she'd regret it.

As casually as she could she stood up and moved toward the back room, where she assumed the ladies' lounge would be. She shot smiles in every direction, and when she crossed paths with the barkeep, he pointed in the direction of a door. Through the door she went, into a closet of a bathroom, where she bent toward the sink and spit the whiskey out. For a moment she thought she might be sick, and she held on to the sink with both hands. But then it passed and she looked into the small shaving mirror that had been nailed to the wall and smiled at her reflection. *This certainly was an adventure*, she thought to herself, and decided that while she was very impressed with herself for braving Barry's Tavern so long, the experiment was over and she was ready to go someplace with comfortable seats.

That was when the door opened behind her. She saw a man over her shoulder in the reflection, and she fixed her gaze on him. "If Charlie sent you to bring me home, you can tell him I don't need him anymore."

But she didn't get to see the reaction on his face, because that was when the burlap sack came down over her head.

Almost before The Vault opened its doors, it was predetermined to be a success. This had been decided by all the chattering about the young lady who was said to be in charge of the place, and then by the chattering about the handsomeness of the building itself. It was decided by the reputation of the Greys' liquor and the reputation of the Greys themselves, who might have fizzled away like so many criminal enterprises when their leader had gone, but had instead grown stronger, more brazen, and then had made themselves into hosts. It was decided by the newspapermen, who had taken a liking to Cordelia when she went out and found that she made good copy, and by the children of the night, whose limousines inched down Fifty-third Street, honking in their eagerness to be already at the center of everything.

Although Charlie had told Cordelia that the droves would flock to her if she opened a club, she could still not quite believe what she saw, even right there in the middle of it. The place pulsed, the whole room swaying to the exuberant band.

The mosaic tiles on the floor were impossible to see, because girls in their newest and chicest dresses and boys in suits were packed in next to every type of person: sportsmen and card players and tourists and writers and fortune tellers and politicians. Men who had never worked a day in their lives, shoulder to shoulder with those who had been working since they were tall enough to see over the counter at the candy store.

As she moved through the crowd, in a pomegranate dress with voluminous sleeves and a devastatingly low back, the guests reached out to grab her by the arm. There were kindly gentlemen who wanted to tell her a story about her father, and girls who hoped she'd lend them some of her light by pausing at their tables. Soon enough she discovered that there were people who wanted to know about private stores, and whether they could have the *really* special champagne, and also those who had lost their precious tickets, and wanted them replaced free of charge. These soon learned that her youth did not make her easy.

Cordelia had just departed the table of a sharply dressed man who claimed to have run liquor down from Canada with Darius in the early days of Prohibition when she was stopped by a throaty female voice saying, "Hey, doll."

Mona Alexander wore a plum velvet evening dress, the V-neck of which went nearly to her navel. She was sitting at the bar with men on either side, and when Cordelia saw her she went straight over.

"What a place you put together," Mona said, patting the waves of her black hair. Her eyes were droopy and heavily made up, and her cheeks were flush with her own celebrity. "Your daddy would be proud of you. I'd say you have a little of him in you, even."

Cordelia beamed. "Is the barman being good to you?" she asked, and Mona bobbed her head exuberantly and lifted her Ball jar of champagne in Cordelia's direction.

"I'll see she gets what she needs," said the man next to her, who was dressed in a deep green suit that almost shimmered in the low light. He gave Cordelia a nod and drew the singer back into his conversation.

Already that night Cordelia had overheard a few of her guests speaking in awestruck tones of "the legendary Mona Alexander," and so she was grateful for the lucky coincidence of meeting her only weeks ago. Of course, these days, luck seemed like nothing less than her due. But there was much to see to, and she was happy not to dwell on the events that had led up to this moment. Without fanfare, Cordelia moved on, along the bar that flanked the old teller windows.

A line had formed by the hat-check girl, and she paused there to see why. The girl was a wisp named Connie who had come in yesterday asking for a job, and now she was run off her feet, her bowl filled up with bills.

"Connie." The girl was wild-eyed, and Cordelia had to call out to get her attention.

"Is everything all right?" Connie asked as she hurried toward her boss.

"Put the bowl behind the window. You never know which one of these fellows is going to run off with everything."

"Yes, ma'am. Oh! And this came for you."

Connie bent and retrieved a paper box, the lid of which she pulled back with a smile. Inside was a corsage of white orchids set in crimson tissue paper.

"I hope you don't mind that I peeked," Connie explained shyly.

Despite the fact that Cordelia herself had visited a florist earlier that day and ordered flowers to be sent, she was taken aback now by how lovely it felt to receive a gift of that kind. No one had ever sent her flowers before. She glanced over her shoulder, as though expecting to see the sender. When she looked back, Connie had already fastened the corsage to Cordelia's wrist.

Because she didn't want to show how much this gift affected her, Cordelia gave a curt nod, turned around, and began walking out into the crowd, moving between the tables, checking to make sure that glasses weren't piling up and that drinks were full. Her eyes flickered over the sea of faces, wondering which one of them had wanted to pay her special attention. She was just coming to the conclusion that it must be a random admirer when she saw Charlie talking to the guards at the door. A number of men were stationed in that vicinity, vetting any would-be revelers, and watching out for any retribution on the Hales' part, too. The big fellow with the hat pulled down over his face nodded, and then Charlie stepped away from him and began to walk toward the back of the club. *Of course*, she thought, *Charlie sent it to congratulate me.*

She turned around and began to walk in his direction, but he was moving faster, almost pushing people aside. His big slab features were frozen in concentration, and his eyes were dark and fixed straight ahead. She had to almost run to catch up to him and was nearly at his side when he careened into a petite girl decked out in yellow sequins.

"Ooooooo!" she wailed, when she realized that her cocktail had been knocked out of her hand.

"Hey, you!" the man next to her yelled after Charlie, standing up fast so that his chair fell away behind him. Cordelia saw the attention of the surrounding tables follow Charlie, and she hurried to apologize to the sequined girl and her fellow.

"Here," she said, pulling a few red tickets from her sleeve and handing them to the girl. "Enjoy yourselves, please."

Whether or not the girl appreciated this gesture, Cordelia had no idea. There was a stone in her belly. Something had gone terribly wrong. She had seen it in Charlie's face, and now she was pushing through the crowd to find out what. The band was playing loud and everyone was shouting, but as soon as she went through the big copper doors that led to offices and dressing areas, she heard Charlie's voice over the rest of the din.

"How the hell did this happen?" he yelled. He went on yelling as she lingered, frightened, in the doorway.

20

THE NIGHT AIR WAS FULL OF MIST WHEN LETTY ARRIVED
on Fifty-third Street, and she felt momentarily shy about going
to Cordelia's club when she saw the activity outside the old
bank. Girls dressed exquisitely, in jewelry and satins fit for a
ball, huddled waiting to get in, and across the street men with
big cameras mounted with flashbulbs leaned against the sides
of their cars, as though hunting some elusive prey. She wished
that she had heeded Cordelia and worn the red dress that the
Greys had bought for her the day that the three of them went
into the city for matching bathing costumes. But there was
nothing to be done about the dusty pink sleeveless dress she'd
put on that morning before taking the train. It was another of

Astrid's old things, and had to be belted because it was slightly large for her, as was the fawn-colored cardigan she wore to cover her shoulders.

With small, timid steps, she went forward to the entrance. She could hear the noise from within, and yet the doors themselves were closed and gave no indication that they would be welcoming. Letty swallowed, raised her fist, and knocked on the metal door. The noise this made was louder than she had anticipated, and she stepped back, embarrassed at having called attention to herself.

A curly-haired girl wearing a tiara glanced at Letty over her shoulder, scowling. "They're full up right now," she said through her nose.

"Oh." Letty turned back around to face the door and hoped that Cordelia would be the one to open it, so that this girl would feel a fool when Letty was whisked in. "Thank you."

A few seconds of agony followed, during which it seemed she would be standing outside forever. But then the door did swing out, and though Cordelia was not the one to do it, the girl standing there was almost as welcome a sight.

"Paulette!"

The taller girl's hair had a new marcel and her dark red lips opened wide when she saw Letty. She bent to kiss both of Letty's cheeks, and then drew her inside, toward the noise. The door slammed behind them, and Letty smiled in satisfaction to think that the girl in the tiara was still out there in the sticky night, and had been taken down a peg or two.

Inside was a riot of color and laughter. Across the vast floor, people were crammed into tables, leaning over the backs of their chairs to flirt and gossip, turning their faces up toward the stage, buying cigarettes from girls dressed all in gold as though they were the bank's currency itself. The big man with the hat who'd been at the door the day before was there, along with a few other men of his type, and they seemed to be scanning the crowd for trouble. On the right side of the building, the band was set up on the stage, which had been built out in front of the old teller windows with some of the same mahogany wood. On the left, Letty could see what Cordelia had been describing the day before. A girl checked hats in the first teller window, and in the next one another girl sold tickets. After that the bar began. Men wearing bow ties took orders from the customers who lined up there, then turned to the teller windows behind them, where some invisible person would produce the requested beverage.

"That's so if there's a raid, the liquor won't be out in the open," Paulette whispered, as she drew her onto the floor. "There's an old system back there for dropping deposits down to the basement, and we figure if federals ever come in, we can drop the hooch down to the basement and cover it up quick."

Letty nodded and bent her neck back to look at the ceiling

with its tarnished, celestial murals. She couldn't believe how packed and frenetic and gigantic the place was—perhaps not so much more wild than Seventh Heaven used to be, but far more incredible, because it was the work of a girl she'd known forever.

"Thanks for telling me about this place. Your friend Cordelia is a real solid broad—soon as I told her I knew you, she said I could have a job overseeing the cigarette girls."

"I guess she is," Letty replied with a shrug. The mention of Cordelia reminded her that she hadn't really come to marvel at the scenery or drink cocktails, but to show her old friend that she wasn't sore about not being the nightclub's singer. "Where is Cordelia, anyway?"

Paulette pushed up on the balls of her feet and looked out across the room. "I just saw her—hold on, I'll find her. I'm sure she'll want to show you everything herself."

With that, Paulette forged forward into the crowd. Unsure whether she was supposed to follow, Letty hung back, smiling shyly at the doormen and occasionally trying to catch the view between the shoulders of the various men, all taller than she, who loitered at the edges of the room. It was through this partial view that she recognized a young man and woman who had just come in. Grady wore a tuxedo, just as he had the night he'd wanted to take her to dinner with his parents, and his sweet and attentive eyes focused on the girl around whose waist his arm draped. The girl wore a marigold-colored Grecian-style gown with one shoulder, and her strawberry-blond hair was cropped short, and tucked behind the ears, the simplicity of which only highlighted the aristocratic features of her face. On her wrist, she wore a cuff of diamonds that looked like fire in the low light.

Letty's feet were heavy and her chest felt like one big days-old bruise that keeps getting kicked. She wished for two things in that moment: that she had gone home to get some rest, and that Grady had any girl but Peachy at his side. For the sight of her long legs had always made Letty seem short, as her rich dress made Letty feel poor, and the length of her neck and the way she carried her head perched on top of it could reduce Letty to nothing. The bruised sensation spread outward from her heart to the pit of her stomach and up to her temples, and she began to take in the full scope of her loss.

Because seeing Grady escort Peachy—the lovely girl that his parents had always wanted him to marry, according to Astrid—across the floor, did not make Letty yearn for lim- ousine rides or dinner at the Colony or diamond bracelets. It was the way his hand rested like a feather at the small of her back. Even at a distance, she could practically feel that touch, gentle and without lasciviousness, but with a decided pressure that said over and over again *I am at your side.* She stared at his hand, which was so close and yet would never reach out to reassure her again, and thought how recently it was that he had seemed willing to do anything for her. That was the third thing she wished for—that she'd been born smarter, so that she could've held on to Grady when she had him.

Letty knew she ought to look away from the couple by the door, but she couldn't help but go on watching as Peachy whispered something, and Grady inclined his head to better hear her over the raucous sounds of young people at play. He nodded and his eyes went across the room and landed on Letty.

Instinctively, she brought her arms up over her chest and stepped away. He stared at her, his face only slightly changed by the recognition, and she retreated further, faster this time, as though she could walk straight backward out of his line of sight. Before she began to worry about the fact that there wasn't really anywhere to go, her foot caught on something, and she fell, landing hard in the lap of a man she'd earlier noticed brushing noses with the girl beside him. The table hit her elbow, which smarted, though not as badly as her pride.

"What in hell . . . ?"

"Terribly sorry!" Letty gasped as she leapt up. Keeping her head down, and refusing to look back in the direction of Grady, she began to make her way through the tables, deeper into the club. The tables were tight together, and everyone was crowded around them, so this involved a great deal of stepping over legs and leaning against tables laden with cocktails in Ball jars, but she was determined to move as fast as she could and not to get stuck. As she passed the band, the guitar player looked down on her and grinned, and then she knew what a spectacle of herself she was making. But she didn't care. All she wanted was to emerge at the other side of the club, safe out of Grady and Peachy's view, and find Cordelia. For Cordelia, despite her indifference as of late, was the only person in the world who knew how low down Letty could get, and also how to build her back up.

When she managed to get past the last table and emerge on the far side of The Vault, she saw the two great copper doors that she'd gone through to see Cordelia the day before. Now she was finally granted a wish, because the man standing in front of them was Anthony, one of the guards she knew from Dogwood, and he opened a door for her without a question, ushering her into the inner sanctum.

The sound of the telephone receiver being put down into its cradle was as loud and shocking as a gunshot. Charlie stood with his broad back to Cordelia, saying nothing. Her scalp was cold and her throat was hot, and she watched him with unblinking eyes and waited for him to speak.

"They have her."

"Who?"

"Astrid. The Hales." He glanced at her wrist, at the tiny white flowers that adorned it. "What are those?" he asked reproachfully.

"You didn't send them?" She looked down at the corsage as though she'd never seen it before.

"Those are from Landry's. Expensive. I've ordered flowers from there plenty times. But those ones aren't from me."

"Oh." Cordelia's face burned as she examined the corsage in a new light. Slowly it began to dawn on her that the only man she knew who was capable of sending rare and expensive flowers was Thom. The hatred that had been simmering in her for weeks, and which she had acted on that morning, shifted slightly. His face when she conjured it in her thoughts was still repugnant to her; but then another picture of him eclipsed it, the way he had been at the place with the mattresses on the floor, how jittery he had seemed that night, and how strangely sincere. With the swift certitude of a premonition, she knew that he had been trying to warn her of what was to come tonight.

Cordelia stepped toward Charlie and put a hand on his back. "How did it happen?"

He shook his shoulder, knocking her hand off, and leaned forward, putting his fists against the big desk and resting his full weight on his arms. "They got her in some West Side dive. God knows what she was doing there." He spit out the words, and for a moment, Cordelia couldn't tell if he was angry at Astrid or at the Hales.

"What do they want?" Cordelia's mind raced. She was afraid for Astrid, but she felt certain that if they acted quickly, no harm would come to her. In all the many newspaper columns she had read about Darius Grey and his kind, she'd never seen a mention of a special lady friend or a child harmed, and it seemed likely that if they kept their heads they could have her back soon.

"Damn that girl!" he yelled again.

"Charlie," Cordelia said in a firm voice. She put her hand against his shoulder again, and though she could tell that he bristled at the touch, he did not this time immediately shake her off. "What do they want?"

"They want us to say we're sorry," he sneered.

"That's all?" Cordelia replied in the same even tone. She could hear the caustic quality in his voice, but refused to be scared off by it.

"They want us to say we're sorry with dollars, lots of dollars. They want us to back off their territories in Manhattan. They want all the business we took from 'em. They want us to lay low for a while, and crawl around on our hands and knees, and act like monkeys."

"All right." Cordelia took a deep breath. "All right, we'll tell them we'll do that, then."

"Damn her!" Charlie yelled, his voice raw with fury. "Why'd she have to go and get herself in trouble? Why'd I have to fall in love with such a little fool?"

"Charlie, you're going to have to calm down. Now, where's

Jones? Let's get Jones on the line. He'll know how to talk to them, and he'll have everything arranged, and once she's back and safe with us, then we can decide what to do from there."

Charlie didn't reply, he only bristled, and she knew that if he'd had hair on his back, it would have stood on end.

"Charlie, where's Jones?" she repeated, stepping forward and picking up the phone.

But he snatched the phone roughly from her hand and put it back in the receiver. The desk shook again, as did the silver tray where a half-drunk bottle of champagne sat beside four champagne glasses. Earlier, a long time ago it seemed, before any customers had come, they had toasted to their family.

"We're not doing it Jones's way tonight." Charlie stared at the tray with enlarged, bloodshot eyes before picking it up and hurling the whole thing against the wall. Glass shattered to the floor and a spray of champagne alighted on Cordelia's face. Cordelia had seen Charlie like this only once before, the day their father died, when he had followed her up to the third floor of Dogwood with a stare that seemed to intend her harm. He was like that now, except even less in control of himself, and it sent a shudder down her spine. "I'm in charge, and I don't want to play Jones's little chess games tonight."

Just then there was a light knock on the door, and both Grey siblings turned slowly. When Cordelia saw Letty, her face as pale as the moon, she raised her finger to her lips so that she would know not to say anything that might inflame Charlie. A moment of still quiet followed, and Cordelia's heart rate began to slow, and she thought maybe now that Charlie had broken something he would calm down enough that she could talk some sense into him. But the phone rang, cutting into the silence, and he ripped the receiver from its cradle.

"Who is it?" he snarled.

Cordelia waited, her eyes wide and dark, to see what Charlie would say. But she knew pretty quickly from the way his face distorted in anger that it wasn't going to be pretty. "I won't negotiate with you," he screamed. "I won't negotiate with you!" He repeated himself three times, his voice louder and faster with each iteration, and then he ripped the phone from the wall and threw that across the desk, too.

When he turned to leave, Letty shifted out of the doorway. She seemed to know she might otherwise be trampled. Cordelia reached for her hand and grasped it as she moved after Charlie through the door, squeezing once before she let go and began to chase her brother.

On the main floor the noise had reached a riotous pitch. Everyone reached out to grab her attention. She batted them away and tried to keep up with Charlie. Halfway down the bar, Roger, her press agent, was the first to succeed in blocking her path.

"Where's Mona?" he demanded, unsmiling. "She was supposed to be on an hour ago and everyone is asking about it.

All the writers want to be able to say the legendary Mona took the stage at midnight, and she's nowhere to be found!"

"Then find her," Cordelia answered, in a quiet but forceful tone, and pushed past him after Charlie.

When she stepped onto the sidewalk, she saw that the streets had become damp and were reflecting the orange light of the streetlamps. The photographers waiting by their cars stood, and the flashes began going off, so she held up her hand to hide her face and went to Charlie. He was standing at the center of a cluster of his Dogwood gang, men who had been on hand that night in case there was trouble.

"This is payback for what happened this morning," she said, coming to stand beside him.

"Yes." Charlie shook his head angrily, but he seemed not as crazed as he had before.

"Where are you going?" she asked.

"Go back inside."

"No, Charlie, I'm coming with you. Astrid is my best friend and she's in danger and I'm coming with you."

"No." Charlie had her by both shoulders and he was steering her back toward the door of The Vault. "No, you're not."

"But it's my fault. I should never have told you about the submarine. I should never have . . ." She felt helpless and angry with herself, and she wanted badly to do something that would make Astrid safe. "And Thom—I saw Thom, and he told me, he told me to be careful, but I thought that was just idle talk. I should have told you. I should have told *someone*."

"It's not your fault." Charlie had pushed her against the door, his brown eyes wide beneath a tensed brow. "Just go inside for now and take care of our business."

The memory of what violence could do to a body was fresh with her, how it could tear up and make fragile a person who had walked around for years with a swaggering air of impenetrability. She nodded until Charlie let her go, but she did not immediately do as he'd instructed. She stood there in the murky street, watching bystanders and photographers and debutantes who were ignorant of the hardships of life and wanted nothing so much as they wanted to get inside her club. She was struck by how summery everything seemed—the bare shoulders of girls, the bright colors of their gowns, the flowers they wore in their hair—because inside of her it had turned cold and wintry.

Poor Astrid, who seemed never to consider the fact that the world might do her harm, and was so careless about everything, except when it came to friendships, where she had always proved herself fiercely loyal. Cordelia was furious with herself for being so selfish and thinking that Thom's comment was directed at her alone. So she lingered awhile longer outside, made immobile by the thought that tomorrow morning she'd wake up with the blood of two loved ones on her hands.

21

IN THE MAHOGANY HALLWAY IN THE BACK OFFICES OF
The Vault, a petite chorus girl stood shivering in a dress that
hardly fit her. She could not go back out into the club, where
birthdays and first kisses and youth itself were being loudly
toasted, and where a millionaire who lived on pennies was
escorting a girl from his own tribe to their table. But she had no
reason to stay where she was, and her current location held no
appeal, for it was the place where Cordelia had abandoned her
yet again. Nothing could have been so predictable.

Just as Letty was about to slide down the wall and crumple
into a ball, a diminutively sized man with a loud bark came in
from the main floor and demanded to know where Cordelia was.

"Don't know," was all Letty could get out.

His nose twitched like a rabbit's. "Who are you?"

"Letty Larkspur."

"That's a good name, kid, but I don't know who you are yet, so get out of my way."

He straightened his suit jacket and brushed past her and knocked on the door. "Mona?" he called out. "Mona, honey baby?"

For some reason—Was she suspicious of this stranger in Cordelia's empty office? Was she curious? Did she simply have no place else to go?—Letty followed the man as he pushed through the door and into another wood-paneled room, where a leather fainting couch had been installed, as well as a vanity table and mirror. She smelled the acrid bile before she fully comprehended the scene within, and it was not until the rabbit-faced man knelt to the ground and repeated the name *Mona* that she realized what was happening.

The pretty woman she'd witnessed strutting through the club yesterday was lying half on and half off the fainting couch, her hair bedraggled and her dress askew. She had been sick all over herself, and all over the floor.

"Mona," the man said again, lightly slapping her face.

She groaned and managed to get one of her eyes partially open. "Roger?" she gasped.

"Mona, I told you not to drink tonight!" he shouted, and then let her limp body fall back where it lay.

"Oh, God," she said, and Letty had to turn away, because she realized that the woman was going to be sick again.

In the hall she saw Paulette, rushing toward her from the main room. "Oh, Letty, there you are! The band is asking for Miss Alexander, have you seen her?"

Letty made a face and inclined her head toward the sorry scene in the makeshift greenroom.

"Christ," said Paulette, once she'd seen for herself. "Mr. Tinsley, what are we going to do?"

"Get me some coffee . . ." he said, standing. "No, get me an ice bucket . . ." But this must have seemed likewise inadequate, because he covered his face with his hands and began laughing hysterically.

"Are you all right?" Letty whispered to him.

"All right? Of course I'm not all right, my reputation is about to be ruined! I'm in hell," he snapped. Then he rested his hand against his hip and stopped laughing. "Letty Larkspur—you make that up yourself?"

Letty shrugged.

"Then you must be—what? A singer, a dancer, a chorus girl extraordinaire?"

"I just had my first night at the Paris Revue."

The man let out a sigh of despair and turned away.

Letty gulped and stepped into the room so that the press agent couldn't look away from her. She had listened to enough radio to know that all a girl needed was one little twist of fate. Suddenly it didn't matter to her that it was Cordelia's club, or that Mona Alexander had just drunk herself out of the spotlight that Letty herself had once coveted. It didn't matter if Grady was still out there and only had eyes for Peachy Whitburn. There was an audience, and she was the girl to entertain them. That was all.

"Let me do it." She fixed her big blues eyes on Roger so that he couldn't look away. "I'm your girl."

"Mr. Tinsley, she really does have a beautiful voice," Paulette said.

His eyes went from Paulette back to Letty, and his nose twitched. "Take that terrible dress off," he said, pulling a slinky black column from the place where it hung by the wall.

"Oh, I . . ." Letty mumbled.

But Roger only rolled his eyes. "Believe me, honey, I'm not interested."

So she pulled the pink dress over her head and let Paulette and the press agent dress her in the black. They powdered her face and put lipstick on her mouth, and then Roger came back from the dressing table with a gold headdress that covered her hair like a cap and dangled along her ears and neck, as though she had on a bobbed wig of glittering metallic threads.

"So what's your angle, kiddo?" Roger asked.

"I told you, I'm a chorus girl at the Paris Revue."

"There have been a thousand of those." He bent to press

fake eyelashes onto her upper lids. "Can't you give me something better?"

"Cordelia and I were best friends in Ohio. Union, Ohio. That's where I was born."

"Forget it." He let out an exasperated sigh as he applied white powder to her nose with a soft poof. "I'll just make something up to tell the boys from the press."

"You look gorgeous," Paulette said. Letty batted back her big, new lashes and glanced at herself in the mirror. Earlier in the evening she had played the tiny backing role, but now she looked almost as much the diva as Lulu.

"Don't get weepy," Roger quipped. "You haven't done anything to write the boys back in Ohio about yet."

Flanked by Paulette and Roger, she went through a door and into a hall that ran along behind a row of teller windows. On this side of the room, the windows had been covered from the inside with parchment paper, but she could still see forms moving out in the room and hear the general din. At the end of the hall there were a few steps that led to the stage, where she could see the profiles of the musicians as they came to the end of a song. She took a deep breath and didn't consider looking back. Her destiny was right there, and she was ready to grab it with both hands.

At first, Astrid thought it was the scratchy fibers of the rope around her feet that would do her in, but now she knew it was the slow drip-drip-dripping of some leak high above her. The chair she was sitting on was pretty bad, too, as was the sack over her head. Wherever she was, it had an unpleasant fishy odor. But the incessant dripping was the real torture.

"Hello?" she yelled. She hadn't heard anybody for what felt like a long time, although she knew that the men who had taken her from the tavern were still close by. She'd only seen the face of one of them in the bathroom mirror. Then he'd grabbed her, one hand over her mouth and the other gripping her around the front, so that he could drag her backward and another man could lift her by the feet. She had kicked furiously, but they were stronger than she was, and after a minute the second man had managed to tie her ankles together with rope. She had struggled against them, but then they put her in the backseat of a car and the motor started up.

At first the men had talked a lot in low, threatening tones. That had been to get her to stop screaming, she guessed. After that they talked less, though when they went over the bridge, one of them began making some bland remarks about base-ball. She didn't know how long they had driven, only that there were more men wherever they had taken her, and that more rope was used to tie her to a chair. By then she knew that it wasn't Charlie's men who had nabbed her, because Charlie's men would have been warned not to be so rough. After that she became terrified they would gag her, the way she'd seen a girl gagged in a movie once, and so she kept quiet. But now she hadn't heard anyone's voice in a long time, and she was afraid that the drips from the ceiling might make her lose her mind.

"Hello?"

The next thing she heard were footsteps that echoed across the room, and splashing as someone walked quickly toward her. She shrank as he got closer, and then she felt the sack ripped off her head.

"What is it?" sneered the man, whose onion-and-pickles mouth was close to her ear.

Astrid's eyes blinked and she saw that she was in a big dark warehouse, only partially lit with bare bulbs. Its walls were lined with large crates and there were puddles across the floor, which were possibly the source of the putrid smell. Her dress had been dragged through the dirty water; it was badly stained around the hem.

"Well, what?" the man repeated, drawing back and showing her his teeth. He had a face like the butcher's least choice cut of beef.

"I wonder if you might do something about that damned dripping?" she demanded, trying to seem as imperious as possible.

The man put his big greasy hand on her cheek and then drew it back over her hair, which was already damp with fearful sweat. He smiled in a way that conveyed the opposite of an ordinary smile. "This ain't the Ritz, dolly."

"Hey, go gentle on her!" a voice from the opposite end of the warehouse called.

Both she and her antagonist bent their bodies to see who it might be. To her surprise, she recognized the second man, who was standing in the doorway from another adjoining room.

"Thom Hale, get me out of here!" Astrid yelled, but she saw immediately that this tack would do her no good, for Thom stiffened at the implication that they'd known each other socially. He was wearing a pewter suit and a starched white shirt, and she wondered if he had begun his evening thinking he'd get a glimpse of Cordelia's new endeavor.

"Aw, Tommy boy wants us to be nice to his swank friends," the man with breath like onions and pickles said.

"Don't be a moron," Thom returned. This time his voice was hard, and he refused to meet Astrid's eyes. "We don't need to hurt her, we just need them to think we might."

"But what does it matter anymore if Charlie says he's not negotiating?" the man yelled back.

"What?" Astrid gasped.

"I told Duluth this was the wrong idea. You don't bring girls into revenge." Thom sighed in a way that briefly filled Astrid with hope, but then he went on in a defeated tone: "Do what you want. I'm leaving."

The man put his big hand over her mouth and leaned in close to her ear again. "Guess you're going to shut up now, huh?"

For several terrifying seconds the skin of his hand continued to press against her face, but when he walked away, she found that her fear of being left alone, and what came after that, was worse. "Wait!" she cried. "Call my stepfather, Harrison Marsh. He'll pay your ransom."

"We don't want your money," the man said. The door had slammed behind him, but the word *money* was still echoing off the walls as Astrid closed her eyes and began to choke quietly on her own tears. Earlier that day she had thought herself very brave for going to an old shack on the waterfront, but now she knew that she was not brave. She had disregarded Charlie, and now he was going to let her die, and the only thing she could do was shed salty tears all over her ruined evening gown.

When Cordelia did finally gather herself enough to return to the club, she was surprised to find that the general clamor of the place had died down. The music was not so jittery, either. It had become sweet and lilting, and it was now accompanied by a female voice that she knew well. She couldn't see the singer onstage, but she knew immediately that it wasn't Mona Alexander. People who had already retrieved hats and coats were lingering by the door, as though entranced by a lullaby, and she had to go around them, making her way along the bar to get a look.

In a black dress, with her face framed by a gold headdress, Letty was a vision of a much more experienced performer. Her eyes danced across the audience and she raised her arms, slow and sure, as her voice swelled. Cordelia thought of her when they first became friends, when they were still girls and Letty blushed when anyone said even the most casual thing to her. It was incredible that this was the same girl. If Cordelia had told any of the men along the bar watching Letty, rapt, that she was just seventeen and had only arrived from Ohio in May, she knew they would have fallen off their stools in surprise.

For a brief moment Cordelia saw a panorama of everything she had come to New York to find. There was good company, a whole menagerie of types, all joined together under one roof by a determination that a day should not end with a balanced meal and an early bedtime, that life should be very glorious and gay and full. Outside was a world of fear and violence and disappointment, and no one knew what bad news awaited them when they left this spot—least of all her. But for the time they remained here, they got to witness a petite girl emerging, as if from a chrysalis, to become everything she'd ever dreamed for herself.

When the song ended, Letty bowed her head. The applause was deafening. Cordelia watched as she turned to the band and whispered something, and smiled to think that Letty's practicing had not been for nothing. The next song was a fast number, and Cordelia had reached the other side of the room, but she had to duck into the back area behind the bar, where even the dishwashers had ceased their labor to listen, because by then tears were streaming from the corners of her eyes.

22

ASTRID HAD NOT IN RECENT YEARS BEEN IN THE HABIT of praying. But she did begin to pray in the dark warehouse. Not audibly, because she could still hear the voices of her kidnappers in the next room, like the hissing of a radiator in winter, and she did not want to call attention to herself. She could not decipher their words, but they seemed to be disagreeing, and that could not be a good thing for her. By then she'd gotten used to the smell, although every time a drop of water hit the concrete floor, the sound had become increasingly more terrible. Her pretty red dress was stained with sweat, and her hair had come undone. It was limp and damp and hung in her face. All these discomforts had at first seemed like indignities thrust upon her by a pack of rogues, but they were coming to seem like only the smallest hints of the vast and as yet unknown peril she was in.

So she prayed. She prayed that if she sat still her heart would stop making such a frightful racket. She prayed that Billie had seen the car pulling away from the tavern, and had followed, and was even now waiting outside with a fleet of policemen. She tried to tell herself magical stories, in which a humble farmer comes along, smells something amiss, and breaks into the warehouse, defeating one man after another before reaching the captured princess. Of course he would be handsome, and of course they would fall in love and be married, their story proclaimed with banner headlines: HEIRESS WEDS HUMBLE HERO IN FRONT OF HUNDREDS OF HER CLOSE PERSONAL FRIENDS.

After that she tried making deals with God. She had been vain and stupid and she could see that now. Going to that tavern had been a mistake, and she had been frivolous and silly to think that it would have made an interesting story, or that she was bold or original for going there. And she had defied Charlie because she was angry with him for not paying better attention to her, and she had been trying to teach him a lesson. It was all very childish, and she could see that now, and she promised God that if he would just send someone to save her, anyone, she would be always dignified, the way Cordelia was, and not pout ever.

When this produced no results, she turned against Charlie in her mind. Because he had been lousy and she had been lovely, and she had shown him that she wasn't going to suffer lousiness in the only way she knew how. He had cared too much for the bootlegging business, and too little about her, and now she had been caught up in his war. She, who'd never hurt anyone, and only wanted life to be always exquisitely airy and delicious, and who loved nightcaps and her friends and long summer days. The man with the hacked-up face had said it clear enough: Charlie wasn't negotiating. They didn't want money, they wanted something else, and whatever it was, it was more important to him than she was.

That was when she began to see that she was truly lost. Her mother was a selfish woman who wouldn't notice her absence until it was too late, and Charlie had given up on her. By now she could sense the collecting of moisture on the roof, and she had a wretched premonition of the next drip. Her breathing became short and her pulse quick. The tips of her fingers tingled, and numbness spread over her hands. Though she was still breathing quickly, it was all of a sudden impossible for her to get any air into her lungs. Above her the drop had formed—it hung for a moment, suspended in air, laughing at her predicament, and then it fell to the ground, slowly as though it didn't have a care in the world. The impact when it hit, however, was so great that Astrid felt it over her whole body. The sound ricocheted against the walls and she screamed and screamed until her throat ached.

A metal door banged against the wall and the footsteps came toward her quick.

"What?" the man with the hatchet face snarled. "What?"

The way he'd smelled before seemed benign to her now—pickles and onions were the result of the everyday task of eating, and she longed for that. Now his mouth smelled like nothing so reassuringly common, just vaguely of something that had been rotting for years. His mouth was close to her face, and he put his big hand on her throat, and though she had closed her eyes and begun to tremble, she could feel that he was looking her up and down.

"If you don't shut up, I'll make you shut up." His breath was hot on her ear. "Your boyfriend's dropped the line, and I was getting awfully tired of you, anyway."

"No, I'm not—I didn't mean—please—I won't—" she stuttered. For some reason it seemed right then that if she explained about the drip that might help. "It's only the dripping. The dripping is crazy-making. If you could just stop the dripping . . ."

"Shut up," he repeated, in a tone that made her never want to speak again.

She'd been listening for a long time, and she knew that it was too soon for enough moisture to have collected on the ceiling for another drop. But another noise came then, hor-rifically loud, and the man's hand tightened on her throat. It wasn't until she heard more gunfire that she knew it had been a single gunshot, and not water from the roof. The man kept holding on to her throat—tighter than was comfortable, but not so much that she couldn't breathe—and listened. She knew he was scared, too, from the way his eyes went glassy. There was shouting and a staccato firing of bullets in the next room, and she could hear car motors starting up. Then she heard another voice, and for the first time in hours she began to hope.

"Get your hands off her," the voice said. She could tell he meant it.

Both she and her assailant looked, and at first she didn't recognize the man holding the gun. He was wearing a well-tailored deep red suit and his hair, which had once been care-fully arranged, was now pushed back at strange angles. He was big, and his brow tensed in a ragged line, and he was breathing heavily through his mouth. It was Charlie—she knew that in her mind. He had Charlie's features and Charlie's voice. But he looked like a stranger.

"Get your hands off her," he said again.

The man moved, putting her body between himself and Charlie, and gripped her throat with both hands. "Put your gun down or I'll kill her right now."

"Get your hands off her!" Charlie screamed, and she heard him coming toward them.

"Stay back!"

More footsteps. "Get your hands off!"

"I'll kill her!"

Then everything happened at once. A gun went off; a spray of hot blood hit her face; the man groaned and his hands tensed around her neck; she writhed in his grip, not very successfully, until all of a sudden he let go and fell back hard into a puddle. There was a splash, and Astrid closed her eyes. Behind her, Charlie began to hack at the rope that bound her hands to the chair with a sharp object. When he was done with that he went to work on the rope at her feet. It came off quickly and he put away his knife, but though she was free she could not make herself move.

Charlie bent and scooped her up and began walking quickly toward the door. He was still breathing through his mouth in the same heavy way, and she was so frightened of everything that might have happened, and ashamed of having brought herself to this place, that she couldn't look at him. Instead she put her face under the protective cover of his jacket and began to sob. The tears wet his fine shirt, but he only pressed her tighter to him, as though encouraging her to go on until the shirt was entirely soaked through.

She did not dare to peek from under his suit jacket until

he had carried her outside. The place where she had spent the worst hours of her life was nothing more than a row of warehouses, with boats up on scaffolds, and though she couldn't see the sound, she knew from the smell that it was close by. They were moving away from a building where two men lay lifeless—one slumped against the wall by the door, the other face down in the gravel. Victor was waiting by Charlie's car wearing a grave expression. He nodded at Charlie and then got in the car and started up the engine. A second car started up its engine, too.

As they came around to the passenger side, she saw that Danny was in the backseat, his mouth open and eyes closed, as though he were asleep. She had always liked Danny and she was relieved that he was there, until she saw the blood on the other side of his face and realized that he wasn't breathing. She curled back in against Charlie's chest, as he slid into the front passenger seat and closed the door behind them, and tried not to think about what had happened to Danny.

"Don't you ever do that to me again," he said, once the car had begun to move and they were traveling fast over country roads. His voice was stern, and she knew how scared he'd been.

"I won't, Charlie," she sobbed.

"From now on you are not leaving my side."

"I won't." She bunched his lapel in her hand, and held on to it tight. "I'll stay at Dogwood and do as I'm told, I promise! Only don't ever leave me."

"I promise, I promise I'll never leave you." Charlie was smoothing her damp hair back from her forehead, and he strengthened his grip on her, and kissed her forehead. "I want to be with you always, and I want to tell the priest as much as soon as possible. Tomorrow. Tomorrow we're getting married, and we're never going to be apart."

The road was uneven beneath them, and Victor was driving as fast as he could. "All right," she heard herself say. "All right, Charlie, whatever you say, only please, don't ever leave me alone."

23

IT IS A FACT OF BIG CITIES THAT ONE GIRL'S DARKEST hour is always another's moment of shining triumph, and New York is the biggest and cruelest city of them all. So it should not be surprising that beloved socialite Astrid Donal's lowest depth of misery should coincide with the sparkling ascendance of her new friend Letty Larkspur.

Had Letty been nervous when she first stepped onstage? That seemed like a long time ago, and though she smiled at the memory, she could no longer remember the way she had felt then. In the space of an hour she had been transformed. There were certainly no remnants of nervousness when she finished the last of the songs she had practiced a lifetime ago and took a low, sweeping bow. The audience stood and their applause drowned all the other noises out. When she stood up again, she turned and pointed to the band members who had so nimbly backed her up, one by one, so that the audience could clap for them, too. Then she blew a kiss to the room, pulled back the skirt of her gown, and stepped down off the stage.

A path opened up for her and she went through it toward the bar, smiling with somewhat disingenuous bashfulness at the gentlemen who were clapping for her. "Bravo," some of them called, and a few reached out for her. To those she extended her hand so that they could kiss it. She had no real destination, but this didn't seem to matter anymore once she saw Paulette, who took her by the arm and led her to the most private corner of the bar, where a seat had been cleared for her. In fact, it seemed quite natural at that moment that she should take a step into the world, and that the world would rise to take care of her. By then the audience had begun to talk again, and the general hubbub returned her to a kind of anonymity.

She sighed happily and perched on the stool.

"And to think," said Paulette, with a disbelieving shake of her head, leaning into the bar on a long arm, "you were just some girl I felt sorry for one night at Seventh Heaven."

Letty smiled back in the same awestruck way. "Some girl just off the train from Ohio, you mean."

"Right, just off the train from Ohio." Here Paulette bent

close to her and lowered her voice to a whisper. "Although I wouldn't repeat that too loud. I think Mr. Tinsley may have told everyone you grew up in an orphanage in the Bronx, because your parents were somehow killed in a deal of Grey's gone wrong, but when he found out he adopted you, or something like that. You'll read it in the paper tomorrow, I guess."

"All right." Letty laughed at the absurdity of this, and took the golden headdress off, and smoothed her helmet of dark hair over her forehead. "Where is Cordelia, anyway? Did she see the show?"

"Yes, she saw the show." Paulette paused to straighten Letty's bangs for her. "But everyone was ordering champagne when you were singing because they wanted to celebrate their new discovery and we ran out of bubbly, so she had to go into the basement with the head barman to show him which to open next."

"Oh." That seemed like a fine thing, for her voice to be an inducement to ordering a drink as fancy as champagne, and she smiled again, even if she did feel almost lonely, sitting in the corner of the room when a minute ago everyone had been looking at her.

"In fact, I should probably go see what else we're out of. Looks like a lot of people are about to ask for a lot of every-thing."

"Oh . . . are you sure?" Letty whispered.

"Don't worry, this gentleman will take care of you. He asked that you be sat next to him once your set was over."

Paulette moved away from the bar and across the room with a hawklike watchfulness, and Letty saw that all the while there had been a man on the other side of her that she knew well. She smiled, relieved that she had not been left alone, and said, "Hello!" in a loud and happy voice. Then she began to blush, because she realized that despite his familiar face, she had never actually met him before.

"Hello, yourself," he said, his slender lips parting beneath a pencil-thin mustache. "My name is Valentine O'Dell."

"I know—what I mean to say is—" Her hands had risen involuntarily to her cheeks. "It's awfully nice to meet you."

He was wearing a white dinner jacket and a white bow tie, and his hair, which appeared so raven-colored in the pictures, was in fact a warm chestnut brown, combed from one side to the other. His eyes flickered from her face to her dress for a moment, after which he extended his hand for her to shake. "And your name is?"

"Letty Larkspur."

"Letty Larkspur," he repeated, holding on to her hand another minute. "Letty Larkspur, I'd like to be the first to tell you that you are a star."

All she could manage in response to this was a faint squeal. Her gaze went across the room, and though some people did glance back at her, none of them seemed to think it was incredible that she was sitting with Valentine O'Dell, who had played the lead role in at least twenty motion pictures. They seemed only to want a better view. When her attention returned to him, he was still staring at her, almost into her, with such warm steadiness that she felt certain no one had ever really understood her until this moment. Then he sat back onto his stool and let go of her hand so that he could signal the bartender.

"You must let me buy you a drink." He was smiling at her in the same way that he smiled at Sophia Ray onscreen, from the corner of his mouth and with a certain light in his eyes. In fact, Letty felt as though she herself had drifted onto a big screen—she felt projected large and not quite real. Sitting there, at a nightclub, next to a movie star seemed like the kind of scene that was reserved for the pictures. She knew that in such situations you were supposed to pinch yourself to make sure that you weren't dreaming, but she was too afraid that Mr. O'Dell would notice, and if it was a dream, she wasn't ready for it to end yet. "You were incredible, you know that, don't you?"

"Was I?" she replied breathily, even though she certainly had suspected, because of the enthusiasm of everyone else in the room.

"Exquisite." The barman approached, and Valentine turned toward her solicitously. "What will you have, *ma chérie*?"

"Champagne, I guess." She didn't really feel like drinking

anything—she was drunk enough on the way her evening kept mounting one miraculous turn upon another, but she liked the way it felt to say *champagne*.

"We'll have a bottle of Pol Roger, the 1911 vintage," he said to the barman. Then he returned his attention to Letty, and his eyes had that same blazing intensity.

"I wasn't supposed to perform, you know," Letty said, because it did seem incredible to her that if she had not wanted to show Cordelia that she was all right, and Mona Alexander hadn't drunk herself into a stupor, and if Paulette had not insisted that Letty could sing, then she would not now be sitting here with Valentine O'Dell.

"Indeed—I was told Mona would be the chanteuse tonight. That lady is a sad case—I can imagine what transpired there, how it happened to be that you had to take her place. But you know it is like that with all of us." He issued a quick wink, and she knew that when he said *us*, he was including her. "A door opens by chance, somewhere in our vicinity, and we walk through it, and we begin to dazzle for everyone to see."

Letty, blushing, was relieved to see the barman approaching with two glasses and a bottle of champagne. While the barman popped the cork and poured them each a glass and stored the rest of the bottle in a large silver bucket, Letty kept her eyes averted, and it was not until Valentine picked up one of the glasses that she dared turn her eyes to him again.

"Here's to the future of Letty Larkspur," he said. She raised her glass toward his and took a sip of the sweet, fizzy liquid.

The sip made her feel dizzy and bold, and when she had set her glass down, she fixed Valentine in her gaze and murmured: "It's so strange to sit here, just talking to you . . ."

"You mean, because you've known me as my screen self, and it's odd to see I'm made of flesh and bones instead of celluloid?"

Letty didn't know what celluloid was, but she nodded anyway. "I guess that's it."

He laughed and took another sip. "You feel like you know me, and yet you don't?"

"Yes, exactly like that." She was vaguely aware of women off to the side staring at her jealously, but she didn't care anymore. They were staring because she and Valentine made a very glamorous picture, and though she couldn't blame them, she was starting to believe that her rightful place was in the picture.

"But I feel the same way about you," Valentine went on, leaning his elbow on the bar. "As though I know you somehow, even as I'm meeting you for the first time. I felt that when you were on the stage, you know, this—*familiarity*."

The way Valentine looked at her, his very presence seemed a confirmation that she was the most gorgeous girl in the room, as though her skin were made of gold dust and flower petals and her eyes were pure sapphire. It seemed as though he was about to tell her that their meeting here tonight had been written in constellations, that it didn't matter that he was married to Sophia Ray, that they were two separated halves of one creature, divided long ago and seeking each other ever since.

"Like destiny, you mean?" Letty whispered.

But Valentine only laughed, not unkindly, and shook his head. "No, of course not, nobody believes in destiny anymore."

"Oh," she faintly whispered. For a moment she had been willing to believe in any outrageous fortune—a million dollars had been left to her, the Raja wanted her to come ride elephants with him, a movie star was her one, true love.

"Except when they go to the pictures, of course, or when they forget themselves in a dark theater," he went on, apparently not noticing her fallen face. "That's because of stars, performers with the talent to make them feel that life is beautiful and magnificent and built upon a cosmic scheme. I hope you won't find me immodest for saying that I have a little of that— it's my only skill, really, and it's allowed me to make a handsome fortune in the show-business racket. You have it, too. *That* is what I saw up there."

If Letty was disappointed to realize that Valentine O'Dell didn't think they were destined for each other, her disappointment didn't last long. That would have been too good to be true, anyway. He recognized in her a talent comparable to his own, and that was worth much more in the long run.

"I want to propose something to you," he said, refilling his glass from the silver bucket. "And you must not think that I am lascivious. I am married, as you may know, to the actress Sophia Ray, so you can trust that my motives are purely those of a gentleman and a comrade. I would like to mentor you. I think you have something that one in a thousand, one in a million girls have, and I think with some training, I could turn you into a screen star."

"You mean you want to put me in the movies."

He smiled, in the way she had seen him smile at children in his films. "Yes. You do need some training, but natural talent you have in spades. What I propose is this: Come live with Sophia and me on Park Avenue. We'll get you dance lessons and acting lessons and we'll round off your edges, and then we'll see what Mr. Warner thinks about you."

"You mean Mr. Warner of Warner Brothers?" Letty gasped.

Across the room the same people who had watched her sing onstage were teasing and flirting and pushing back and forth as though this were just any old night. The low, orangey light in the place flattered their features and softened their scowls, and Letty was gratified to see that it was a glorious night. Beyond them, by the door, she caught a glimpse of red, and realized that Cordelia was standing there. Her head was bent listening to the big man with the hat over his face. Afterward, she quickly said something in return. Though Letty watched her for several seconds, Cordelia never looked her way, and then she disappeared amongst the crowd.

"So, Miss Larkspur, what do you say?"

Letty's small mouth spread wide, so that Valentine could see all her pearly teeth. If she hadn't woken up yet, then it must not be a dream, and her own life really had become just like a Valentine O'Dell picture. She felt so flush with promise that she wondered if her small frame could possibly contain the joyful spirit within.

"Yes, absolutely," she said. "I can't wait."

24

IT HAD BEEN SUCH A LONG NIGHT THAT BY THE TIME Cordelia returned to Dogwood she was almost wide awake again. For hours her heart had been gripped by fear for one best friend; but then the sight of her other best friend as she stunned a jaded Manhattan crowd with her singing opened it up again. Over those hours, she had sold hundreds of bottles of champagne at a criminal markup and paced so much that her feet had swollen and she'd had to remove her shoes for the long ride home. By then the news had reached her that Astrid was all right, but the worry and guilt Cordelia had experienced during the kidnapping did not immediately dissipate. A sense of calm, or something like it, returned to her only when she entered the Calla Lily Suite and saw Letty sleeping soundly in the big bed there, her hair like a blackbird laid against a white pillow.

On tiptoes Cordelia had gone into the dressing room and washed her face and taken off her makeup. Not wanting to wake her friend, she lay down on the plush white couch by the window. Her mind was so busy that she feared she wouldn't be able to sleep for a long time. But she must have fallen asleep quickly, because that was all she remembered before waking up, curled on the same couch. The windows were open and clean sunshine was streaming in, and Letty was not where she had been when Cordelia's eyes had drifted shut.

Cordelia was still wearing the red dress from the night before, and an orchid corsage was crumpled and wilted on her wrist.

"Oh," she moaned, and put her forehead in her hands for a moment. Then she took off the corsage and decided that it didn't really matter who had sent it, or what it was supposed to mean. A tray of breakfast things had been left for her, and when she saw that, she found the will to cross the floor and pour herself a cup of coffee. Newspapers had been brought up with the pastries and juice, and she took the society page with her into the dressing room and read it idly as she repinned her hair.

MANHATTAN'S NEWEST STARS was the headline, and the article went on breathily:

Last night, at the spot everyone has been talk-
ing of for weeks, the city's beautiful things came
out decked in getups that ranged from elegant to
whimsical and back again, to laugh and meet one
another, to see and be seen, and in the end were
treated to the great spectacle of a star being born.
Miss Letty Larkspur, an orphan from the mean
streets of the Bronx, rose to the stage, a nightingale
of jazz, under the roof of an old bank, at the center
of a room cheekily made up in homage to the all-
mighty dollar . . .

Cordelia closed the paper and regarded herself in the mirror. She looked another year older than she had yesterday at this time, but it had been a success, and she ought to be happy. Perhaps she was just tired. She took another sip of black coffee and then went downstairs.

"Cord!" She heard Charlie call out before she had even made it to the second-floor landing. He came out of the billiard room and toward her, wearing a dove gray suit and an ivory collared shirt, with a wild light in his eyes and purple creases under his eyelids. The man she'd seen last night throwing glass against the wall and pushing aside customers was gone. Now he wore the happy expression of a boy who has just received his first bicycle for Christmas, which was especially winning in a man of his size. He came striding toward her with his arms wide open. "Cord, we did it. We did it."

"You think Dad would have been proud?" she asked as he folded her into an embrace.

"Sure bet, Cord, that's a sure bet."

"We made a lot of money last night, didn't we?"

"Yes, we made a lot of money." Charlie stepped back and held Cordelia's shoulders with his hands so that he could assess her. It was remarkable to her how his face, which last night had seemed so tough, could in the light of day appear so broad and full of childlike wonder. He held her gaze with his brown eyes, and said, "Would you do something for me?"

"Anything."

"I know it's going to sound funny, but I know you've been hanging around with that Billie Marsh, so maybe it won't be strange after all. Would you be my best man—or, I don't know, my best lady?"

Cordelia took a breath. "Then everything is all right between you and Astrid?"

"Everything is all right. I made a nice contribution to the little church on Main Street this morning, and we're going to be married there this afternoon."

"This afternoon?" Though this seemed precipitous, she couldn't help but beam back at Charlie the way he was beaming at her, reflecting his delight.

He nodded.

"Of course I'll be your best man. And you don't have to change the title for me, I don't even know if I deserve to be called a lady anymore."

Charlie put a kiss on her forehead, punctuating it with a big smacking sound. "Good. Now will you take care of these?" He handed her a small black velvet ring box. "I'm so nervous I keep thinking I've lost them. I was going to wake you up, I was so worried I'd do something dumb. But now I'm glad I didn't. At least now one of us will've got some sleep."

"Okay, Charlie."

"Go downstairs, would you? I think they're waiting for you in the ballroom. I told her I'd send into the city for a dress, but she had her own ideas. Just go make sure it's all fine, would you?"

"All right." Cordelia stood on her toes and kissed Charlie on the cheek. "But go take a cold shower or something, you're making me nervy, too!"

On the threshold of the ballroom she paused. Inside she could hear the excited, wispy breathing of girls at work. None of them were talking. She peeked around the door and saw Astrid standing on a wooden crate, her yellow hair brushed and shining around her heart-shaped face, her wishbone cheeks glowing as healthily as ever, her eyes closed as Milly stood in front of her, making careful stitches. Kneeling at her feet was Letty, who was carefully making adjustments at the hem. The bodice was sleeveless and made of some gold fabric, with an Egyptian pattern that ran along its U-neckline and up its thick straps. The skirt appeared to have been made out of a filmy white sheet, which had been wrapped around her from the back so that the two sides crossed over her front like two drapes, falling away so that when she walked a hint of knee would be revealed.

"Cordelia," Astrid said.

Cordelia, surprised because she hadn't realized that her friend's eyes had opened again, came forward from the doorway with a smile on her face. "Good morning," she said.

Letty looked up from the floor and smiled, and Milly gave a brief, harried nod of acknowledgment.

"Does your mother know?"

"Oh, yes," Astrid replied with obvious satisfaction. "I told her myself this morning and even now she's scrambling for a getup worthy of the occasion. Of course, after my ordeal last night, she can't say no to me. Dear Billie spent all night trying to locate her, to tell her that I'd been nabbed, but she couldn't be found until after it was over and naturally she feels wretched. Or is pretending to, at any rate."

"You look so happy."

"I am so *very* happy. What a long night it was last night. Anyway, Charlie and I, we realized that life is short, it passes in the blink of an eye really, and you never know what's going to happen, so we thought we had better stop playing games and start calling each other man and wife, just as we were always meant to."

"Congratulations." Cordelia gave her friend a soft smile. "Can I help?"

"Yes, you could make a bouquet for me and Letty. I hope it won't make you sore, but I asked Letty to be my maid of honor, because Charlie was so adamant that you ought to be his best man. I know that sounds horrific really, but he's so headstrong about everything this morning, and I really couldn't convince him otherwise."

"No, I don't mind, I think it's perfect." Cordelia went over to the white piano, where she began dividing the calla lilies and tying them with twine.

"Do you like my dress? I thought of it myself," Astrid went on, as though it calmed her to talk about something. "The bodice is from this old dress I found in Darius's closet—must have been one of his old girls'—and I had Milly cut the skirt off, which was a horrible purple thing, and now this is just some sheet I found, but isn't it going to be divine?"

"It's perfection."

"Yes, I thought so. The only hitch is I haven't got a veil . . . and a sheet won't do for *that*, I'd be tripping all over myself."

Letty's blue eyes rolled up in Astrid's direction and her hands ceased their activity. "I know what you could use—there must be some mosquito netting around, don't you think? It'll look just like a veil."

Then she turned her gaze on Cordelia, as though the full reason that this idea existed in her mind had not occurred to her until now. For a moment, both girls were thinking of a dusty day back in Union when Cordelia had worn mosquito netting, and of the hopeful face of the boy she'd left behind.

"I'm sure there's some in the attic." The pain of this memory was so great that Cordelia had to look away. "I think I saw some there once. We'll have one of the boys go look."

I'm sorry, Letty mouthed, although there was nothing for her to apologize for. Whatever unpleasant feelings were stirred by the mention of mosquito netting were Cordelia's fault alone.

Me too, Cordelia mouthed back. She wasn't sure which of her many sins, small and large, she was apologizing for, but it felt good to say it, and Letty seemed to understand. They smiled at each other in a way that they hadn't in a long time, and then both went back to work. After that, Cordelia didn't think about the terrible thing she'd done to John Field in order to come to New York, and instead got caught up in what needed doing for the union they would be celebrating in a few hours.

A dinner would have to be ordered, just something simple in the spirit of the day, cold cuts and meatball sandwiches and potato salad from the delicatessen on Shore Lane. They would set up a table on the lawn where Darius used to have his parties, and those guests who could make the ceremony would be invited over afterward to mingle on the lawn. At least one reporter would have to be notified—the Marshes might prefer everything hush-hush, but Astrid certainly did not. Cordelia knew that the first sentence would read, *Bootlegger's son, Charlie Grey, who on Saturday night made his first foray into the nightclub business, was wed Sunday afternoon to White Cove socialite Astrid Donal.* She had a business to see to now and had to think of such things.

By the time the redbrick church on Main began to chime in anticipation of the ceremony's beginning, a reporter and a photographer were on hand, and they exuberantly documented the arrival of the bride, by limousine, at half past three. She stepped from the backseat of the Daimler and paused, giving them a radiant smile as though she had been expecting them.

Once Astrid knew that they had their shot, she continued up the curved path to the church, where Cordelia and Letty were waiting for her on the steps, Cordelia in a simple long-sleeved black boatneck dress that must have been punishing in the sunshine; Letty in a lavender chiffon with little fluttering sleeves and mother-of-pearl buttons down the front, in which she looked slightly less like a waif than usual.

"Are you ready?" Cordelia asked, fixing the mosquito netting that fell away from Astrid's head before turning and going to stand beside Charlie. When she reached the front of the church, the organ music started up, and Astrid knew it was really happening. First Letty began to walk that slow, purposeful march, and then finally it was Astrid's turn. She stepped into the modest little church and walked at her own buoyant pace up the aisle, not bothering to turn and look at any of her family or friends, who even at such short notice had packed the pews. Her eyes were fixed on Charlie, and his on her, and when she reached the altar, she handed her bouquet off to Letty without hesitation and reached out to grip Charlie's hands.

His eyes glittered, and hers glittered back, and then the priest began to speak. She barely heard a word he said, so engrossed was she in Charlie's face, his big grin, the sweet way his eyes were spaced far apart under that defiant brow. Once or twice she did let her gaze drift over the guests. There was Willa Herring, under a broad, flower-bedecked hat, trying to look happy instead of jealous that Astrid had upstaged her wedding by going small and sudden, instead of big and with much fanfare. There was Billie, her chin lifted in a dignified way, wearing red lipstick and a black brimmed hat rather reminiscent of those worn by horsewomen in Seville. She shook her head slightly, and Astrid knew that she really had given poor Billie a bad scare. Beside her was Virginia Donal de Gruyter Marsh, who was flashing smiles to anyone who might possibly glance her way and wearing a very brave face. Astrid knew, however, that she was steaming inside to see her only daughter wed not at all in the way she would have chosen, and with very little pomp. But this was among the day's minor joys.

Mostly there was just Charlie, looking down on her with a smile that neither flood nor famine would have been capable of wiping away. There was the priest's voice, droning and calming, finally arriving at those magical words: "I now pronounce you man and wife."

Astrid, still grinning, stepped forward and threw her arms around Charlie's neck, and he put his lips to hers and bent her back theatrically as the organ began to play again.

Later, she was unable to recall much of what happened after Charlie kissed her, only fleeting images: the whole church standing up, her smart-set friends mixed in with Charlie's boys, their faces more pockmarked and their suits flashier; her mother clinging to her elbow and saying, shrilly, how happy she was over and over; the photographer's camera going off again when she came outside; the thumping of cans, which someone had tied to the back of Charlie's roadster, as they drove back along Main Street toward Dogwood with the breeze in their faces. The only thing that felt real to her anymore was Charlie, and Charlie's strong arms, which had carried her out of that dank and cruel warehouse, where she had known she would die, and safely home to Dogwood.

Other cars trailed them, and though she saw that a reception had been arranged on the lawn, neither she nor Charlie really considered paying attention to anyone but each other. At the threshold, he scooped her up in his arms and stepped into the house that was her house now, too. As he climbed the stairs, she could feel his heart through his thin ivory shirt and knew that hers had quickened, too. She reached up, taking his head in both her hands so that he would keep bringing his lips, which felt so pleasantly warm and soft, to hers all the way up to the third floor.

At the top of the stairs she felt a wave of trepidation pass through her, and she wondered if Charlie would feel it, too, and guess that she was scared. But she had already promised to be his forever, and the grin he was wearing seemed to indicate that he hadn't noticed anything amiss. He carried her into his bedroom and lay her down on the big brass bed. One by one his buttons came off, and she heard each one as though it were a rhythm beaten out on a drum. Then she felt his weight on top of her, the smell of his skin and the oil he used in his hair filling her nostrils, and there was nothing left to do but wrap her arms around his neck.

"Are you mine?" he asked.

"Yes," she whispered.

"Are you ready?"

She smiled and put her fingers through the hair at the base of his neck. "Yes," she said, pronouncing it as though it were the most beautiful word in the world.

25

OUTSIDE TRINITY CHURCH, THE SUN WAS BRIGHT AND the air was full of dust. The bride's more traditional friends called after her and threw handfuls of rice, and her newer friends stood slightly apart and waved. White Cove had been a kind of nirvana in Cordelia's mind, a place she had been trying to reach for a long time, but she could not help but notice with a wry smile that this wasn't so different from a wedding in Union, where the ceremony also was usually performed in the church on Main Street, and the groom, if departing in a hurry, was liable to kick up the dust of a country road.

"She looked happy," Letty said.

"Charlie, too," Cordelia replied.

Both of the calla lily bouquets were still in Letty's arms, and as the crowd began to disperse, she glanced down and took note of this. "Astrid never threw her bouquet!" she exclaimed.

"I guess you're the next to get married, then."

"Not me." Letty shook her head with a firmness that surprised her old friend. Perhaps she sensed Cordelia's confusion, because she added: "I have things I have to do first."

"I know you do." Cordelia waved at Willa Herring and her husband, who had spent quite a lot of money at The Vault last night, as they glided to their waiting car. "Did you read the papers this morning?"

"Yes, can you believe it? That news might even reach home," Letty marveled in her wide-eyed way. "They really actually think I'm good."

"They think you're much better than good." Cordelia pinned back a few loose strands of hair and watched another group of wedding guests depart for Dogwood. "I do, too."

"Oh, but you always thought that." Letty gave a small wave of her hand.

"Yes." Billie descended the stairs of the church on her father's arm, and she sent a subtle wink Cordelia's way before climbing into the Marshes' chauffeured Duesenberg. "Letty, you remember how I said I was sorry earlier?"

Letty turned her blue eyes up at Cordelia, and had to squint because of the sun.

"Well, I'm sorry that I told you you couldn't sing at the club, but it's not just that. I'm sorry I didn't know that you would be the best singer for the place all along—I'm sorry that I hadn't planned it that way from the beginning." She took a breath and her dimples emerged as she smiled. "From now on, I'd like to bill you as our main act."

The last guests pulled away, and there was only Cordelia's car waiting to take her back to Dogwood. Letty shielded the sun with her hand and for a number of seconds wouldn't meet Cordelia's eyes.

"What do you say?" Cordelia tried to make her voice sound enthusiastic, but she could tell that even in the cloudless sunshine of a summer afternoon, Letty was turning a hard thing over in her mind.

"A few days ago, that was all I wanted . . ." she began slowly. "It was my very best dream." Letty pressed her lips together and tapped the toe of her heeled Mary-Janes. "But what those people said in the paper is true. I have something, I've always known that. Now is my chance to use it. I got a job all by myself, and now Valentine O'Dell wants to turn me into a star." When she said his name, her cheeks turned pink, and she tried to hide the fact that she was smiling over it by turning her face away. "He wants to give me the training that will make me the most polished version of myself. He's going to teach me the things I *really* need to know."

Shrugging, Letty finally let her eyes drift back up and meet Cordelia's. Her blue irises had a coldness in them, and Cordelia realized that she was not the only one who'd grown up with the events of the previous night. A different girl would have gloated about her good fortune, but Letty seemed almost sorry to be standing there telling Cordelia that she didn't need her job after all, thank you very much.

"Mr. O'Dell sounds nice," was all Cordelia could manage to reply. She wished that she could say more, but she had become so accustomed to Letty needing her, and it was such a shock to see Letty become so suddenly independent that she couldn't quite think straight.

"Yes, he is. He and Sophia Ray are taking me out for supper tonight, after the show." A big sigh passed through Letty's small frame, and then she shook off whatever sadness had arisen within. She handed the bouquets to Cordelia, removed the straw cloche from the place where she had been keeping it tucked under her arm, and fixed it over her hair. "And speaking of the show, I had better hurry, or I'm going to miss my train."

"Well, get in, I'll give you a ride," Cordelia said, gesturing at the car. The driver, seeing her point at him, started up the engine.

"It's such a pretty day . . . I think I'd rather walk." Letty pressed up on her toes and kissed Cordelia on the cheek. "I'll see you," she said, squeezing Cordelia's hand. When she let go, she turned immediately and began walking toward the station.

"Hey, good luck tonight!" Cordelia called when Letty was a short way down the road.

"You, too!" Letty called back, raising her arm but not turning around.

With her hand on the hot metal of the door handle, Cordelia went on watching until Letty's silhouette became very small and turned the corner. Though she knew she ought to be happy for Letty, and happy for Astrid, she couldn't help but feel a little lonely now that her two best friends had gone off into their glittering futures and she was left without a boy to even imagine herself falling in love with.

That was when she saw the plain black car loitering across the street, and the muscles of her face constricted. She let go of the handle and walked swiftly toward the mysterious car before her driver would notice she was gone. In a matter of seconds she had rounded the passenger side and slid into the front seat.

"You can't be looking for me," she said.

Max stared at her for a long time, but she couldn't be sure what he was thinking. Was he admiring the way her dress fit her, or was he mentally rehearsing some final insult? In the end, he never did answer her question directly. "Did you get the corsage?" he asked.

"That was from you?"

"Did you like it?" he pressed, in that same even tone, with his eyes focused on her. With a flutter of surprise, she realized that he was nervous. That he wanted to be sure he had given her the right thing. In his plain white T-shirt and brown utilitarian pants, it was easy to see that sending the right flowers was not something he'd ever thought much about.

"Yes, it was beautiful." She smiled at the memory of how it felt to be given orchids. Across the street, her driver had noticed that his charge was gone and had stepped out of the car. Without thinking, Cordelia lay down on Max's lap. "If you want to talk more," she said, looking up at him, "you had better drive."

So he steered the car nonchalantly down the road. Once they'd turned and he told her it was all clear, she sat up. He gave no indication that he planned to stop driving now. She waited for him to say something, to explain his hurtful denial, or at least his coming there today. But he offered nothing and met her eyes only briefly.

In the silence, all the confused emotions that Max had inspired in her over the course of their short friendship rose up again, and she was trying to decide how to tell him to take her home when he finally spoke.

"Do you have time for dinner?" he asked.

"No, I couldn't, I—"

"I don't mean dinner like your set does it, five courses and a show. Just something simple and wholesome. Come now, you've got to eat."

She regarded him. "What do you want from me?" she said eventually.

"I want you to have dinner with me," he replied, in a practical tone, ignoring the yearning in her voice. "At the same place I have dinner every Sunday night."

She would have said no, except that she didn't want to go back to Dogwood, where the celebrating would be going on for hours, and Astrid and Charlie would have eyes only for each other, and Letty's absence would be quite acutely felt.

"All right, but you have to drop me at the club when I'm done."

"It's a deal."

"And let me call Charlie's man Jones quickly. Otherwise my driver will be in trouble for letting me get kidnapped, too."

By then it seemed clear that he wasn't going to explain why he'd told the newspaper people he didn't know her, nor was he going to be very elaborate or romantic about what he wanted from her now. So she let them sit in silence and didn't try to think up bits of conversation that would only have sounded silly in that context. It was a familiar drive, and she enjoyed seeing the other motorists out on Sunday, and the boats cluttering the East River, and the well-dressed women walking poodles on Fifth Avenue. Children holding balloons came in and out of Central Park, under the shade of dense, green foliage. Soon they had passed the park, and she realized that the streets were no longer numbered in the nineties, but in the hundreds.

"I didn't know the streets went up this high," she said,

twisting to scan the tops of the buildings in the new part of town they had drifted into. The limestone mansions were behind them; here the apartment buildings and townhouses were made of brick.

Max laughed.

"What's so funny?"

"I didn't mean to offend you," he said. "It's only that you do seem to know everything, and it surprises me when I find a chink in your armor."

"Oh." Cordelia paused, unsure whether this was an insult or a compliment.

"Welcome to Harlem," he said.

"Harlem?" She knew what Harlem meant—that was where nightclub aficionados went to hear race music—and when she raised her eyes again, she realized what was different about the neighborhood. The streets here were just as populated, and the people were doing all the same things that people on the other part of Fifth Avenue were doing, but here their faces were black.

She was so surprised that he would take her here that she didn't think to ask another question until he had parked the car and come around to open the door for her. "You've been here before," she said, as he led her toward a redbrick townhouse and nodded hello to the children playing on the stoop. They smiled up at him, not as though he were the great Max Darby, but as at someone kind and familiar.

"I told you, I have dinner here every Sunday night."

They went in the front door and down a dimly lit hallway. As her eyes adjusted, she saw that the walls were covered with felted wallpaper, and that a number one had been painted on the door to the parlor-level sitting room. Max beckoned to her, and they began walking up the carpeted stairway with the polished mahogany banister. On the second floor, he knocked on the door where the number two had been painted, then turned the knob and went in.

"Hello!" he called as he walked into the living area of a small apartment. Cordelia, following behind him, saw that a simple chandelier hung over a square table set for two. Through the doorway, she could see a neatly kept living room, with old Victorian-style furniture and a view of the street.

"Hello!" Max called again, and then a woman came out of the kitchen, wiping her hands on her apron, and embraced him.

"Shhhh, you'll wake the neighbor's baby," she said.

"I want you to meet someone," Max said, stepping aside and putting his arm around the woman's shoulders. "This is Cordelia Grey. Cordelia, this is my mother."

The woman's face was the color of milky coffee, and though her eyes were tired, Cordelia could see that she had once been beautiful. Max had inherited some of her features, she could see that now, but it still stunned her that Max, who seemed so natural amongst his white, Protestant patrons, should be related to this woman. Her hair was not like the hair of the black women who lived in Union—it had been treated with something that made it straight, and it was arranged like Cordelia's, in a low bun at the nape of her neck. She wore a brown housedress, which was smartly tailored and fit her well.

When Cordelia became aware that she was staring, that it had taken her too long to respond, she stepped forward and offered the woman her hand.

"I'm Rosemary Darby," the woman said, shaking Cordelia's hand warily as she glanced at Max.

"It's nice to meet you."

"It's nice to meet you, too," she replied, although her posture seemed to say she wasn't sure. Cordelia couldn't help staring another moment, and Mrs. Darby looked back at her in a precise and undaunted way that made Cordelia ashamed of always peering at people, wanting to figure out what was going on in their minds. *None of your business*, Mrs. Darby's eyes seemed to say, in her quiet dignified way.

"Do you smoke?" Max's mother said eventually, breaking the silence, but not the air of suspicion.

"No." Cordelia hated to lie, but she decided this time it was all right. She could see this was an important point for Mrs. Darby, and she decided that if she was sure that she would never touch a cigarette again then she could get away with a little white lie this once.

"Good." Mrs. Darby clapped her hands and the mood lightened. "Are you staying for dinner? I'm afraid I only have two steaks, although I have plenty of potatoes and greens, and I always get a big cut for Max, so there's really plenty of meat for three, and if he wants you here that badly, he'll be willing to share."

So Max set another place, and the three of them sat down and talked for an hour or more as they ate Mrs. Darby's cooking. At first Cordelia talked about Ohio, and how she had come to New York, trying to be vague about her father and her family's current line of work. But this proved easy enough, because Rosemary Darby seemed perfectly happy whenever the conversation returned to her son, of whom she was very visibly proud.

"Has he taken you up in the airplane?" she asked, as they were picking up their plates to bring into the kitchen.

Cordelia nodded.

"You must be special then."

Cordelia smiled at that, and looked to Max to see if it were true. But he gave no sign. He only said, "I'd better go, Ma. I asked Cordelia to come over last minute, and she has somewhere she has to be."

"Thank you for dinner, Mrs. Darby. Everything was delicious," Cordelia said, as she began to follow Max toward the door.

"Come back soon, Cordelia. You're a long way from

home, and this is a city that will wear you down if you don't put a home-cooked meal in your belly once in a while."

"Thank you. I will."

Cordelia waited in the hall as Max embraced his mother and said a few parting words, and then they walked to the car and headed in a downtown direction. By then it had grown dark outside, and a half moon was hanging over the silhouettes of the buildings, and a cool night air that smelled like summer touched the skin of her face. There didn't seem to be anything to say until he turned the car onto Fifty-third, and parked halfway down the block from The Vault. She could see that already people were gathering out front, and that photographers were waiting in the street as they had been the night before.

"You wouldn't be able to fly anymore if they found out, would you?"

"Not the way I do now," he said. "Maybe they'd let me be a boxer. But not a flyboy."

"I'm glad you introduced me to your mother," Cordelia replied.

He was as handsome to her as ever, and it made her feel pleasantly weak having his serious gaze on her again, and at such close quarters. The anger that she had felt toward him had evaporated—she could see now why he made himself difficult to know, and why he had resisted pursuing her the way another boy might. All his celebrity and all his opportunities depended on him seeming like a very specific type of person, and he couldn't risk seeming like another person for even an instant. Too much was at stake.

She knew that when she got out of the car she might not see him again, and so she sat quietly and looked straight ahead and reached out for his hand. They interlaced their fingers and listened to the other's breath grow steady. Everyone had secrets, Cordelia saw now; she was not alone in that.

"Well, good-bye, I guess," she said after a while. The phrase made her heart hurt.

"Bye."

She squeezed his hand and got out of the car and began walking toward the club. She was glad that it was there and would keep her busy for many hours to come. The crowd would pour in, and there would be brutes and beauties, and it would be a whole pageant for her to watch. She had come all this way to see spectacles like that, and now they were hers to view every night, but she had never been so grateful for them as right now.

One of the cameramen had spotted her, and she heard a flash go off. Someone ahead of her called out her name, and she smiled. Then she heard her name from the opposite direction, from over her shoulder. She turned around and her smile dropped away.

Max was standing on the sidewalk in his white T-shirt

with a look on his face that made her want to cry. She took a step toward him and then stopped, unsure if he only wanted a final glimpse of her and was hoping to remain unrecognized. Then he began to stride toward her on his strong legs, his face as determined and serious as it had been when he was flying the plane. When he reached her he put one hand on her waist and one hand on the back of her head. He brought her mouth up to his and kissed her for the first time. She could feel the strength of his jaw in the kiss, and as her heart floated upward, she pressed back with equal force. Another bulb sizzled behind her, but still he let their breath mingle for a few seconds more.

"Can I see you soon?" he asked when he pulled back. There was such uncharacteristic yearning in his voice.

"You know how to find me," she said simply, and gave him a wink.

All was briefly calm on the street; he flashed her that exquisitely rare smile once and then he was gone. She could hear him running back to his car and the motor starting up, but she had already turned around and lifted her arms to greet the gathering crowd. There would be singers looking for a big break and debutantes in tiaras who wanted special tables and newspapermen begging for quotes. The taste of Max's mouth was still on her lips, but she couldn't dwell there. The day had been beautifully long, but it was going to be a longer night.

ACKNOWLEDGMENTS

I am very grateful to have such wonderful friends and editors in Sara Shandler and Farrin Jacobs, who work so hard to turn these books into the best versions of themselves. Many thank-yous also to Joelle Hobeika, Josh Bank, Les Morgenstein, Elise Howard, Catherine Wallace, Kristin Marang, Sasha Illingworth, Beth Clark, Marisa Russell, Christina Colangelo, Lauren Flower, Liz Dresner, Aiah Wieder, Melinda Weigel, and Laura Lutz. And thank you, Hawkes, for the use of the spare house in old rum-running country to write in.

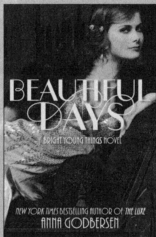
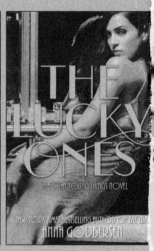